Starlight Wedding

Frank Thomas

This book is dedicated to my loving parents, Frank and Dorothy, who always encouraged me to follow my dreams.

Copyright © 2015 Frank Thomas
All Rights Reserved

All rights reserved. No part of this publication may be reproduced, stored in a retrieval system, or transmitted in any form by any means, electronic, mechanical, photocopy, recording, or otherwise, without the prior permission of the publisher, except as provided by U.S. copyright law.

This book is a work of fiction. All characters appearing in this work are fiction. Any resemblance to real persons, living or dead, is purely coincidental.

eISBN: 978-0-9961412-0-8
Paperback: 978-0-9961412-2-2
Library of Congress Control Number: 2015903337

Cover design by Alisha @ www.damonza.com

Thomas, Frank, 1971-
    Starlight wedding / by Frank Thomas.
    pages cm
    LCCN 2015903337
    ISBN 978-0-9961412-2-2 (paperback)
    ISBN 978-0-9961412-1-5
    ISBN 978-0-9961412-0-8 (eISBN)

    1. Weddings--Fiction. 2. Man-woman relationships--Fiction. 3. New York (N.Y.)--Fiction. 4. Love stories. 5. Humorous stories. I. Title.

PS3620.H62785S73 2015   813'.6
                                  QBI15-600088

CHAPTER ONE	1
CHAPTER TWO	15
CHAPTER THREE	23
CHAPTER FOUR	29
CHAPTER FIVE	45
CHAPTER SIX	66
CHAPTER SEVEN	81
CHAPTER EIGHT	95
CHAPTER NINE	111
CHAPTER TEN	133
CHAPTER ELEVEN	145
CHAPTER TWELVE	154
CHAPTER THIRTEEN	167
CHAPTER FOURTEEN	182
CHAPTER FIFTEEN	194
CHAPTER SIXTEEN	212
CHAPTER SEVENTEEN	228
CHAPTER EIGHTEEN	248
CHAPTER NINETEEN	265
CHAPTER TWENTY	274

CHAPTER ONE

THE RING WAS EXACTLY as Amanda imagined. A brilliant, two-carat princess cut beauty swimming in a sea of pave diamonds on a platinum band from Tiffany's. It was, in a word, exquisite. Of course, it should be since she was the one who had picked it out. Not one to leave anything to chance, especially the all-important procession from engagement to ceremony, Amanda had made it perfectly clear exactly what she would accept from Carl if he planned on marrying her. It had to be two carats, it had to be princess cut, and it had to be from Tiffany's. It wasn't that she was a snob, it was that she believed in having a plan; not to mention, weddings were her business. After a lifetime of dreaming about her own wedding, working in countless bridal shops, and coordinating other's weddings, Amanda had scrimped and saved to open her own bridal shop, Starlight Weddings, to give advice to other soon-to-be Manhattan brides. And if they were going to listen to her, she had to live by example. If it had to be a two-carat example, who was she to judge? And now here it was in the box between her fingers. Everything was going exactly according to plan.

As Amanda stood there gazing at the ring, a tear streamed down her cheek. It was finally happening. Her dreams were coming true, and the proof was sitting in the box in front of her: the box she had mistakenly found while attempting to leave a love note in a drawer in Carl's bedroom. Of course, Carl didn't know she was there. The note was supposed to be a surprise when he got back from his weekend visiting his parents' house upstate. And she'd be long gone before he came home. Amanda set down the box and checked her watch. How long had she been there? It seemed an eternity since she had first seen the iconic blue Tiffany's box sitting in the corner of his top drawer next to a pile of neatly-folded black socks. Amanda let out a sigh as she saw the time. It was already seven thirty. She'd better go in case Carl decided to stop home before work and found her rifling through his drawers. Yet just as she thought it, a sound emanated from the kitchen. Or was it the living room? "Carl!" Amanda whispered to herself. Amanda slammed the box shut and threw it back in the drawer, wedging it next to the neatly-folded black socks, just getting the drawer closed as Carl's dog, Max, trotted in the room.

"Max!" Amanda exclaimed, relieved, catching her breath. "You scared me half to death!" Amanda bent low and took Max's overly fluffy ears in her hands and kissed him on the head. "I thought you were your master, and that would not have been good!" But of course it wasn't

Carl, Amanda realized. It was Carl's fuzzy sheepdog. The whole reason she had come. She had promised to water and feed Max before work while Carl was out of town. The note had been an afterthought. And a good thing too or she wouldn't have found the ring—that wonderful, precious ring.

Giving Max one last pat on the head, Amanda stood and opened the drawer again, hoping to take another look. Should she try it on? Of course she should try it on, she determined! What was she thinking? She had been so caught up in the surprise at seeing it that she hadn't even tried it on to see if it fit. Unable to resist, Amanda pulled the box out again and flipped it open. Within seconds, the ring was between her fingers, shining miraculously in the morning light. How could it possibly have gotten more beautiful in the last few minutes, she wondered? As Amanda slowly slid it down her finger, a smile grew on her face as the ring made its way down. "And it's all mine," she thought. Yet as the ring reached the base of her knuckle, something odd seemed to be happening—it wasn't going over. That can't be right, she thought, somewhat confused. She was sure Carl knew her ring size, so Amanda pushed a little harder, calmly turning it a bit, sure the ring would make its way to where it belonged. When that didn't work, she pushed harder, eliciting a shock of pain in the joint of her finger. "Ow!" she cried. Desperate, Amanda licked her knuckle, sure she must just be swollen from one too many cupcakes the week before. Yes, that must be it, since she knew for certain she had given Carl the right ring size. Yet as she tried it again, it didn't budge. A cold shiver went down

Amanda's spine as she realized it was no use. The ring would not go down. It was then Amanda knew her perfect ring, bought by her perfect man, for her perfect wedding—was too small.

***

"You did what?" Amanda's best friend and coworker, Margot, exclaimed from behind the Starlight Weddings cake counter. In the middle of putting the finishing touches of icing on her latest multi-tiered masterpiece, Margot freed a hand long enough to put it on her hip and gave Amanda one of her best disapproving glances. Amanda's best friend since junior high, Margot knew exactly the right look to get her friend's attention. It was a look Amanda had seen many times. There was the time she skipped class in seventh grade to kiss eighth grader Jimmy Hargrove behind the school bleachers and got caught by the janitor. Then there was the time she decided to bleach her hair platinum blond. And, of course, Amanda's least favorite memory, the not-so-brilliant decision to jump in a public fountain with the rest of the seniors in an all-white outfit on her senior trip to Washington, D.C., unwittingly giving the entire class and an unsuspecting Benjamin Franklin statue a muted view of her unmentionables. The first two were mortifying. The fountain was disastrous beyond words. And now she was getting that look again.

"Nothing!" Amanda replied. "It was just a peek! I had to see what it looked like. And it's a good thing I did, because..." Amanda stopped, realizing she'd gone too far.

"Because what?" Margot returned, already shaking

her head in disapproval.

"Amanda? What aren't you telling me?"

"Nothing, except... Well it's a good thing I did because it wasn't the right size," Amanda finished.

"And how did you know that?" Margot asked, knowing full well what was about to come. "Did you try it on?"

Amanda's face grew crimson. "Maybe." Then, after a moment, "Oh, of course I tried it on. How could I not?"

"Amanda!" Margot shrieked.

"Well! I couldn't help it! You know I like to be sure of things! Everything has to go according to plan!" Amanda said, throwing her arms up helplessly.

"Oh, not the plan again!" Margot retorted, setting the icing bag on the counter.

That's all she'd heard about for years, Amanda's perfect wedding plan, which she had been working on since Amanda discovered her first *Modern Bride* magazine on a magazine rack when she was too young to be thinking about such things. And it had only gotten more and more ridiculous as she got older. Amanda was determined to have the perfect wedding, and Margot knew she was willing to do anything to achieve it—and that's what scared her. Margot readied another disapproving glance. "At least tell me that was all."

"Of course that was all! I'm not crazy," Amanda said, taking another step around the cake in an attempt to block herself from Margot's glaring eyes. "Besides, what more could I have done?"

Margot finally relaxed. "Oh, thank God."

Amanda took another step around. "Except..."

"Amanda?" Margot quickly followed. "What did you do?"

Amanda bit her lip. She was caught. And knew she was about to spill everything. Amanda cast a glance to the floor, rethinking her decision to tell Margot. Of course she wouldn't understand. People never understood all she went through to make sure things worked perfectly in her life. But she couldn't help it. It's who she was. But Margot was her best friend, and frankly, she couldn't keep it in any longer. "Except..." Amanda continued, digging into her pocket as Margot watched. Finally, she pulled out the blue Tiffany's box, holding it like the contraband it was, her face wincing from the reaction that was about to come. "I got it resized."

Margot stared incredulously at the box held in her best friend's hand. "You are going to hell."

"I know! I just—I had to," Amanda replied. "I couldn't tell him. And I couldn't let him give me a ring that didn't fit. What would that say about our future?"

"That he's not marrying a crazy person?" Margot replied.

Amanda laughed. "He'll never know. Besides, he just sent me a text. He's coming in tomorrow now. I'll return the ring before he knows, which makes me perfectly normal in his eyes."

"If only he knew," Margot smirked, taking the ring box to look it over.

Amanda laughed again. "He's a man. He'll never know until it's too late. The wedding will be over, I'll be Mrs. Carl Firestone, and he'll be none the wiser. Then I'll unleash the crazy."

"Lucky him," Margot replied dryly.

"Yep. And he'll love it, and me; we'll have two point one kids, and we'll live a life of perfect happiness. So do you want to see this thing or not?" Amanda asked, eyeing the box.

A smile cracked through Margot's facade as she looked at the box holding the symbol of her friend's future happiness, unable to resist. "What do you think?"

"Yes!" Amanda screamed.

Margot started to open it but stopped to wave a definitive finger. "But then you are taking this ring back where belongs!"

"I promise," Amanda assured.

"Good!" Margot replied, returning her eyes to the box. "Then let's see this baby!" And with that, she flipped it open.

***

Amanda strolled through the folded tables of food set out by her store chef, Eduardo, plucking out delicious entree samples as she went along. As usual, Eduardo's samples looked to die for, and she had no doubt they probably tasted the same. From a small Guatemalan town, Eduardo had taken to New York quickly upon his arrival as a teenager. He had worked in practically every restaurant in the city worth mentioning before starting his own catering company, E Street Catering, which catered to New York residents of all backgrounds, giving every prospective bride unforgettable catered meals no matter her price range. It was this love for people, along with his amazing skills in the kitchen that kept him booked throughout the year and helped him develop into one of Amanda's most requested caterers.

Amanda winked at Eduardo as she weaved her way through the gaggle of brides huddled around the tables sampling Eduardo's creations and stuffed her favorites into a Styrofoam container until it was so full it was nearly spilling over. Satisfied she had secured enough food to feed a small army, Amanda somehow managed to close the lid of the overflowing container and made her way over to Margot's cake section, where Margot was setting out plates of sugar-filled masterpieces to a group of excited brides and mothers. Amanda quickly filled a much smaller container with slivers of both chocolate and carrot cake before turning to her Margot, barely able to contain her excitement.

"Carl called. He's coming back tonight! And he wants to meet for dinner at Tivoli's! He said he has something important to ask me!"

"Tonight?" Margot's eyes shot open in realization. "This is it! You're getting engaged! My best friend's getting engaged!" Margot grabbed Amanda's hand, happy to share this special moment with the person she'd known forever. "So tell me—are you still going to wear the dress?"

The dress she was referring to was Amanda's grandmother's wedding dress—and of course, she was going to wear it. It had been the plan from the beginning. A vintage lace dress with inlaid pearls along the collar and sleeve, it was the dress her grandmother Rose had worn on her wedding day, and she and Amanda's grandfather had been married fifty years. It was good luck. Amanda had heard the story a million times as a little girl and she had always imagined herself in that dress. Of course, she had gotten it altered to fit her frame and had added a bit of modernization to it to keep up with the times, but the dress was essentially the same. And when she walked down the aisle to meet Carl at the altar, there was no other dress she wanted to do it in. Not to mention the veil.

"The veil!" Amanda remembered, "I forgot to unpack it when I moved. I need to get it cleaned."

"You've got time," Margot responded.

"Of course I do," Amanda returned nonchalantly.

Margot eyed Amanda warily. "You're taking it to get cleaned today, aren't you?"

Amanda shrugged helplessly. "Well! You know I can't leave anything to chance! I'm a planner. I can't help it."

Margot laughed. "Oh, I know. God help poor Carl. He doesn't know what he's getting himself into."

"He'd better!" Amanda returned. "He's been with me long enough. Too long! He nearly gave me a coronary waiting this long to propose."

Margot lovingly put her hand on her best friend. "Don't worry. Your Starlight wedding is going to happen. And it's going to be beautiful. The most important thing is that you're with the man you're supposed to be with."

"In the perfect dress," Amanda said.

"Well, of course in the perfect dress!" Margot exclaimed. "I'm not a cave woman!"

As the two broke into laughter, Amanda moved around the counter, shutting the lid to her dessert samples. Locking it in place, she grabbed her purse from the floor and hurried to the front door, calling out, "Lock up!" behind her as she made her way outside.

Stepping onto the sidewalk, Amanda scanned the nearby alley for signs of Henry, the ever-present homeless vet she'd gotten to know after years of being in this location. Having a heart for those less fortunate, Amanda loved living in the city, but always felt a twinge of regret she couldn't do more for the thousands living on the fringe of society sometimes through no fault of their own. She reasoned it was probably her Catholic upbringing.

So Amanda did what she could, giving what extra food and money she could afford, and found unlikely friendships with many of those in need. But her favorite was Henry, a war veteran who had fought in Iraq before finding his way to his current residence, the alley behind Amanda's shop. Always polite and surprisingly clean, considering his disadvantages, Henry always offered a smile and a hello to anyone who passed and rarely asked for money. But like everyone, he appreciated a hot meal, especially a meal made from Eduardo's kitchen.

It was then she saw him, just a few yards away. Henry turned, a smile immediately forming on his face as she neared.

"Good morning, Miss Amanda, you're looking lovely today." Always up for a lengthy discussion about the Yankees, her favorite team, Henry asked, "Did you see the game last night?"

Amanda shook her head. She guessed he hadn't either but had read about it in one of the discarded papers one of Wall Street's early risers had left behind.

"No, I had to work late," Amanda replied. "But I heard

we won."

"Yankees won three to two," Henry responded. "Sounds like it wasn't pretty, but we got the win."

"I'll take it," Amanda replied. In a hurry, Amanda held out the boxes for Henry. "Hey, Henry, got you something. From Eduardo."

"You are the best!" Henry's eyes lit up as he took the containers, eyeing them greedily. "Any sweets?"

Amanda knew sweets were Henry's weakness. "Henry! Sweets are bad for you! I told you I'm not bringing you anymore."

Henry grumbled, then opened the lid of the smaller container, discovering the delicious slivers of cake. "Ha! I knew you couldn't resist."

"But this is the last time! You hear me, Henry!" Amanda waved a finger in emphasis.

Henry laughed. It's what she said every time. "Whatever you say, Miss Amanda."

"I'm serious." Amanda did her best serious impression, but they both knew she didn't mean it. "Well, I've got to go. I'm late and there are some things I've got to do. Enjoy your day, Henry. And your last dessert," she said with a wink. With that, she was off, hailing a cab.

"Will do. Good luck, Miss Amanda," Henry called from behind. "God bless you."

***

Amanda stared at her reflection in the full-length mirror of her bedroom. The wedding dress was everything she remembered. Despite the twinge of sadness that came from missing her grandmother,

Amanda knew Grandma Rose was watching down from heaven, smiling her approval. Amanda stepped back, whistling to herself at how amazing the dress actually was. The combination of vintage craftsmanship, combined with the modern touches Amanda paid to have added, made her look spectacular. Heck, with the deeper plunging neckline showing a hint of cleavage, Carl might not be able to wait until after the ceremony to say "I do." Not to mention the shoes. Jimmy Choos may not come cheap, but they were worth every penny. Yes, everything was coming together. By the next morning, she would be engaged to Carl as she had planned, and the wedding procession would begin. And though Carl didn't know it, it would be just in time. Despite believing in honesty, especially in her relationships, there was one thing Carl didn't know and wouldn't find out until tomorrow about their upcoming nuptials. Sure he knew they'd be getting married at St. Patrick's. And he knew they were having their reception at The Plaza. Those were deal breakers he'd agreed to long ago. What he didn't know was that the date was set—September twenty-fourth—and it was only four months away.

It was the day her mother had gotten married thirty years earlier and her grandmother thirty years before that. It was the day the Starlight Comet would awake from its thirty-year nap and make its way through the sky just like it had on both her mother's and grandmother's wedding nights before disappearing the next morning for another thirty years. Amanda had always planned on marrying on that day and to delay any nuptials if she found the right guy earlier, but fate had intervened until it looked like she might actually miss it. And she certainly couldn't wait another thirty years. That would put her in her fifties. Talk about a December wedding. Yet, for her, no other date would do. Amanda had decided that shortly after the car accident that had taken both her parents. But she didn't want to think of that now. This was a time for celebration. And this would be her way of including them and Grandma Rose on the most special day of her life. She had nearly given up until Carl showed up and swept her off her feet with his great job, winning smile, and the way he treated her over the year they'd been together. Of course, they'd had their fights, but on the big things, they seemed to agree. It didn't hurt that he came from money. She liked security like every other girl. Despite her own success, it was important she have a man who could take care of her if need be. Something about losing two parents makes you immeasurably more practical on matters such as that. But lately, since he'd been so busy working longer hours and had been constantly out of town, she had started to question their relationship. Yet then she had discovered the ring—her precious ring. Now nothing would get in the way of her Starlight wedding.

Of course, it hadn't been easy keeping her plan a secret. Not wanting to suffocate Carl, Amanda had tried to casually prod him along without giving him a timeline. Telling a man where you wanted to get married was one thing. Telling him the date was quite another. She always knew she'd have to wait at least until they were engaged to tell any man about her secret; she just never imagined she would cut it this close. Amanda shook her head, wiping away the tears forming in her eyes before they got away and ruined her makeup. She couldn't believe it was finally happening. So what if it only gave her four months to prepare? This was her field and something she'd spent her lifetime planning. She had a stuffed wedding scrapbook hidden in the closet to prove it. Not to mention, four months was practically a lifetime for someone like her. With Eduardo's catering and Margot's cakes, the reception was practically already planned. Which reminded her, she hadn't looked at her wedding gown in ages, or her veil, though she'd had each for years. She'd better take them to get refitted and cleaned ASAP.

Amanda turned to get one last glimpse of herself in the mirror. Carl was going to love this dress so much, and tonight he was going to propose. Then she was going to have her Starlight wedding, and they would live happily ever after. Amanda sighed. Sometimes life seemed so perfect—and after the difficulty of losing her parents, she deserved it. At least she hoped so. But that wouldn't stop her from planning to make it a reality. She was going to have her Starlight wedding with Carl, and nothing was going to get in her way.

CHAPTER TWO

DANIEL MOVED AROUND the giant stone, which was glowing in the dim light of his loft, admiring his work. Though incomplete, the head of what was to be a fallen angel for a local church had started to take form. It wasn't the largest thing he had done, or the most impressive, but when complete, it would be the highest paying. Sure it would barely cover the cost of the stone, not to mention a fraction of the rent in his rent-controlled apartment, but it would be stunning. And he would have earned the money doing something he loved. At least he hoped it would look good. One mistake of his chisel could ruin the entire slab. That was one of the thrills of working in stone. But he wouldn't trade it for anything. It had been over a decade since he had discovered art in high school and dedicated his life to it, and he couldn't imagine doing anything else. Of course, it didn't always pay the bills. Come to think of it, it never had. But seeing the look on people's faces when they saw his creations was worth it, not to mention the joy of forging something out of nothing, of turning a giant unformed rock into something to be admired.

Daniel stopped to take in the head from a new angle. His high school art instructor would be proud of how far he'd come. He'd learned so much since his first attempts in that freshman art class. If only Daniel's father shared in that sentiment. To him, it was a waste of time—and worse, money. He had wanted Daniel to take over Evelyn's, the family dry cleaning business he'd named after Daniel's mother, when he got older and never let a shared moment pass without relaying his disappointment. It seemed all the women Daniel had dated felt the same. Oh, at first it was always romantic. And with his chiseled looks and brown hair he had no problem finding a woman. Women practically threw themselves at him. They'd brag to their friends about dating an artist. But inevitably there'd be the talk. Could he make more money doing something else? Or why couldn't he just work more for his father and sculpt in his spare time? Yet Daniel could think of nothing more loathsome. In here he felt alive. Every day brought a new adventure, whereas time at the dry cleaner might as well be time in prison. And so inevitably the relationships would end as the women moved on to better prospects. He just needed to find someone special, someone who appreciated him for who he was, someone who knew the importance of doing what you love. Then he might tell her his secret. The secret he hadn't told any of the others. He wasn't poor. He never had been. The truth was he was worth millions.

STARLIGHT WEDDING

***

The alarm on Daniel's phone buzzed, reminding him he needed to go. He had deliveries he needed to make. That was part of the deal. Daniel's inheritance would remain intact as long as he put time in at the cleaners. Revolted at the idea of pressing shirts all day, Daniel agreed to do deliveries for one of the nearby locations. At least on the street he felt free. In exchange, his father didn't completely disown him and paid whatever shortfall he accrued each month. If he ever "came to his senses," in his father's words, and agreed to work full time, the waiting inheritance would be his. Daniel hoped it would never come to that. He hoped to make it on his own.

***

Daniel drove through the city in the delivery van with the windows down, feeling the wind gust through his hair. All around the bustle of Manhattan was in full swing.

People in suits hurried back and forth on their lunch breaks, coffee and sandwiches in hand, as taxis filled the streets, shuttling passengers to their destinations. The city was positively electric. Daniel smiled, appreciating the excitement as he careened to a stop in front of his first delivery, a postal shop, as a line of customers exited the front door.

Grabbing a load of freshly-pressed uniforms, Daniel headed inside. He hadn't even made it to the door when his phone rang. Daniel's heart lurched when he saw the name. It was his mother—and his mother never called him at work. Something must have happened.

"Mom?" Daniel asked, putting the phone to his ear. "Is everything all right?" He hoped he was just being paranoid, but the heavy breathing on the other end told him otherwise.

"It's your father," she declared. "He's had a heart attack. We need you now."

***

Amanda hurried down the sidewalk cradling the box, with her grandmother's veil in one hand and her phone in the other. With little time to get to the dress shop before traipsing across town in time for dinner, she knew she was cutting it close. But it couldn't be helped. She needed to know the task was done. She'd have too much to think about in the coming days, and she didn't want to have to worry about the veil. Yet as she walked, her phone began to ring. Amanda glanced at the lit up screen. It was coming from St. Patrick's. Perfect—just what she needed. More trouble. They'd been hassling her ever since they'd discovered she didn't have a groom. And with the date fast approaching, it had only gotten worse.

Amanda looked up to heaven, her version of saying a quick prayer before answering, and then pressed the talk button. "Hello?" Amanda spoke, cradling the phone on one ear, as she kept pace with the pedestrians around her. "This is Amanda." She was attempting to sound as confident as possible though her insides were turning.

"Miss Jones," the person on the other end of the phone began, "this is Donald Mayberry, from St. Patrick's."

"Oh, great," Amanda thought. It was him. Now she was sure she'd have to explain herself all over again.

"Miss Jones, the reason I'm calling is—"

"I know why you're calling," Amanda interrupted. "You're worried there won't be a wedding. But if you wait just one more day, I'll be engaged, and I'll be able to relieve you of your concerns."

Mr. Mayberry didn't seem convinced. "So you admit you don't have a fiancé?"

"Not yet," Amanda responded. "But the proposal is happening tonight, so there's nothing to worry about." She did her best to sound convincing.

"Tonight?" By the skepticism in his voice, it didn't sound like Mr. Mayberry believed her, nor cared. "Miss Jones, you do realize how in demand St. Patrick's is?"

Amanda crossed the street, picking up her pace. "Yes, sir. It's a lovely church. That's why I chose it."

"Well let me remind you," Mayberry continued, "with only four months remaining, our policy at St. Patrick's is to terminate any contract we deem unreliable."

"Sir, I assure you I'm well aware of your policy," Amanda broke in before continuing, "as I've had the date booked since the first day it was available."

"Then you are aware we may cancel at any time with reason," Mayberry reminded.

"I'm aware, sir." Amanda stopped in her tracks. "But if you give me just one more day, I'm sure it will no longer be an issue."

Amanda waited for what felt like an eternity of silence.

"Very well," Mayberry conceded after some time. "Let me know when you've secured your man. Good luck tonight, Miss Jones."

"Thank you, sir." Amanda hung up, taking a moment

to relive the conversation. Secured her man? Who says that? Well at least he hadn't canceled. For a moment, Amanda had been worried she would have to find another church. But to her, there was no other church. St. Patrick's was the best in Manhattan and where she had always dreamed of having her wedding. Of course, in her dreams, there wasn't a Mr. Mayberry calling to harass her. Regardless, even if she wanted a different church, none would be available. Amanda wondered what the real reason was for Mayberry's call. No doubt some wealthy patron was trying to steal her date for a relative at the last minute and offering an enormous sum. Well, it wasn't going to happen. Tonight she was getting engaged, and both Carl and the church would be hers. Amanda snapped from her revelry to glance at her watch. "Tonight! I'd better go!" Stuffing her phone in her pocket, Amanda took off down the sidewalk as fast as she could with the box.

***

Daniel burst through the door of the post office to the street outside. Just minutes before, everything had seemed okay. Yet, after the call from his mother, his whole world seemed to be spinning out of control. Daniel's mind raced with fears of his father's imminent demise. Was it a heart attack? How serious was it? Would he be okay? Would he make it to the hospital in time? Caught up in his emotions, Daniel didn't notice the woman with the box heading directly at him. By the blank stare on her face, she didn't see him either—and ran straight into him.

Upon impact, both Amanda and Daniel looked up at

the same time, each snapping a mental picture of each other as they crashed and fell to the ground. Amanda's box and Daniel's keys went flying as both braced for impact. Within a moment it was over, and Amanda found herself sprawled on the pavement next to him.

Daniel was the first to speak. "I'm so sorry," he said as he stood, offering his hand. "Are you okay?"

A small crowd had begun to form. Embarrassed, Amanda used her arms to get up on her own and quickly brushed herself off. "I'm fine. But what were you thinking?"

"I wasn't." Daniel stared at Amanda, stunned by her perfectly shaped eyes. "That is to say, I didn't see you."

"Well next time pay attention," Amanda hissed. "You nearly got me killed."

It wasn't like her to be mean, but this stranger, okay, this handsome stranger, she admitted to herself, had gotten in her way and made her even later than she already was.

"I know. I'm sorry. I was preoccupied," Daniel continued as apologetically as possible. "I didn't mean to crash into you. I should have been paying attention."

Daniel continued his gaze, taking in every inch of Amanda's face. She'd be perfect for one of his upcoming projects. How he'd love to sculpt that face. Her cheekbones and dimples were adorable. And her hair... She'd make such a great angel that, for a moment, Daniel lost himself thinking about the possibilities.

"Hello? Are you there?" Amanda asked, growing annoyed. "Why are you staring at me?"

Daniel snapped out of it. "What? No, I wasn't. I was

just thinking about something at work." Daniel broke his gaze and noticed Amanda's box, now crumpled and lying on the ground. "Is this yours?" Daniel picked it up, attempting to fix it.

Amanda's heart sank as she looked it over. The box was crushed. The veil was probably ruined. Amanda fearfully opened what remained of the box and looked inside and her heart sank. It was worse than she had imagined. "My veil... It's ruined!"

Daniel looked on, dumbfounded. "I am so sorry." As Daniel spoke, he saw what looked like the beginning of tears forming in Amanda's eyes. "My family owns—I mean, I work at a dry cleaner. If you'd like, I'm sure we can fix it."

Daniel reached to take the box from Amanda, but Amanda quickly jerked it away. "Just stay away!" Amanda cried. "You've done enough. Just stay away from me!" With that, Amanda ran through the crowd, eager to get away.

Daniel started after her. "Wait! I never got your name!" Daniel even took a few steps then stopped, standing on his toes to see through the crowd. But it was too late. She was gone.

CHAPTER THREE

AS THE TAXI SLOWED TO A STOP IN FRONT of Tivoli's Restaurant in midtown, Amanda could hardly control her excitement. Within hours, she would be engaged to Carl and just a few short months away from being Mrs. Carl Firestone and hosting her dream wedding. Just the comfort of knowing her future seemed to shine through the dark events of the day and give her peace. Her plans were finally coming together. It helped that the dress shop assured her they could repair her ruined veil. Once that was done, it was one less thing to worry about, no thanks to that Neanderthal who had run into her. She hoped to erase his hideous face from her memory forever. So what if he was passably handsome? That didn't make him any less revolting. Regardless, she decided, there was no need to muddy her mind with him. She would be meeting Carl in a minute, and her new life would begin: a life of excitement, planning, and hope. It was time to focus on that and making sure tonight was memorable, as she'd be telling the story to her girlfriends, and anyone else who would listen, for the rest of her life. Amanda stepped through Tivoli's entrance and saw Carl as soon as she walked in the door. Still in his work suit, Carl looked positively amazing. She could tell he was nervous. "Poor guy," Amanda reflected. He'd probably be beside himself the whole dinner. She imagined the bulge in his jacket where the ring pressed firmly against it, waiting for him to break it out after dessert. As she did, Carl neared, ever the gentleman, and offered a kiss.

"You look beautiful," he exclaimed, sounding somewhat surprised.

Amanda chose to ignore his surprise and smiled, offering her cheek. "Thanks. So do you."

Just then, the host stepped up and offered to take them to their table. As they moved through the restaurant, Amanda took in their surroundings. It was a nice place she admitted, though perhaps a little less than she had imagined. She would have chosen something a little fancier, given the occasion, but she was certainly not going to complain. She was more than happy to be here. She would have met him at McDonald's if it meant going ahead with her wedding.

The waiter slowed in front of a four-top in the center of the room by the kitchen. Even before they neared it, Amanda knew it wouldn't do. First of all, it was too big—and definitely not romantic. Then there was the matter of the clanging dishes coming through from the kitchen, which could be heard clear across the restaurant. They would definitely ruin the proposal.

Amanda put on her best smile for the host. "Excuse

me. I hate to complain but is there another table away from the kitchen? I'm sorry to be a bother; it's just we haven't seen each other in a while, and we'd prefer something a little less noisy." Amanda turned to Carl to gauge his reaction. "Is that all right, Carl?"

Carl shrugged and nodded his approval. "Fine by me."

By the look of it, Carl was playing coy. Good. He was clearly none the wiser she had seen the ring, and if he was, he wasn't letting on. Carl followed Amanda as the waiter led them to a much more intimate table in the front of the restaurant and sat them down. Upon sitting, Amanda realized there was another problem. The table was fine, but she was staring at an exceedingly odd painting across the room. In it, a large man was smiling while getting hit with a fish. Nope. That was not something she wanted to remember for the rest of her life. Amanda immediately got up.

"What's wrong now?" Carl asked with a hint of annoyance.

"Nothing," Amanda responded, attempting to sound calm. She didn't want him to have second thoughts. "I just felt a chill." Amanda pointed to where Carl was about to sit. "Do you mind if I sit there?"

Carl smiled and shook his head, "Not at all," then immediately stepped out of the way and took a seat in Amanda's chair. For a moment, he eyed Amanda with a look of confusion. "Are you all right?"

Preoccupied, Amanda rearranged the silverware in front of her before moving her wine glass to be perfectly in line with Carl's. "What was that?"

"I said, are you okay? You seem..." Carl didn't know

how to finish. "I don't know...distracted."

"Really?" Amanda responded, laughing nervously. "No, I'm fine. You know me. I just like things to be perfect."

It seemed like forever before Carl responded unflatteringly, "Oh, I know."

Was he upset? All she'd done was requested to switch tables. And chairs. Oh, and rearrange the silverware. Okay, maybe that was a bit much. Now she was driving herself crazy thinking about it. She'd have to do better in the future, or she'd drive herself mad. Lucky for her, the waiter showed up to take their drink order. She was more than ready for that.

For Amanda, the actual dinner proved uneventful. To her, it seemed Carl was just nervously muddling through until the main event. He talked about the weather so much Amanda began to wonder if he was about to tell her he was switching careers to be a weatherman rather than propose. Yet, at last, it came time for dessert. In fact, the waiter had barely cleaned their plates before Carl reached across the table to nervously take Amanda's hand.

"Amanda," he began, "I'm glad you could meet me here because there's something I want to say."

Yes! Amanda thought. Here it comes.

Carl continued. "I've thought about this long and hard, and I don't want another day to pass without getting this out."

Amanda's heart lurched inside of her. She could already feel the tears forming in her eyes. This was it. It was really happening.

Carl continued, "We've been together over a year now, and in that year, we've shared some amazing times. And I'd like those times to continue..."

"Oh, me too!" Amanda interjected. Her first tear tried to force its way out. It took everything Amanda had to hold it back. She knew, if one escaped, the entire dam would burst, and she'd be a mess before he could get the ring out.

Carl squeezed her hand harder. It was time to say what he had to say. "Coming here tonight, seeing you with the waiter and the whole table thing and your love of perfection, it just reminds me of how special you are. And how special the man you end up with will have to be. But..." Carl took a deep breath before continuing, "I know for a fact it isn't me."

"What?" Amanda blurted, sure her ears were playing tricks on her. Suddenly the world seemed to freeze around her. Her heart seized within her as if in need of sending every last bit of blood to her brain to process what she believed she had just heard. This couldn't be happening. This wasn't happening. Amanda pulled her hand back, using it to steady herself on her chair.

"I'm so sorry," Carl continued. "I was having doubts. And the truth is... Well, the truth is, I'm seeing someone else." Carl winced as if bracing himself for the impact of what he was saying. "I didn't go to my parents this weekend. I was with Rachel. She's amazing. You'd really like her. It's only been a month, but we're getting married. I'm sorry."

"Sorry?" In an instant, Amanda saw her entire future collapse. Everything. Gone. Her wedding would never happen. She would never get married. She would never have a family. She would grow into an old maid. Amanda made a mental note to stop by the pet store in the morning to start looking at cats. She hated cats, but she would have to get used to them, as they were going to be her only companions for the rest of her life. If all that weren't bad enough, it was what Carl said next that really killed her.

"I'm so sorry to ask," Carl began, "but there's one more thing. If you don't mind, I'd like to use the ring you picked out to give to Rachel. It's such a beautiful design and I know she'd really love it."

Amanda started to feel lightheaded. It was the kind of tingling sensation she knew preceded passing out. If Amanda had to listen to one more word, she was going down. Unfortunately, Carl didn't stop.

"I was going to propose to her this weekend, but I knew that wouldn't be fair to you," Carl admitted. After that, Carl reached into his pocket and pulled out her beautiful blue ring box and looked it over. "Amanda, would you mind if I proposed to Rachel using our ring?"

That's when everything went black. Amanda fell from her chair and landed with a thud on the floor. It was over. She'd never get her Starlight wedding and she'd never get Carl. What's more, she'd just passed out in front of the entire restaurant and was now lying on the floor for everyone to see. For a while, this is where she remained, until the darkness receded long enough for Amanda to open her eyes before returning her to unconsciousness. Of course, the last thing she saw was the painting—that stupid fish painting—before everything went dark again. Great, now she was going to remember it forever.

CHAPTER FOUR

BY THE TIME MARGOT GOT to Amanda's apartment the place was unrecognizable. Clothes and magazines were everywhere. The usually pristine kitchen looked like an ice cream truck had exploded, leaving empty cartons and spilled pools of melted cream everywhere. Margot counted the empty cartons on her hand until she ran out of fingers. How could one person, especially one as thin as Amanda, eat that much?

"Hello? Amanda? Are you in here?" Margot called out as she worked her way down the hall. "You'd better not be feeling sorry for yourself!" Not getting a response, Margot started to worry. "Amanda? Make a noise if you're still alive."

A muffled groan emanated from the living room. Upon entering, Margot saw Amanda's wedding scrapbook, on a pile of dirty clothes on the couch, move.

"Amanda?" Margot asked. "Are you under there?"

"Go away," Amanda's muted voice responded from somewhere below the pile.

"Amanda!" Margot shook her head as she made her way to the couch. "What are you doing?" Grabbing at clothes, Margot threw them aside, revealing Amanda's face and more empty cartons.

"Too much light..." Amanda groaned, shielding her eyes. It had clearly been awhile since she'd moved. Margot felt sorry for her friend. To go through what she had gone through, on a night that was supposed to go a completely different way, was unimaginable. But she knew she couldn't let Amanda wallow for too long, or she might never recover. "Amanda, you can't stay like this. It's been two days. You have to come back to work."

Amanda groaned. "It's no use. My life is over."

"No, it isn't, Miss Melodramatic," Margot reassured. "It's just the beginning of a new chapter."

But Amanda wasn't listening. She was too far gone, playing out the remainder of her life in her head, over and over, with little to hold on to. "And now I have to get a cat!"

"You're not getting a cat!" Margot took Amanda's hand, doing her best to sound reassuring. "Everything's going to be okay. I promise."

Amanda frowned, giving Margot the saddest face she could possibly make. "You can have my BMW."

"You don't have a BMW. You live in the city." Margot corrected, "You don't even have a car."

"But I would have!" Amanda demanded, falling back into the couch. "And a wedding, and a husband—and now they're all going to Rachel!"

Margot hated to see her best friend unravel. It was heartbreaking to see, yet Margot didn't know how to stop it. "Hey, what's this? Is this your wedding book?" Margot said, picking up Amanda's scrapbook. Margot knew exactly what it was, as she'd seen the book a million times, but she was desperate to get Amanda's mind on something other than self-pity. Margot turned a few pages to get Amanda's attention, and it seemed to work. Amanda was at least taking notice.

"Yes. Not that I'll ever need it, because no one's ever going to marry me. I'm demanding and I eat too much ice cream," Amanda grumbled. "That's what Carl said."

"He said you ate too much ice cream?" Margot pictured all of the empty cartons she'd come across since entering the apartment. If he had, she totally understood.

"No," Amanda admitted. "But he did say I'm demanding. And he's right. No one's ever going to marry me." Amanda put her hand on the scrapbook she'd had since childhood. "This was just a complete waste of time."

Margot didn't know how to respond, so she went with the old standby, "You just need to find the right guy." To further emphasize the point, Margot turned to a page in Amanda's book holding a collage of hot men, clippings of models and movie stars she'd taken out of magazines. Margot pointed to a photo of a handsome doctor with a winning smile. "Like this guy." Doctors were always an easy sell with Amanda, as with most girls. They were clean, efficient, and helped people get better.

Amanda's curiosity piqued. "He is rather handsome." Amanda couldn't remember finding, let alone including, the handsome doctor in her wall of men, but she had to admit she had good taste. Yet any excitement Amanda mustered was short lived. "But it's not going to happen. Besides, it's already too late. September is only four months away. I'll never have my Starlight wedding." With that, Amanda dropped back into the couch and covered her face again.

"You'll have a wedding someday," Margot explained, doing her best to sound positive. "And it'll be beautiful. The most important thing is that you find the right person. It's not about where you're married or what day it's on; it's about whom you share it with."

"You're right. Of course you're right," Amanda agreed, unconvincingly. "I guess I'll call the church tomorrow and tell them the wedding's off."

"That's probably for the best." Margot knew how hard this must be for Amanda. It wasn't just the ruining of her wedding but the disappointment of losing her chance of doing something to make her feel connected to her family again. It was a chance she'd never get back. Margot took Amanda's hand and squeezed it. "Don't worry. Everything's going to work out."

"Of course it is," Amanda agreed, but by the look on her face, Margot knew she didn't believe it.

***

Amanda stared at her phone, unable to make the call. It was already halfway through her first day back at work, and she couldn't bring herself to dial the number.

Something about the finality of canceling her booking at St. Patrick's ripped her heart out every time she remembered it. She knew it had to be done. There was no way to make it a reality. Planning a wedding in four months would have been difficult but doable. Doing it without a groom was impossible. Her mother would be so disappointed if she were still alive. They'd spent countless nights talking about how wonderful her Starlight wedding would be. Back then, it had seemed there was so much time left, Amanda hadn't considered the possibility of not making it a reality. Of course, back then, everything had seemed possible. She was a teenager, and the next Starlight appearance was light years away. She had been sure she had plenty of time — and then everything had changed. Her parents had been taken away in an instant, and Amanda would never see them again. The next few years had been a blur. Grasping for ways to hold on to the memory of her parents, like naming her business Starlight Weddings, was natural but ineffective. Amanda knew the memories of her parents would fade. This only made Amanda more determined to carry out her and her mother's plans. But now those plans would never come to fruition. She would never share a Starlight wedding with her mother and grandmother. Just like the rest of her life after her parent's passing, she'd have to go it alone. Amanda slid her phone back into her pocket. She wasn't ready to call St. Patrick's. She would, but she'd have to make the call later.

***

Daniel raced through the hospital searching for his father's room. Room four thousand and nineteen had to be here somewhere. He was sure the nurse he'd asked had pointed in this direction, but every room he passed seem further and further away from where he needed to be. Still, Daniel continued moving forward, hoping to find it in the never-ending labyrinth of hospital hallways. As he passed room after room of sick people, Daniel wondered what life would be like without his father should the worst happen. Their relationship had always been tenuous, but he was still his father. Daniel couldn't imagine life without him.

Daniel rounded the corner in time to see a nurse exit his father's room. Sliding in behind her, Daniel took a deep breath and made his way in. On the bed, his father, Jack, sat with tubes and wires coming out of him. For the first time in his life, his father appeared vulnerable.

"Daniel! Finally!" Daniel's worrying mother, Evelyn, exclaimed. "Thank God you made it."

"Hello, Mother." Daniel gave her a kiss then looked at his father lying comatose beside her. "Is he alright?"

"I'm fine," Jack responded, opening his eyes. "It's nothing."

"He had a heart attack," Evelyn corrected. "He nearly died."

This description didn't sit well with Jack, who bristled at the idea of appearing weak. "I'm fine. Don't worry the boy." Jack turned his attention back to Daniel. "I'll be back to full health in no time."

Daniel didn't know how to respond. "That's good. So when do they expect to let you go?"

"Within the week," Jack responded sourly, "so there's no reason for you to worry."

"He's here to support you, Jack. The least you could do

is talk to him," Evelyn demanded. "Surely there's something you have to say?"

"Actually, there is," Jack began. "The doctor has advised me to slow down a bit, which means I'll be taking a little time off work. And since it would be good for you to know more of the family business—"

"No," Daniel interrupted. "I'm not working for the business any more than I have to. While I'm happy you are well and applaud your decision to take time off, you've got people in place..."

"People I don't trust," Jack demanded. "If this setback has taught me anything, it's that you need to be prepared for anything. If and when I die, you'll need to know something about how things run. Therefore, I want you at the office while I'm away."

"You know I don't want that," Daniel protested.

Jack bristled. "Fine. Then I'm stopping your allowance. You're a grown man. You can pay your own way—that is, if you can make due on delivery money and art."

"I guess I'll have to," Daniel retorted. Daniel didn't think it was possible, but he didn't see a way around it. Once his father made up his mind, there was no turning back.

"Then I guess you've made your choice," Jack challenged.

Daniel gulped. The knot in his stomach grew the more he considered on it. He'd have to take more deliveries not to mention how much it would cut into his sculpting, but he refused to give up what he loved. "I guess I have."

***

Daniel closed the door to his loft and let the peace of the space overtake him. It had been a trying day, first with the girl from the sidewalk and then with his father. Luckily, it was nearly over, and his favorite time of day had begun—the blue hour: the magical hour between day and night when the world and everything in it took on a bluish hue. Being in the loft always gave Daniel a sense of peace, but it was extra special during this time. Flipping on a spotlight for illumination, Daniel strode to the statue he was working on, slipped off the cover, and stared at his creation. The angel was nearly complete. The wings stretched out behind it had been filled with the most intricate of detail. The leg and arm muscles looked amazingly real, with every bulge and striation accounted for. All that was left was the face. Daniel knew he just needed inspiration and the willingness, and his hands would do the rest. Daniel ran his fingers over the statue, feeling the details, when it hit him—the girl from the sidewalk. Who was she? Where was she from? And why couldn't he stop thinking about her? Once in his mind, he couldn't let her go. As enigmatic as she was, there was something about her. She had an inner strength he'd rarely come across—along with a sadness he couldn't quite place. He'd seen it in her eyes the second they'd met. She was upset when he ran into her, and for good reason, but there was something else—a searching. Something he couldn't place. Daniel lost himself thinking about her—then picked up his chisel and began to work. Before he knew it, it was midnight. The hours had melted away in what felt like minutes, as always happened when he worked until he completed what he worked on. Wiping the sweat from his brow, Daniel stepped back to look at his creation. In a few short hours, the face had come together. The excess stone had been stripped away, and the details had emerged. It was a perfect resemblance. It was the girl from the sidewalk.

***

Daniel loaded the next batch of deliveries into the van and shut the door. Sliding into the driver's seat, he went over the events of the morning in his head. It had been surprisingly okay. Sure it was monotonous, and he would much rather have been in the studio, but the time had passed quickly, just like in his loft when he had been thinking about the girl. Was that it? Was it the girl? Daniel realized he'd been thinking about her all morning. What was happening to him? Why couldn't he get this stranger out of his mind? Daniel started the van, pulled onto the street, and rechecked the address of his first delivery. It must be a new client, he decided, as he didn't recognize the address or the name of the business. Starlight Weddings? Well, at least it was close. Daniel turned on the radio, suddenly finding himself in the mood for love songs.

***

Amanda stood in the Starlight kitchen and poured what felt like her tenth cup of coffee. It was already noon, but considering how little she'd slept since Carl's great reveal, as she'd begun calling it, it may as well have been midnight. Sleep was at a premium, and what little there was seemed filled with painful replays of that terrible night she'd rather forget. Men! Why did they always have to be so difficult? As she finished pouring, she heard the bell to the front door. Someone must have come in. Her coffee would have to wait. With Margot and Eduardo at lunch and her shop girl Chloe out sick, there was no one to greet anyone who entered. Well, they could wait. She'd only be a minute. She was in no mood to be greeting anyway. Her decision made, Amanda opened the refrigerator and pulled out a carton of creamer.

Daniel entered the front door of the shop with a delivery of uniforms slung over his shoulder. For a wedding shop, he'd guessed there would be more people—at least a few workers, maybe a bride or two. Not that the place didn't look nice. It's just no one was there. He figured they must be on their lunch break. "Hello?" Daniel called out to no one in particular. At a loss, Daniel looked at the tag on the shirts he was carrying. The delivery was for an Amanda Jones. "Amanda? Anyone?" Not getting a response, Daniel grabbed a cookie from a tray sitting on a decorative stool and took a bite. Must be for customers, he decided. Moving on, he headed for the back hall, hoping to find someone to sign the receipt. Still not seeing anyone, Daniel took another bite of cookie and went into the first door he came across—and slammed directly into her.

"What is wrong with you?" Amanda exclaimed, holding the now empty cup in her hand. Amanda couldn't believe what had just happened. The guy from the sidewalk was there and had run into her again, and now practically the entire floor was covered in coffee! Luckily she hadn't dropped the cup, but that hadn't stopped its contents from escaping and going everywhere. Most had landed on the floor, but a few drops had landed on her white blouse, essentially ruining it. Amanda stared at the intruder in disbelief. What was he even doing here? How did he know where she worked? And why did he keep running into her?

"I'm so sorry. I have a delivery for an Amanda Jones," Daniel blurted out defensively. He didn't know what else to say. He still couldn't believe he was talking with the woman from the sidewalk, the woman he had been thinking about all day.

What were the odds? He also couldn't believe he had run into her again. What was wrong with him? Why did he keep doing that? "I'm sorry. Again," he reiterated. "There was no one out front and I thought..."

"You thought you'd go snooping in the back?" Amanda accused.

"What? No!" Daniel protested. "I just needed a signature."

Amanda didn't know what to say. Why was he here? And why did he have crumbs on his face? "Is that my cookie?" she asked, eyeing the half-eaten cookie in his hand. "The cookies we leave out for clients?" What was it about this man that made her so angry? It was probably the way he kept running into her, ruining her things. And that dumb look on his face every time he did it. He probably thinks he can get away with it because he's attractive.

Daniel didn't know how to respond. He looked down

at the half-eaten cookie, then back at Amanda, speechless. "I believe so."

"What is wrong with you?" Amanda said a little too dramatically. She was already having a bad week. The last thing she needed was to be dealing with this guy. "Fine. You know what? Keep the cookie. Just give me my dry cleaning and go." Amanda took the dry cleaning from Daniel and stalked off to her office and slammed the door.

Daniel stood in the hall, dumbfounded, for what felt like a full minute. What had just happened? She had run off again, that much was sure. This time it was to her room, and she'd shut the door without signing her receipt. Should he leave? Should he go and leave her alone? He needed her signature, but she was clearly in no mood for company. But what if he never saw her again? And what would he do without the receipt? Left with little choice, Daniel stepped to her door and gently tapped. "Amanda?" he said, assuming that was her name. Daniel listened and for a moment he believed he could hear crying.

"What?" If she was crying, she wasn't letting on.

"Are you okay?" He didn't know what else to say.

"I'm fine! Go away." She clearly wasn't in the mood to see anyone, least of all him.

Daniel tried to think of the best way to continue. "There's just one thing," he began, "The receipt. I need it signed before I go."

The receipt. Amanda realized she had taken the clothes and hadn't signed for them. "Fine. Come in." Amanda dabbed her eyes with a fresh tissue, then quickly grabbed the receipt stapled to the clothing. By the time Daniel had made it all the way in, she had the receipt signed and was holding it out to him. "Here," she said. Now hopefully he'd leave.

Daniel took the receipt, taking note of the used tissue overflowing from the trashcan as he put it in his pocket. She was clearly going through something, and it wasn't just running into him. "Okay, well, thank you," Daniel said, turning to go. Why was this so hard? Why was he having so much trouble leaving her? Upon reaching the door, he knew he couldn't go through with it. He had spent an evening putting her resemblance on a statue and the entire morning thinking about her. He'd always regret not saying anything, even if he were clearly getting shot down. Unable to continue, Daniel stopped, and then spun around to Amanda. "Would you like to have dinner?" he asked. "I know it sounds crazy given what just happened and what you must think of me, but I haven't stopped thinking about you since the other day. I'm Daniel by the way."

Amanda couldn't believe what she was hearing. First this guy ruins her grandmother's veil, then he spills coffee on her, and now he wants to ask her out? Men! He had a lot of nerve, this Daniel, especially after what she'd been through. Amanda could feel her anger rising. "I'm sorry. I'm not dating you or any other delivery guy. I have standards." She knew it sounded harsh, but that was just how she was feeling, and someone needed to pay for Carl's mistakes. He was just the unlucky person who'd stepped into it. "And that's not part of my plan."

"I see," Daniel responded. He didn't know what else

to say. Though he'd gotten his answer, he still didn't want to leave. "And just what is your plan?" As he waited for a response, Daniel noticed a scrapbook on Amanda's desk that was open to a page with pictures of models and movie stars and at least one picture of a doctor. "This?" Now it was his turn to be blunt. He'd dated enough women who only wanted one thing and was tired of seeing how quick they were to jump at anyone who could offer it and disregard the rest. No wonder the divorce rate had gotten so high, he determined. People were more in love with other people's things than they were with each other. Frustrated, Daniel turned his gaze to the trashcan of used tissues—tissues he imagined were spent crying over one of those guys. "How's that working out for you?"

If Amanda was angry before, though misplaced, this brought it to a whole new level. Seething with anger, Amanda nearly jumped over the desk to strangle the intruder. "It was working," she said. "Everything was working. My life was perfect. I had a plan and everything was going great until you bumped into me! Ever since, it's all been downhill! You're like a bad luck charm!" Amanda had to admit, it was a bit much to suggest he was the reason for all of her problems with Carl, but everything was going great until he'd run into her on the sidewalk. That part of it was true.

Daniel pointed to the scrapbook of suitable men. "Well if this is what you call perfect, you've got a lot to learn."

"Really? And what do you know about love?" Amanda asked.

"I know when you find the right person, none of that

stuff matters," Daniel responded. "I know all that other stuff is just details. I know life is messy and unpredictable, and you can't plan happiness. If you were lucky enough to find the right guy, you'd get married in a sandwich shop in SoHo, and it'd be the best day of your life!"

"Says the dry cleaning delivery man," Amanda retorted. "How convenient. You probably buy your underwear online just to save money." Her blood boiling, Amanda rounded the desk to further make her point clear. "And your shirts at Walmart!"

Amanda almost had to laugh. Had she really just said that?

"Maybe I do!" Daniel had never even been to a Walmart, but her closeness had unnerved him. "And I'll do it again in the future."

"That doesn't surprise me!" Amanda wanted to say more to further put him in his place, but now that she was close to him, she didn't know what else to say. "And while you're there, next time maybe you should get some cologne!" She wasn't sure where that had come from. He actually smelled nice. But she sure as heck wasn't telling him that.

"Yeah, well..." Daniel raised his arm, ready to point a finger to emphasize his next point, but realized all he wanted to do was kiss her. So he did—right on the lips. It was messy and awkward and awesome. There she was, standing there looking all beautiful and vulnerable and angry, and he just lunged forward and planted one right on her mouth. He could tell she was shocked, but she didn't back away. In fact, she'd responded. Her lips had parted. It was only for a moment, but it was positively electric. Pushing him off, Amanda backed away, frazzled and unsure. At first she was speechless. Then she was angry. She was not falling for this. Or him. No way. Back in control, her mind had to overcome whatever false emotion she'd had. "No," Amanda said, determined to put a stop to it. It didn't matter how good it may or may not have felt for that brief moment, she would not let herself go there. Not with the delivery guy. Not with stupid, always running into her delivery guy. Gathering her senses, Amanda pointed to the door. "Get out!"

Of course, the Neanderthal didn't move. He just stood there with that dumb look on his face expecting more. In the silence, Amanda heard voices in the other room. Margot and Eduardo must have returned from lunch. Amanda was certain she did not want them to see him in here. It was bad enough he had kissed her, but she didn't want to have to relive it a thousand times. Amanda emphatically pointed to the door. "Now!"

Daniel opened his mouth to speak. He wanted to stay or at least apologize for what had happened. More than anything, though, he wanted to ask if she had felt what he had. But he knew better than to stay when a woman asked him to leave. So Daniel nodded and said, "Okay. I'm sorry to have troubled you," and left.

CHAPTER FIVE

MARGOT COULDN'T BELIEVE what she was hearing. "He did what?" she asked Amanda in complete shock. Why did the good stuff always happen when she was at lunch?

"He kissed me," Amanda exclaimed. "The jerk kissed me. Do you believe that?"

Margot couldn't remember the last time she had been kissed, jerk or not. In fact, she could really use having some of Amanda's jerk problems right now, especially if the guy looked anything like the guys in Amanda's book. "So? How was it?" Margot asked. "Tell me everything! And don't leave anything out."

"Awful!" Amanda exclaimed.

"Awful?" Margot returned, shocked. "Why? Did he have bad breath or something?"

"No."

"Then what?" Margot looked at her friend, stumped. "Did he have one eye? Walk with a limp?"

"Come to think of it, I think I did notice a limp!" Amanda exaggerated.

"You are such a liar! He did not!" Margot knew Amanda was holding out on her. "Come on, tell me! What does he look like?"

Amanda was having trouble thinking about the moment. She just wanted all memory of it to go away. "I don't know. Average."

"Average?"

"You know...six-foot, square jaw, nice hair."

"Yeah, sounds like a real troll," Margot responded, rolling her eyes.

"I know, right?" Amanda agreed, ignoring Margot's sarcasm. "He's definitely no Carl."

"Thank God for that." Margot was glad Amanda's mind was at least temporarily off Carl, even if it wasn't exactly for the best reason.

"And he's certainly no doctor," Amanda continued.

"Few are," Margot agreed. "Well too bad. If he's that hard up, you could have roped him into your Starlight wedding."

"Ugh!" Amanda made the most disgusted face she could think of. "I'd rather eat dirt." No way. Amanda was not going to let herself think about the possibility.

But Margot wasn't so sure. "Come on; tell me you didn't at least think about it?"

"Marrying the delivery guy?" Amanda laughed so hard she nearly snorted. "Absolutely one hundred percent not!"

"Why? What's so wrong with him?"

"Everything!" Amanda exclaimed. "Not the least of

which is being able to walk without running into me!"

"He can learn to walk," Margot implored. "And you can learn to not be so judgmental."

"I'm not judgmental!" Amanda reasoned. "I just don't want him."

Margot threw up her hands in defeat. "Fine. Have it your way. I guess you'll just have to say goodbye to your Starlight wedding."

Amanda frowned at the depressing reality. Margot was right. It was past time that she accepted that her wedding wasn't going to happen. It was time she called Mayberry. "You're right," Amanda admitted. "I guess I'd better call St. Patrick's and tell them the wedding is off." And with that depressing truth, Amanda skulked back to work.

***

Amanda slumped in her chair temporarily defeated. The emotional roller coaster since her dinner with Carl had been more taxing than she'd been prepared for. Up one minute, down the next...it was getting hard to forecast her emotions throughout the day. And then there was the issue with St. Patrick's. She knew she needed to call. Any delay at this point was unfair. Some other girl who actually had scored a last minute fiancé could really use her day and would be delighted to have hit the wedding lottery by landing such a great place at such a late date. So why couldn't she call?

What was the point of holding on to something that was never going to happen?

Amanda took her phone out and scrolled through the

list of numbers until finding St. Patrick's. She bet Donald Mayberry wouldn't be surprised. He had probably given her a few days out of necessity but probably never had really believed she was getting engaged to begin with. She didn't look forward to telling him he had been right. Dialing the number, Amanda waited as Mayberry's phone rang, wondering if they'd ever let her book there again. She'd probably have to change her name. She wondered if she'd be the first prospective bride to give a fake name to book a church. She figured probably not. It would just mean she'd be going to hell for being a bad person. All those years of praying and going to church would be wasted. But she probably shouldn't think of that now. She'd have all of eternity to think about it as she suffered in misery next to the other sinners like serial killers and Mets fans.

Mayberry's machine picked up, pulling Amanda back to the present. "This is Donald," Mayberry's outgoing message began. "I'll be out of the office for a few days. But if you'll leave a message, I'll get back to you as soon as I return." He wasn't in. Well at least that was something. She'd go ahead and leave a message, but at least she'd have a few days before her shame. "Mr. Mayberry," Amanda began after the beep, "It's Amanda Jones. I just wanted to update you about my fiancé. Can you give me a call when you return?" Having said it, Amanda hung up. At least that was done.

Well, half done. The hard part was yet to come. But at least she had tried. Maybe if the good Lord decided to take her away sooner rather than later she'd only spend eternity suffering with the pickpockets and thieves. One could only hope, she guessed.

Well, at least she had something to hope for. Lucky me, Amanda determined, as she got back to work.

***

Amanda leaned back, letting the spray of the water overtake her. This was more like it. After a long, frustrating week, a few hours at the salon was exactly what she needed. As the water flowed through her hair and the technician, Naomi, worked shampoo into her scalp, Amanda was starting to feel like she'd died and gone to heaven. Maybe crying over a man was overrated. She could just go to the spa every day and be treated like a princess and not have to worry about pleasing anyone. The spa would never run off with Rachel or ask to use the ring she had picked out. It would love her forever. And she would certainly love it.

But of course, before she knew it, it was over. Naomi had included a scalp massage with her shampoo, but inevitably, the water had stopped, and Naomi was waiting to take her to her next station. "We're ready, Miss Jones. If you'll follow me, I'll take you to your chair."

Amanda groaned. She didn't want it to end. "You have no idea how much I needed that."

Naomi smiled at her satisfaction. Amanda was sure the girl must have heard that a million times a day. Once at the chair, Naomi left Amanda with a stack of magazines.

Looks like it'll be awhile, Amanda mused. Her stylist Wendy was good, but that meant she was always juggling multiple clients. Amanda skimmed the articles and pictures of the first magazine before reaching for the next. She had gotten through two whole magazines, and there was still no sign of Wendy. She'd practically read every article on celebrities and hairstyles imaginable and was down to the last magazine. Oh well, Amanda accepted, opening it. That's the price of beauty. Once again, Amanda worked her way through the articles until she was about halfway through, when she saw him. It was the doctor from her scrapbook—Mr. Perfect Doctor. Right there on page twenty-two. That must be how she had found him the first time. He had a column in the magazine in addition to working at one of New York's premier hospitals. Amanda's insides did a somersault. The hospital! All this time she had wasted with Carl, and her dream guy was waiting around the corner. Amanda buzzed with excitement. She had to take action. She had to tell Margot. This was beyond coincidence. It was fate. She needed to get back to the shop right away. Stuffing the magazine in her purse, Amanda raced for the door. "I need to reschedule! And I'm keeping the magazine!" Amanda called out as she flew past the reception desk. Amanda got more than a few stares with her wet hair and inappropriate running, but she didn't care. This was way more important. She had found the doctor!

***

Margot was with a client when Amanda arrived. Racing over, Amanda grabbed Margot's hand and yanked her away, yelling her apologies to the young woman as she dragged Margot to the back hall. "What's going on?" Margot demanded, dying to know what this was about.

"Margot, I found him!" Amanda exclaimed as she reached inside her purse for the magazine. "The doctor!" Amanda could hardly contain her excitement. "He's real! His name is William Grant! And he's in Manhattan!"

Amanda flipped through the pages to the doctor's article and showed it to Margot.

Margot stared at the photo, unsure what to say. "So?"

"So, I'm going to find him," Amanda declared. "And I'm going to marry him!"

She was so sure of herself Margot hated bursting her bubble, but the truth still remained. "You don't know him."

Amanda wasn't going to let reality ruin her excitement. "It doesn't matter! He's a doctor! And he was in the book. It's fate."

Margot wasn't so sure. "It's crazy is what it is."

"I know it's crazy," Amanda admitted. "But I have to try. I have to do something!"

Margot hated to go against her friend, especially after what she'd just been through. "It's certainly something."

"So you'll help?" Amanda said hopefully.

Margot looked at her friend, who was practically humming with excitement, then down at the photo of the handsome doctor. He was certainly good-looking. And knowing Amanda, there would definitely be a good story to tell when it was all over. What could it hurt, Margot thought. "Every pilot does need a good wing-woman."

"So?" Amanda pressed.

Margot rolled her eyes, and then finally nodded her consent. "So let's go snag ourselves a doctor!"

***

Amanda applied a fresh coat of lipstick as she waited for Margot to get off the phone. The plan was set. They would make an appointment with the doctor, and then Amanda would show up looking hot, land the doctor, and everyone would live happily ever after. What could go wrong?

Margot hung up the phone and frowned. "Bad news. They won't let you make an appointment."

Amanda stopped what she was doing to digest the painful news. "What? Why?"

"Apparently your hot doctor is booked up for months," Margot explained. "They'll only see emergencies."

Amanda frowned at the unwelcome news. "So we'll make up an emergency. I do feel a cold coming on." Amanda attempted a fake sneeze. Yep, she was going straight to hell.

"Nope. Not going to work," Margot began. "I tried that. He's a trauma doctor. It needs to be real."

"Like a backache?"

Margot shook her head. "Like blood."

"Blood?" Amanda was willing to go through a lot, but this definitely put a crimp in her plan. She thought for a moment. "Maybe if I hit my head..." Amanda moved to the wall and gave it a gentle tap with her head. "Ouch!" Okay, that was not going to work. Pain was really not her specialty. "Or maybe if I threw my shoulder out..." Ever since a mistimed jump on the Central Park ice rink threw her shoulder out in the fifth grade, Amanda had always been able to count on it popping out at the worst time.

It was time to use her weakness for good. Amanda threw her shoulder against the wall, nearly buckling from the pain. "Ah!!!" Amanda cried out in pain. She tried again, but it was no use. The stupid thing must have finally healed.

"Well?" Margot asked.

"It's not working," Amanda lamented. "Just my luck. I'm finally normal."

"I wouldn't go that far," Margot commented with a smirk.

Amanda paced back and forth. What they needed was a guinea pig. Someone she wouldn't mind seeing with a little blood. Too bad Carl was unavailable. "Any ideas?"

It was at that moment Chloe entered with a bouquet of flowers. "There's a Daniel here. He said to give you these and to tell you he's sorry and wants to start over."

"Tell him to get lost," Amanda responded. She had too much going on to deal with the likes of him. As Chloe retreated, Amanda resumed her concentration. Chloe was already practically out the door before it hit her.

"Chloe, wait!" Amanda yelled. "I changed my mind. Send him in."

Amanda had a plan, a plan she was so eager to get started she was practically licking her lips in anticipation.

Margot looked questioningly at her friend. "Amanda, what are you doing?"

"Well, I'm already going to hell," Amanda responded matter-of-factly. "Might as well make it worthwhile." Amanda fluffed her hair and gave her breasts a quick lift. "If it's a guinea pig we need, it's a guinea pig we're going to get."

By the time Daniel entered, both Amanda and Margot were facing the door, waiting. Daniel noticed the woman with Amanda was smiling but the look on Amanda's face was decidedly unclear. Even so, he couldn't stop thinking about the kiss. He wondered if she was thinking about it too.

"What do you want?" Amanda began.

"I just came to apologize." Daniel had rehearsed what he was going to say a million times on the way over, but now, suddenly, standing in front of her and this stranger, he started to feel unsure. "I know we got off on the wrong foot," he continued.

"And you want to start over?" Amanda interjected. It wasn't so much a question but a statement of fact.

Daniel responded anyway, "Actually, yes."

"Fine," Amanda quickly accepted.

"Fine?" Daniel couldn't believe what he was hearing. While happy with the response, he was starting to feel like something was going on here he wasn't aware of. Whatever it was, he was certain it was not in his best interest. At least he'd be closer to Amanda, he determined. Still, something didn't add up.

"Oh, this is my friend Margot, by the way," Amanda said, turning to Margot.

Daniel smiled, offering a hand. "How do you do?"

Before she could answer, Amanda stepped between the two, interrupting the exchange. "It's funny you should ask," Amanda began, "because she's come down with something, haven't you, Margot?"

"I have? Oh, yes, I have," Margot confirmed,

producing the most pathetic fake cough Daniel had ever heard. "Something dreadful."

"Oh, I'm sorry to hear that," Daniel acknowledged. "Is there anything I can do?"

Amanda pretended to think on it for a while. "As a matter of fact there is. It may seem strange, but there's something that would help. She needs you to... punch her in the face."

"Excuse me?" both Margot and Daniel responded at the same time.

"Well," continued Amanda, "she needs a doctor, and she doesn't have an appointment, so she needs you to punch her, so she can get in today."

Daniel could feel the trap springing around him. She wasn't serious, of course. That was certain. Neither he nor anyone he knew would ever hit a woman, especially one they'd just met. "I'm not punching a woman," he made clear.

"Thank you," Margot replied. She didn't know this Daniel, but so far he wasn't so bad.

"You're right it should be you," Amanda agreed, looking directly at Daniel.

"Me?" Daniel couldn't believe what he was hearing. Yet somehow he knew this had been her plan all along.

"You're the man," Amanda continued. "Besides, we have to look nice."

Daniel didn't have the slightest idea what that meant. "What does that have to do with anything?"

Amanda shrugged. "Everything. Now close your eyes. And don't worry. This won't hurt a bit. We just need a little blood."

"Blood?" Daniel stepped back quickly. "No way. I am not letting you hit me!"

"Fine. You are such a girl," Amanda relented. With that, she turned, temporarily defeated. She'd have to find another way to see the doctor. Daniel was too smart to fall for her tricks. Or was he? Amanda's eyes lit up as she turned, once again facing him.

It was her last chance, her last desperate hope. Amanda smiled as she dropped the bomb. "I'll let you kiss me."

It was not what he was expecting, nor was Margot for that matter.

"What?" Daniel reiterated.

"What?" Margot asked.

"You heard me," Amanda responded, looking confidently at Daniel. "So, do we have a deal?"

It was too much to think about. Daniel's mind was racing at the possibility so much all he could get out was a simple, "Uh…"

It was all Amanda needed. "I'll take that as a yes," Amanda said, and with that, she punched him in the face.

***

As they waited for the doctor in the tiny examination room, Daniel looked incredulously at Amanda. The blood had stopped running and now the only remnants of the punch were the dry remains still stuck to his face and hands. He had to admit the hit wasn't as bad as it looked. In truth, he'd barely felt it. As a former football player in high school, he'd endured much worse, but usually it was from two hundred pound linemen, not a one hundred and ten pound woman. He had always been prone to nosebleeds, which is why it bled immediately on contact, but he wasn't going to tell her that. He knew she felt bad about it. She had apologized a million times in the van on the way over and seemed genuine in her apologies. But he still didn't understand why she'd done it.

"I can't believe you punched me in the face!" Daniel exclaimed, looking up from the examination chair.

"You said 'Yes,'" Amanda responded defensively.

I said, "Uh," Daniel clarified.

"I'm sorry. I was just thinking of my friend." Amanda didn't know what else to say. She sure as heck wasn't telling him the real reason.

Her friend? Daniel puzzled. Then why had her friend seemed to make a miraculous recovery once they'd gotten to the hospital? In fact, where was she? She'd gone to the bathroom more than a half hour ago.

Daniel sat back in the chair, trying to make sense of it all. As he did, Amanda leaned down to put her hand on his shoulder.

"Are you going to be okay?" she asked, sincerely. In truth, she hadn't meant to hit him that hard. Had it really been that hard? She felt like she'd barely touched him, and suddenly all hell seemed to break loose. Maybe she had a hidden strength she didn't know about. Maybe she should be an MMA fighter. As Amanda drifted in her thoughts, she felt Daniel take the hand she'd placed on his shoulder. When she looked down, he was staring directly at her. Amanda felt her insides do a little somersault, just like they had in her office during the kiss. Maybe he wasn't so bad. He could really have been angry at what she'd done, but instead of yelling at her he'd gone along with everything, even though he had no idea what she was up to.

Looking up, Daniel felt the connection too. It was the same connection he'd felt after the kiss. For a moment, he could feel her walls finally coming down. He saw the scared little girl inside of her searching for something more. As much as he'd wanted to respond angrily to what she'd done, now all he wanted to do was tell her it was okay, to tell her it was worth it. He was about to say it when the door opened and the doctor walked in. The very handsome doctor, William thought. The guy looked like he belonged in a soap opera.

Suddenly, Daniel could feel the shift in Amanda's emotions. She'd immediately dropped her hand from Daniel's shoulder and taken a step back and now was looking at the doctor with a dreamy look in her eyes. That was fast, Daniel thought, confused.

As far as Amanda was concerned, it was as if she was somehow transported from one dream to another. It was William. She had found her handsome doctor, and he looked even better in person, if that was even possible.

"Sorry to keep you waiting," the doctor began. "We've had quite a busy day. I'm Dr. Grant," he said, offering his hand.

Amanda immediately took it. Dr. Grant was polite, she determined, as she squeezed his hand. Polite and sexy. She bet he'd never run into her and ruin her veil on the street. If anything, he'd save her from falling by holding out one of his perfect doctor hands the second she'd lost her balance, something she could definitely get used to.

Pulling away, William stepped over to Daniel to look him over. "Now, what do we have here?" he began, eyeing Daniel's nose. "Looks like you had a little accident."

"It was nothing," Daniel responded, a little too proudly for Amanda's liking.

"He's always running into things," Amanda interrupted, eager to turn Dr. Grant's attention back to herself. "Sometimes I wonder how he even manages. But it's not my place to question."

William briefly looked up before continuing his examination. "Oh, so you're not together?"

He'd said it innocuously, but Amanda took it as an opportunity to set the record straight.

"Us? Together?" Amanda laughed extra loudly, eager to put any notion of her being romantic with Daniel to rest. "No! God no!"

"Or just no," Daniel responded defensively.

"He's just an acquaintance," Amanda clarified. "A very distant, non-romantic, strictly platonic acquaintance. Like a cousin."

"A cousin?" William responded, intrigued.

"That's right." Amanda smiled her sweetest smile. "I'm Amanda, by the way."

"Dr. Grant," William responded with a smile, "But feel free to call me William."

"Thank you, William. I believe I will," Amanda returned, sweetly. This was going well, she calculated. Now if she could only get Daniel out of the room, it would be perfect. Fat chance, she knew, as his ailment was the whole reason they were even in there. She'd just have to do her thing with him in the room. Not that she knew what that meant. She hadn't done her thing or any other thing in her life. Men had always come to her. She didn't know the first thing about chasing after someone else. She could start by showing she was caring, she decided.

"So how bad is it, William?" Amanda asked, making sure to use his first name. At this point, William had thoroughly examined Daniel's nose and the surrounding area and had already begun wiping away some of the blood.

"Well, it appears to be minor," William answered. "I don't see any structural damage, which is good. If you don't mind me asking, how did this happen?"

"She punched me," Daniel stated.

"He fell," Amanda laughingly overrode. "In his car. I mean, into his car. He fell into his car."

Daniel looked at Amanda. He didn't know what was going on, but something was definitely happening here. Was she flirting with the doctor?

"That's not what happened," Daniel corrected. "She hit me."

"Ha! Shut up, you!" Amanda squeezed Daniel's arm tight in warning while still smiling at William. "He's dizzy. You know, from the blood loss. He's probably seeing visions." Amanda took a step closer to the doctor, hoping some of her overly expensive perfume was wafting in his direction. "So, tell me, William... Are you married? Do you have children? Any animals we should know about?"

William paused from his examination. "Nope. No children," he began. "And unfortunately, this job leaves little time for relationships or pets."

"So no girlfriends, strange habits?"

"None that I'm aware."

"Great. Do you like baseball?" Amanda was in full interrogation mode now, and nothing was going to stop her.

"Actually, I do love baseball," William answered.

"Great!" Amanda expressed, mentally checking boxes off her list.

Daniel looked up awkwardly. "What is this, an interview?"

"Quiet. You'll have your turn," she said, before turning her attention back to William for the most important question of all. "So, William, how do you feel about quick engagements?"

***

Daniel walked out of the hospital in a daze, completely confused as to what had just happened. Somehow the examination had gone from him being looked at to a pre-date between Amanda and the doctor. By the time it was over, he felt he knew more about the doctor's habits than those of his own mother, not to mention the fact Amanda had given the doctor her business card and wrote God knows what on the back of it. Whatever it was, it must have been interesting because the doctor had smiled and put it in his pocket with a nod of affirmation. And now here she was walking beside him to the van with the biggest grin he'd ever seen. A grin he was certain had nothing to do with him. Sure they'd had a connection before William the perfect doctor had made his way in, but then, in an instant, it was gone. The more Daniel reflected on it, the more the whole thing seemed planned. She must have known she would run into him. She must have planned the entire thing, which meant she was just using him as her guinea pig.

"What was that all about?" Daniel finally asked, turning to Amanda on the ride to her shop.

"What do you mean?" she replied as innocently as possible.

"I mean what just happened?" Daniel restated. "You were flirting with that doctor like you were hoping he'd ask you to prom!"

"Don't be silly," Amanda protested. "We're not in high school!"

"You know what I meant."

Amanda could tell he was upset. Good, she decided. Maybe he'd leave her alone now. It's not like he was her boyfriend. Besides, she had never asked him to show up, just like she had never asked him to run into her and kiss her. The sooner he realized that and went away, the happier both of them would be. Now that she'd given her number to the doctor, she had no further use for him. Talk about a guy who couldn't take a hint. So what if he was a passably good kisser. She was looking for marriage, and marrying a guy who delivered laundry for a living was not in her plan. He was probably the kind of guy who would think it was funny to shove cake in her face at the reception. Besides, William just seemed better, like a guy who made good decisions. Not to mention, she could imagine herself as a doctor's wife. Sure, he worked a lot. But so did she. They were both driven and could understand each other. Heck, maybe she could even have her Starlight wedding. She knew it was probably crazy to think about, seeing as it was so near, but with a guy like William, she certainly wouldn't rule it out.

By the time they reached the shop, Amanda had contemplated every possible way she could deflect the oncoming advance she knew was sure to come. She had promised Daniel a kiss in exchange for his services, and she was sure he would demand payment. Yet it was the last thing she wanted. Besides, Margot would be waiting inside to hear all about the doctor. Margot had snuck out at the perfect time at the hospital, as any good wing-woman should, and would be ready to hear all of the juicy details of what had gone on in the examination room.

Finding a spot for the van on the street, Daniel walked Amanda to the front door where she stopped, hoping to deter him from going inside. If this whole kiss thing were going to happen, she'd rather kiss him here and get it over with. No use letting him linger. They had driven almost the entire way in silence after his initial comments, and now she just wanted him to leave.

"Well, thanks for taking me," she said, hoping to bring the whole thing to a close. "And thanks for the, uh...other stuff."

"Don't mention it. I hope it works out for you."

She knew what he meant, but she wasn't about to admit it or get him started. "I don't know what you mean," she said innocently.

"Yes, you do," Daniel responded.

"Fine," Amanda answered, not willing to argue. At least now she might not have to make due on her end of the bargain. Who would want to kiss someone who didn't want to kiss them back? "Then you probably don't want to kiss me."

She couldn't have been more wrong.

"Oh, I still want the kiss. That is, if you're willing to give it to me." He wasn't about to force her.

Amanda rolled her eyes. For a man she wanted nothing to do with, he sure was exasperating.

"Fine. I'm a woman of my word. I'll live up to my end of the bargain."

"Fine," he acknowledged.

"Fine," she said again, wanting to get in the last word.

For a moment, both stood awkwardly, feeling each other out. Was she supposed to make the first move, Amanda wondered? She'd never bartered affection before or whatever this sort of thing was supposed to be called. She didn't know exactly how to go about it. However it was supposed to go down, she hoped it'd be quick. "Well, I guess here goes…" she began, leaning forward.

Amanda never had time to finish. Daniel's lips struck fast. Once again, they were a million miles away, then suddenly pressed up against hers, taking her by surprise. Despite any mental objection, Amanda felt a traitorous shock of desire pulse through her body. Why did he have to be such a good kisser? The jerk had many flaws, but he really knew how to kiss. Before she knew it, her lips were kissing him back. At least she hoped it was just her lips. It certainly wasn't her. Okay, this had to stop, she told herself. This wasn't supposed to be good, or lengthy, or desirable in any way.

Remember the doctor, she reminded herself. Remember the plan. It took a second, but finally her mind won over, and she broke free, pushing Daniel back to keep him from re-engaging. Once disengaged, her walls thankfully reemerged, and she felt her inner strength return, along with the dislike and loathing she felt for him. She could use that, she decided. She could use anything to keep him away. Backpedalling to the door, Amanda quickly slipped inside.

"I hope it was worth it," she said, looking out but still keeping the door as a buffer between them. "Because it's not happening again."

Daniel didn't think twice. "Oh, it was. Thank you," he said with the slightest hint of a smile," making her cringe.

"Well you're not welcome," she answered. It was the last thing she said before slamming the door shut.

CHAPTER SIX

THE NEXT TWENTY-FOUR HOURS were torture. Why did it take so long for men to call, Amanda wondered, as she paced back and forth in her office? And why did women have to wait for them in the first place? It was archaic. Sexist. Who came up with that rule in the first place? A man? Of course it was a man, she decided. Regardless, it was something that needed to be changed. How many torturous days could women have saved since the beginning of time if they hadn't been constantly waiting for men to step up and take action?

As Amanda pondered the question, the door opened and Margot looked in. "Still no call?"

"Nothing. Do you believe it?"

"Give him time."

"I don't have time!" Amanda exclaimed.

"Well, neither does he," Margot answered. "He's a doctor. He's got patients and surgeries and paperwork to deal with."

Though she agreed, it was still frustrating. "You're right. Of course you're right," Amanda accepted. "I just need to relax." Amanda set the phone on her desk and started walking away. She was not going to wait on some man. It didn't matter how perfect he was. She was too good for that. "He'll call when he calls, and if he's lucky, maybe I'll answer because I'm a busy, modern woman who has pride," Amanda said confidently on her way out.

"That's right," Margot agreed.

Just then the phone rang.

"It's him!" Amanda squealed, running back and lunging for the phone. "Hello? Hello? This is Amanda. William?"

Hearing nothing but silence, Amanda hung up, crestfallen.

"Well?" Margot asked.

Amanda shook her head shamefully. "Wrong number."

Margot chuckled, taking Amanda's hand in support. "Well, at least you have your pride."

"That's not funny," Amanda scowled.

Margot laughed. "You're right. I'm sorry. Come on. Let's go eat some icing. That'll get your mind off it."

She was right. Sugar did tend to solve a myriad of problems. Icing from one of Margot's cakes would be the perfect distraction. "I suppose I could eat a little icing," Amanda admitted. "You know, if you're going to twist my arm…"

Margot put her arm around Amanda, locking her in tight. "Good, then consider it twisted." And with that, she led Amanda away.

Even with the sugar buzz keeping her above water, Amanda's day moved at a slow crawl. After spending a few tortuous hours staring at her suspiciously quiet cell phone, Amanda decided to go out into the store. Standing in a corner, she watched as Eduardo and Margot engaged in conversations with prospective brides. How lucky the brides were, she concluded. All of them were past the waiting stage. All had found grooms and were safely headed toward marriage and future happiness. All of their men had stepped up and proposed. Stupid Carl! Amanda thought. How could she not have seen it coming? Sure she was lucky to have not ended up with a man like that. That's what everyone told her. But it didn't feel that way. Up until the non-engagement dinner debacle, she had believed he was the one, which was why her emotions were still raw. He certainly had acted like he was the one. And then he had ruined everything by running off with Rachel. Stupid Rachel. They deserved each other. They could have stupid children together. At least she knew William was upstanding. He was a doctor. He helped people. Not to mention his name was William. That was the name of fairy tale princes and the future king of England. So why hadn't he called? It had been nearly twenty-four hours already. Surely he hadn't forgotten her already. He better not have, she decided, after what she'd endured kissing that Neanderthal. Yet despite her determination to block every ounce of Daniel in her brain, the image of kissing him forced its way in. A tingle went down her spine. Stop that, she told herself. Think of the hot doctor. Switching back to visions of William, Amanda immediately began to relax. Their kids would be so smart.

They'd probably test out of high school or be born with surgical gloves already on their hands. As a smile grew on Amanda's face, her phone vibrated in her pocket. Too afraid to look at it, she let it ring a few more times before her curiosity got the best of her. It was only Daniel, as it had been all morning.

What was wrong with him? Why couldn't he take no for an answer? He was no better than those stalkers you see on Dateline. So why was there a part of her that wanted to answer it? Probably because he was a jerk, she decided, and jerks always get their way. Well not this time. This jerk wasn't getting anything. Amanda waited for the ringing to stop, yet no sooner than it had, it started ringing again. "You've got to be kidding me!" Amanda croaked, causing the room full of brides to look up and take notice. This was getting downright ridiculous. Amanda was about to launch the phone across the room in frustration when she glanced at the number.

It was the doctor! Amanda was sure of it. It was the same number as the hospital. Should she answer it? No, she didn't want to appear too eager. It's not like she had been waiting for it all day. Okay, maybe she had, but he certainly wasn't going to know that. No, she'd let it go to voicemail.

Seeing the look on her face, Margot immediately stepped over. "Well?"

"It's him!" Amanda responded enthusiastically.

"Doctor him?"

"Yes."

"And?"

"And what?"

"Aren't you going to answer it?" Margot questioned.

"I should, shouldn't I?" Amanda wasn't used to having these problems. She wanted to answer, but she didn't want to appear too eager.

"Of course you should!" Margot exclaimed. "Don't play games! You're too good for games!"

"You're right!" Amanda agreed all too eagerly. "Only immature women play games. I'm going to answer it."

"Yes, do it!" Margot nodded in agreement.

Amanda clicked the answer button and put the phone to her ear. "Hello? Dr. Grant, what a surprise! I'd forgotten I'd given you my number," Amanda lied as confidently as she could. "But I'm so glad you called."

Amanda put her hand over the mouthpiece and turned to Margot and whispered, "It's him!" causing Margot to silently jump up and down in support.

"How's my cousin, you ask?" Amanda shot Margot a questioning look before realizing. "Oh, Daniel... Of course! He's fine. Just as blockheaded as usual." Amanda made a face of disgust. Daniel could eat worms for all she cared. "But thank you. I'll be sure to tell him you called."

Amanda held her breath. With the pleasantries over, it was time to get down to business. Was he going to ask her out or not? "What's that? How am I you ask?" Amanda gave Margot a thumbs up. It was happening. "I'm well, thank you for asking. You want to take me to dinner? Tomorrow? To the Savoy? Oh, that sounds lovely. Let me just check my schedule." Amanda covered the mouthpiece again. "He wants to go to dinner!"

Margot nodded her approval as Amanda looked at her watch, waiting for enough time to pass before continuing.

"Looks like you're in luck, William. I am free tomorrow night." And the rest of her life, Amanda wanted to add, if he'd like to go ahead and book that, too. "Eight o'clock? Great. I'll see you there."

"Well?" Margot asked as Amanda hung up the phone. "Mission accomplished?"

Amanda turned to Margot and threw her hands up in victory. "Mission accomplished!"

***

Donald Mayberry stepped into his office at St. Patrick's and took a look around. It had only been a few weeks since he'd been back to work, but it might as well have been an eternity. Spending two weeks in the Caribbean had been just what he needed after dealing with desperate brides all year as St. Patrick's sole event coordinator. How he wished he could just magically reappear back on St. Thomas in his beach chair with a drink at his side and forget about weddings and florists and anything else he was bound to come across on his first day back. From where he stood, he could already see the answering machine blinking with more messages than he could hope to go through in a month from his few weeks out. By the time he had gone through them, he knew his tan would be faded and the grind of his job booking weddings for demanding brides would already be eating away at his sanity. As he moved past the mirror, Donald stopped to look at his reflection, admiring the stark contrast where his tan skin surfaced from beneath the white collar. Sure he could lose a few pounds. His trousers barely fit, and his shirt spilled out over the sides, but at least he was tan. For a few short weeks, every time he looked in the mirror, he would be thinking of a place other than here. A place without difficult brides with their demands constantly messing up his schedule. A place with sand, beach chairs, and a never-ending supply of drinks.

Settling into his chair, Mayberry looked at the answering machine for over a minute, hoping to prolong the vacation as long as he could. He knew that the second he pressed the button on it, his vacation would be over, and he would be lost in the madness of work. Oh well, he accepted—time to get it over with. After a few torturous seconds, Mayberry relented and pressed the button. The first three messages that came in were from the same woman, desperately looking to book a June wedding the following year. Good luck, Mayberry thought. Maybe you can find one upstate, but not in Manhattan only a year out. Mayberry rolled his eyes at her naivety and waited for the next message. Three down and only two hundred to go, he bemoaned. He'd better get some coffee. Standing, Mayberry moved over to his private coffee machine and got it going as the next message started. "Mr. Mayberry," the voice began, "It's Amanda Jones. I just wanted to update you about my fiancé..."

Oh, boy, Mayberry thought, this out to be good. Though he doubted she'd actually gotten engaged, at least she was using the term fiancé. That was a good sign. Maybe he wouldn't have to replace her after all. No, he'd been in this business too long. He knew a last minute flake when he heard one. She was more than likely buying time. Too bad, he lamented. He had plenty of brides willing to give their first born in exchange for a shot to be married in New York's premiere cathedral, especially at such late notice. Pouring water into the machine, Mayberry made a mental note to call her the second he got through all the messages.

***

As Amanda rode in the taxi on her way to meet William, she couldn't help feeling an unsettling bit of déjà vu. It was the first time she'd been to a fancy restaurant since Carl. And just like that night, it was entirely possible her hopes and dreams would be shattered once again. Of course she'd bought a new dress—that was a given, and had her hair exactly the way she liked it, but that didn't stop the pit in her stomach from reminding her of what had happened the last time. Rest assured, she told herself, she was going to find out what made this man tick, and if she saw any red flags, she would be out of there before dessert. She wasn't wasting another year on a man only to have him run off with someone else again. She would be sure to get all of her questions answered by the time the night ended, or else.

"We're here," The Israeli cab driver explained with his thick accent, turning in his seat to face Amanda.

"Oh, thank you," Amanda said, snapping from her thoughts. After paying the driver, Amanda stepped out of the taxi to make her way inside. Wow, she thought. The place was lovely. In fact, it was so lovely she could hardly believe she hadn't been here before. And it looked expensive. Thank God she had borrowed money from Margot in case it was needed, she decided, as she hadn't been able to find her purse since her visit to the hospital. At least now she would be covered in case William had to make an unexpected exit to save a patient's life and accidentally stuck her with the bill.

As Amanda strolled past waiting guests, she saw William sitting in a corner booth talking to a waiter. He stood the moment he saw her, causing Amanda's heart to race with excitement. William was wearing a tie and looked positively sexy. It didn't hurt that he was over six feet tall. She'd always been attracted to tall men. She hoped he was just as attracted to her. By the look on his face as she neared, Amanda felt confident he was.

"Good evening," William began, putting a hand on her arm. "I got us a table by the window. I hope that's okay."

Perfect. As long as it was romantic, she was up for anything. "That sounds great," she replied. Considering how good he looked, the table could have been in the bathroom, and she would have followed him in a heartbeat.

"Excellent," William said, leaning in to give her a kiss on the cheek. "Then I shall lead the way."

As William led her off, a chill ran down Amanda's spine. She could hardly believe her luck. William was sexy and a gentleman. She knew it was too early to get her hopes up, but he was making it really difficult.

"So tell me about yourself, Amanda," William began after the drink order was in. "I want to know everything."

"You do?" The last person who wanted to know everything about her, Amanda reckoned, was her mother. And even she had her limits. Okay, calm down, Amanda told herself. She was starting to think if they were in

Vegas she'd be on her way to the Little Chapel and a wedding officiated by Elvis before midnight. She told herself to remember this night wasn't just about her. She needed to know more about him to make sure he wasn't another Carl. "You first."

"Alright. What do you want to know?" he asked.

"Why did you decide to be a doctor?"

"That's easy. I love helping people."

Perfect, Amanda concluded. Just perfect. "Next question. Have you ever been married?"

"No."

"Children?"

"Not that I'm aware."

Amanda laughed. He was funny too? If William continued like this, Elvis might actually be on the horizon before sundown. "And you really love baseball?"

"I played in school, and I go to every game I can," he said confidently.

"Mets or Yankees?"

"There's only one answer—because there's only one team."

"Which is?" Amanda asked nervously.

"Yankees, of course."

Amanda practically whistled through her teeth. "How are you still single?" she asked, causing William to laugh.

"How are you?" he responded. "You're beautiful, charming, and you run your own business... Why, you're practically superwoman."

Amanda's heart flipped. Thank you, Carl for being such a putz, she thought. Without you, I'd never have met this perfect man who is an absolute dream. She'd have to remember to send Carl a thank you note. She'd still dust it with anthrax, but she'd thank him nonetheless.

William took Amanda's hesitation as a sign to continue. "The truth is, Amanda, the reason I'm still single is I believe in following a plan. And until now, it just wasn't the right time."

"What's that?" Amanda practically choked saying it. Did he just use the word plan? She didn't know anyone who used that word and meant it other than herself. She was starting to think she was hearing things or this really was a dream. It was all too good to be true. Maybe she had died from eating too much ice cream after Carl dumped her and she had gone to heaven.

"Oh, yes, I love to plan. Some say that's my weakness," William continued.

"Impossible," Amanda assured.

"But now that I'm where I need to be at work and financially, all that's missing is finding the right woman. Maybe that's where you come in," he said, taking her hand.

Amanda nearly fell off her seat. In fact, she was still in a daze when she heard her phone ringing somewhere off in the distance.

"Is that for you?" William asked politely.

Crap. She'd forgotten to turn her ringer off before dinner, Amanda realized, snapping out of her revelry. "I'm so sorry," she pleaded, reaching for her purse. "I must have forgotten to turn it off." Whoever it was, they were going to be dropped from her life immediately for interrupting, she promised herself. Glancing at the number, Amanda felt an immediate surge of anger radiate through her body. It was Daniel. What was wrong with him? How on earth could anyone be that dense? That's it, when she got home, she was going to call him and give him a piece of her mind using words her mother would definitely not want to hear.

"Is everything all right?" William asked, sensing her frustration. As someone who was used to getting bad news by phone, he of all people could empathize.

"It's no one," Amanda explained, shoving the now silenced phone into her purse. "Just stupid..." Amanda stopped herself from going there. No, she told herself, she was not letting Daniel shoehorn himself into her perfect date like the rest of her life. "Just my stupid...cousin." Amanda remembered that's how she'd introduced Daniel to William.

"Is he okay?" William asked, genuinely concerned.

"Who cares?" Amanda blurted before she could stop herself. "That is, I'm sure he's fine. He's just..." Amanda needed to sound a little more convincing and sweet. "He's just a little needy. He doesn't have many friends, so he likes to spend as much time with me as possible."

"You're a saint," William said admiringly, reaching over to take her hand again from across the table. "He's lucky to have you."

Amanda sighed inwardly. William's hand was warm and soft. Yes, she could get used to this. She could definitely see a future as Mrs. Perfect Doctor.

"Thank you, William," Amanda returned, genuinely. Amanda squeezed William's hand hoping to move the conversation to anything other than Daniel. "Now, where were we?"

The rest of the dinner went better than Amanda could hope. William was everything she wanted and more. Amanda knew it was foolish to get so enamored on a first date, but in baseball terms, William had knocked it out of the park. Not only that, but he was eager to be married. What more could she want? As they exited the restaurant, William took Amanda's hand and led her down the sidewalk. Amanda felt so light she wondered if she was floating the entire way as they moved along. Together they passed a line of cabs waiting nearby as William led her just out of sight to a private place on the sidewalk and turned to face her. Here comes the kiss, she guessed.

"I had a lovely evening," William began. He was looking down at her, and his head was practically glowing in the moonlight.

He really was an angel, she thought, sent from above.

"So did I," Amanda responded. She would have loved to elaborate, but her mind was already preparing for the kiss. It was going to be wonderful; she just knew it. She was practically already swooning, and he hadn't even done anything yet.

"Well..." William started before cutting himself off to lean forward.

Amanda's heart raced as she watched William's perfect mouth moving toward hers, inch by wonderful inch. Here it comes, she thought, closing her eyes in anticipation. Amanda could feel her pulse quicken. Even with her eyes closed, she could hear everything around her. It was as if her senses suddenly became heightened, like she was some wild animal, with her reactions sent into overdrive by what was about to happen.

The moment William's lips touched hers was positively electric. She felt her insides explode from the sensory overload. Even with her eyes closed, she could picture his face glowing in the moonlight, and all she could think about was how she wanted more. She wanted it to last forever. She wanted to see his perfect doctor face waking up next to her for the rest of her life. She had found bliss, and his name was William. And then suddenly it hit her. It wasn't William's face she was picturing—it was the Neanderthal's.

"No!" Amanda's insides screamed as she attempted to push Daniel's stupid face out of her mind. The realization had hit so suddenly, she had practically gagged while still connected to William.

"Is something wrong?" William asked as Amanda suddenly pulled away.

"No," Amanda lied. "Nothing. Let's try again." Determined to not let Daniel ruin the moment, Amanda practically dove forward and kissed William again. Normally she would not be this forward, especially on a first date, but circumstances demanded it. William was getting her best kiss, and that was all there was to it.

Yet there Daniel was again the second her lips touched William's. And again, she actually liked it. Disgusted with herself, Amanda forced Daniel out of her mind once again and tried to think of William—perfect, planning William. She pictured William at dinner touching her hand. She pictured him across the table. Finally, she pictured him in the moonlight. Yet each time she did, there was Daniel again. The more she tried to wipe Daniel's annoying face from her mind, the more determined it seemed to stay there. There was only one rational thing she could do, she decided. She would have to find him and kill him when this was all over. Yet when she finally stopped thinking of him, William pulled away.

"That was amazing," William expressed the moment they'd parted.

"For me too," Amanda lied. It certainly wasn't as amazing as it could have been, she bemoaned, thanks to the stupid Neanderthal.

"I'd like to do it again," William continued. "I mean the date and the kiss, of course."

"Me too," Amanda agreed.

"Great. How about lunch, Thursday? And perhaps after, assuming Mrs. Johnson's kidney doesn't act up and pull me away, we could catch a baseball game before I start the night shift?"

At the mention of a baseball game, Amanda was back to dreaming of a future as Mrs. Grant. "I do," she answered before correcting herself. "I mean, I do...think that sounds great."

"Excellent," William answered, leading Amanda back to one of the waiting taxis. "Then I shall see you then."

After helping Amanda into the backseat, William gave the cab driver a fifty, kissed Amanda's cheek, and closed the door. As the car moved down the street, Amanda looked back to watch through the back window, and there he was still standing there looking dreamy. Her insides did another somersault just looking at him, yet the second she turned around, all she could think about was how much she was going to kill Daniel.

CHAPTER SEVEN

AMANDA WOKE THE NEXT MORNING with a smile. The date with William had gone wonderfully. He was kind, gentle, he respected her for what she did, and most importantly, he was ready mentally and financially to be married. The fact that he was a baseball fan didn't hurt either. She wouldn't go so far as to say it would have been a deal breaker if he wasn't a fan, or worse, was a Mets fan, but the fact that she could go to the games with him was a huge plus. Amanda knew it may have been too early to expect to pull off her Starlight wedding, but she felt a small sense of hope springing up inside of her. Yes, it was still just a crazy notion, but it was still possible, and for now, she was fine with that. They'd have to fall in love quickly, but after the way he was looking at her at dinner, she knew that it was a possibility. And the feeling was reciprocated. In fact, she got goosebumps just thinking about it. She'd just have to ignore Mayberry until they both had it figured out. Amanda yawned and rolled over and checked the time on her phone. Good, it was still early. She had a few more minutes to lounge in bed, dreaming about her life with William and how perfect it would be before she got up.

Suddenly, a dark cloud moved across Amanda's brain as she pictured Daniel. Everything had been going so well until his constant interruptions. He had invaded her date twice: first with the phone call, then the kiss. Neither had been ideal, but the kiss was unacceptable, despite being in her mind! Amanda could feel her anger growing again. Why couldn't he just go away? Or get hit by a bus for God's sake? Well, the next time she talked to him, he would definitely be getting an earful and would be told in no uncertain terms to get lost.

***

Both phone calls came midday. The first was William, who called just to tell her how much he had enjoyed dinner. He was in between patients, so they'd only been able to talk a few minutes before he was called away. But he'd told her again how beautiful she looked the night before and how much he was looking forward to Thursday. Even through the phone, she could hear his interest, and it made her heart flutter. After she'd hung up, she spent the next half hour in a daze, floating around the office with a smile on her face before returning to her desk to daydream in her chair. Her revelry was cut short by Daniel's phone call. The second she saw the number, Amanda tensed. She wanted to ignore it. She wanted to make him languish in voicemail hell. And she would, but not until after she gave him a piece of her mind.

"What?" Amanda demanded, putting the phone up to her ear. She was going to rip him a new one. "What could possibly be so important that you need to call me a million times a day?" She felt a temporary sense of relief at letting it all out. What was it about telling off Daniel that gave her so much pleasure? It wasn't like her. She'd always been so nice. But this felt really good. It was like crushing one of those stress balls. She heard silence on the other end. Good. Maybe he was starting to get the message. "Well?" Amanda continued. "Are you going to say anything, or are you just going to keep breathing like an animal?"

After a moment, Daniel spoke. "Sorry to bother you," he began, his voice slow but determined. "I just wanted you to know you left your purse in my van on the way back from the hospital."

It took a while for the realization to hit. "I did?" Amanda tried to remember. He was right. She had been in such a daze after meeting William that she'd left it on the floor of Daniel's van. That's why she hadn't been able to find it, and that's why he'd been calling so much. Daniel was still annoying and a complete Neanderthal, but as least he wasn't as much of a crazy person as she had feared. "Oh. Thanks," Amanda continued, pathetically. Crap. Now she felt terrible. Here he was trying to help her, and she'd attacked him for it.

"No problem," Daniel continued. "I can drop it off in the morning."

Stop being so nice, you jerk, Amanda thought. He had still ruined her date, even if the phone call was for a good reason. She wasn't going to let herself fall for his pretend niceness. She had William. And eventually, when they actually kissed without Daniel's darn face entering the picture, she'd be able to get on with her life. Amanda felt a sense of peace having a plan. Plans always did that for her. She'd have Daniel drop off her purse, so she could have it before her date, and then get rid of Daniel once and for all.

"Fine. Just bring it by when you can." Amanda felt like she was being too nice, and she didn't want him to get the wrong idea and hang around all day. "But don't plan on staying. I've got a heavy workload."

"Understood," Daniel agreed and hung up.

Understood? Wow, her avoiding his phone calls had really started to work. He didn't even try to talk her into going out with him before hanging up. It was probably a trick. Sure as anything, he was going to show up with flowers or a poem and try to work his way in again. Well it was not going to work. Not if she had anything to say about it.

***

As Daniel hung up the phone and looked around at his loft, he felt a sense of relief overcome him. He had finally gotten through to her and would be able to see her the next day. It would only be for a moment, but he knew every time they were together there was something between them. He'd seen it in her eyes at the hospital, and he had felt it every time they had kissed. Yet after each incident, she had pushed him away and treated him like he was crazy—or worse—like he was a stalker. Maybe she was right. Maybe he had become a little obsessed. Despite something in his gut telling him there was something there, perhaps he was wrong. Daniel looked at Amanda's purse sitting beside him and decided he had to stop the obsession. It was foolish for him to think anything was going to happen. The best thing for him to do was give up and move on. He'd eventually find someone who appreciated him for who he was. And when he did, he'd give her the world.

The first step, Daniel decided, was getting Amanda out of his mind. His decision made, Daniel grabbed Amanda's purse and carried it over to the closet. He'd keep it out of sight for the night and be done with it, and Amanda, in the morning. For the first time in days, Daniel felt a sense of relief. So what if he'd lost his muse? He would find another to replace her. Satisfied, Daniel opened the door to the closet, tossed the purse inside, and slammed the door shut. By the time he'd made it back to the kitchen, he was already feeling a sense of relief. He noticed a spring in his step that hadn't been there a few minutes before. Grabbing a Coke out of the refrigerator, Daniel leaned back to take a drink. That's when he saw it out of the corner of his eye. He couldn't quite make out what it was, but it was sitting on the floor in the same place Amanda's purse had been before he'd moved it. Intrigued, Daniel set the Coke on the counter and moved closer to get a better look at what appeared to be a piece of folded newspaper. What in the world, Daniel wondered, as he kneeled beside the paper and picked it up? It was thicker than he'd originally believed across the room and much denser, and it seemed to be folded up over itself in the shape of a square. It must have fallen from Amanda's purse when he'd moved it.

Curious, Daniel unfolded an edge. To his surprise, a handful of photos fell out and landed on the floor. Some of the photos were in black and white with worn edges. All appeared to be old. Daniel returned his focus to the paper. Unfolding it, he saw it was an obituary for Amanda's mother. Apparently, she'd died in an automobile accident a number of years before with Amanda's father. As Daniel read the obituary, he couldn't help feeling sorry for Amanda. She mustn't have been more than a teenager when it had happened. It must have crushed her beyond words. There were references to her mother's life with Amanda's father, how they had met, and their marriage on the day of something called the Starlight Comet. Moved, Daniel set the obituary down and picked the scattered photos off the floor. After arranging them delicately with his fingers, Daniel flipped through them, taking the time to study each as he moved along. Some were of a young Amanda and her parents, but the majority were of Amanda's parents at various stages of life. Yet it was the last that was the most interesting. It had been taken the night of their wedding. It was the two of them standing and holding each other in front of the church with something in the night sky. At first, Daniel thought it was just a flaw in the photograph, but with the way the photograph was centered on it, Daniel realized it was more than a random flaw. He wondered if it was the comet he'd read about in the obituary. Whatever it was, it was one of the most interesting things he'd ever seen. Daniel felt something stirring inside of him. There was a creation burning to come out. He'd been an artist long enough to know not to ignore the instinct. It's how his best work found its way to life. Daniel looked at his sculpting tool and realized he didn't have a large enough stone to work with. He'd used the last of it for one of the church's statues. He'd have to use paint. It wasn't his preferred method of creation or his best way to work, but tonight it would have to do. A creation was calling from somewhere within him, looking to come out. As an artist, it was his job to listen.

Setting his discovery on the counter, Daniel ran to the closet and pulled out a canvas, ignoring the purse as best he could. That finished, Daniel grabbed the rest of his brushes and the paint that would bring his creation to life, before returning to the part of the room where he did his best work. Within minutes, he had everything set. The easel was up and the fresh canvas was waiting. All that was left was for him to begin. Daniel took a deep breath, knowing that once he started, he would be lost to his creation, stuck in that magical world of dreams until his creation emerged. It was the way with art. Once lost, it was difficult to reemerge, and right now he was about to begin that journey.

Dipping his brush in paint, Daniel took one last look at the empty canvas and began. Suddenly, the world around him immediately slipped away. The only thing that mattered was right in front of him, coming to life with every stroke of his brush. He'd was sure he'd known exactly what he was doing when he began, but the more he worked, the more new ideas sprang from within him. Time flew. Day became evening became night. Yet still he kept working, adding layer after layer until finally, exhaustingly, it was done. Daniel set down his brush and looked at the time. It was six a.m. Morning light had already started to flood in. Sapped of all strength, Daniel stepped back to look at what he'd created. Though he'd looked at it a million times through the night, now that it was finished, it was time to see it with fresh eyes, the way others would see it from a few yards away. Closing his eyes, Daniel attempted to wipe all memory of the painting from his mind and think of nothing. Satisfied, he'd done that, he opened his eyes once again and stared at it in shock. It was by far his best creation on canvas. He'd captured the hope and happiness of Amanda's mother on her wedding day. He'd captured her beauty and excitement. And, just as awesomely, he'd captured the comet glowing magnificently on its march through heaven. Daniel couldn't help but smile. It was a piece to be proud of. It was breathtakingly beautiful. And now it was time for bed.

***

Amanda held the earrings next to her ear as Margot stood nearby, rating each as she went along. It was the day of her lunch date, and she wanted to look perfect.

"Nope. Too dangly," Margot said after the first. "You're going to a baseball game, not meeting the queen of England."

"True," Amanda agreed.

Amanda pulled another pair from her purse. She must

have brought every pair she'd owned to the office in order to get Margot's opinion. "How about these?"

For such a relatively simple task, it was taking a surprisingly long amount of time to decide. William was taking her to lunch, so she wanted to look nice, of course, but since they were also going to a baseball game, she didn't want to overdress. The things we do for men, she thought. Not that she was complaining. In fact, if things continued with William like they were, she could see herself not complaining for a very long time.

Amanda held the new pair to her ears. They were simple and silver and went with everything. Amanda had held them back to see if she could find something better, but she knew they were perfect for what she was going for. And since they'd been at it all morning, she hoped Margot would agree.

"Oh, yeah. Those are the ones."

"Really?"

"Definitely."

Amanda pinned them to her ears and took a moment to look them over. Yes, they would be perfect for a whole range of activities. And now that it was decided, she could move on to other things.

"So, what do you think of the flowers?" Amanda asked, referring to the freshly delivered roses sitting on her desk.

Margot laughed. "The same thing I thought a minute ago."

It was true. Amanda had asked Margot a million times already. William had sent roses that morning, and it had only served to whet Amanda's appetite more for the day that was about to come.

"He's definitely falling for you," Margot commented.

"He is, isn't he?" Amanda happily agreed.

"Two dates in as many days, flowers..." Margot calculated it in her mind. "It's too bad you canceled your church reservation. You might have been able to have your Starlight wedding after all."

At the mention of St. Patrick's, Amanda immediately went silent.

"Amanda?" Margot probed. "You did cancel your reservation, didn't you?"

Amanda shrugged, helplessly. "I tried."

Margot gave Amanda a look telling her she didn't believe her.

"I did!" Amanda exclaimed. "I left a message, but he didn't call me back."

"Maybe it's meant to be," Margot returned, suddenly reflective. "Maybe he wasn't supposed to call you back."

"You think?" Amanda wondered, starting to regain her excitement. While she would have loved to believe that was the case, she wasn't so sure. Things were certainly setting up nicely, but she'd need more time to be convinced. Time she didn't really have. "I did bring my glove, just in case."

Ever since she was a child, Amanda had always fantasized about catching a baseball at one of the games she went to with her father, but it had never happened. Since then, especially after his passing, she'd replaced her father in the fantasy with the man she was supposed to be with. She'd know he was the one if she caught a ball when they were together at the game. Of course it never happened with Carl, thank God. That should have told her something. Stupid Carl! But maybe it would happen today. Amanda smiled just thinking about it. Talk about a miracle. If that happened, she wouldn't even wait for him to ask her to marry him. She'd drag him to the justice of the peace that night.

"If you catch one, you'd better call me!" Margot demanded, buying into the excitement. "I want to know immediately!"

"Can you imagine?" Amanda asked. "Talk about destiny! I'd get married by the hot dog vendor before we got out of the park."

The two were still talking about it when they heard noise in the other room.

"He's here!" Margot exclaimed.

Not wanting to delay, Amanda grabbed her glove and started for the other room. Too bad Daniel hadn't shown up and dropped off her purse already. She'd wanted to give him leeway, but now she'd be without it all day. Margot would have to take it for her and leave it in her office, assuming Daniel even showed up. Neanderthals certainly couldn't be trusted, but at least she wouldn't have to deal with him in person.

***

Amanda's first view of William as she came around the corner was nothing short of amazing. How did he pull off sexy casual so effortlessly? In a form-fitting polo shirt and Chinos, he practically looked like a Ken doll. And he was her date. It was going to be a great day for sure, she told herself.

Upon seeing her, William had smiled, looking at her like she was the only woman in the world. Of course, she'd smiled back immediately.

It was all going swimmingly. That is, until William stepped aside, revealing Daniel behind him.

"Look who I found?" William said proudly. Behind him, Daniel had the purse, and by the look on his face, he was obviously confused as to why William was there. "He was right behind me," William continued. "What perfect timing."

"That's one word to describe it," Amanda responded less enthusiastically.

"Here Amanda was talking about how much she wants to spend more time with you and here you are," William explained to Daniel, unaware.

"She was?" Daniel looked at Amanda questioningly. Maybe he wasn't so crazy after all.

Amanda realized she'd better stop this before it got out of control. Stepping forward, she grabbed her purse out of Daniel's hands, eager to get rid of him. "Yes," Amanda lied. "So it was good seeing you, Cousin." Amanda was sure to emphasize the word cousin. "Now have a good day!" Amanda slapped Daniel on the back, hoping he was smart enough to leave, but of course he didn't move.

"Cousin?" Why did she keep calling him that, Daniel wondered?

"Yes, Cousin, remember?" Amanda smiled, warningly. "Now run along so we can go to lunch."

If only that were true, she wished. He could get the hint, and she could finally go to lunch with William. Unfortunately, William wasn't on the same page.

STARLIGHT WEDDING

"Hey, I have an idea," he began. "Why don't you come with us, Daniel?"

"What?" Amanda blurted in panic. She couldn't believe what she'd just heard.

Did she have the worst luck in the entire world? "Oh, I really don't think that's such a good idea," Amanda argued. "He wouldn't be interested. Would you, Daniel? Besides, I'm sure you have deliveries to make."

"Nonsense," William responded. "We can all go to lunch, then you and I can leave Daniel and go to the game. What do you say, Daniel?"

Daniel turned to Amanda and knew immediately he should refuse. While he would still like to get to know her, being a third wheel was not the way to go about it. "I probably shouldn't," he said finally, "but have a good time."

Daniel could see the relief on Amanda's face.

"Thank you," she said, hopeful that would be the end of it.

But William was not convinced. "I insist," he assured. "That way I can get to know Amanda and her family."

Daniel had been through enough of this family business. It was time to set the record straight, no matter how uncomfortable it might be for Amanda. "I'm not really..." Daniel started to speak but immediately felt Amanda's hand cover his mouth, stopping him.

"He'd love to!" Amanda blurted. "Why don't you lead the way, William?" Amanda waited until William was a few yards ahead before pulling Daniel aside. "Just go with it. Please. I'll do anything."

"Anything?" Daniel looked at Amanda, intrigued.

Amanda knew she was going to regret it, but she didn't want William to find out she'd lied, and she certainly didn't want Daniel to be the one to tell him.

"Yes. Anything. Now shut up and go!"

"Fine." Daniel put a hand up in acceptance. "Then after you, Cousin."

CHAPTER EIGHT

THEY'D ONLY BEEN AT THE TABLE a few minutes when William's phone rang. No sooner had they put their drink order in and watched the waiter scurry off, than William had politely excused himself to take a call from the hospital. Of course, he'd returned with bad news.

"I'm afraid there's been an emergency, and I'm needed at the hospital," William explained regretfully. "It shouldn't take long, but I need to leave."

"Now?" Amanda was seeing her future slip away, and as much as she felt bad for whomever it was in need, she couldn't help feeling a bit selfish.

"I'm afraid so." William was used to giving bad news as a doctor, and Amanda couldn't help thinking he had momentarily slid into that role to answer the tough question.

"What about lunch?" she'd said without thinking before catching herself. It was a fair question, but Amanda knew someone's life was more important than a lunch date, even if it could have a hand in deciding her future.

"You two continue," William answered. "Finish the meal, and when I'm done, I'll meet you at the stadium. Daniel can fill in while I'm gone if that's okay. That way you two can spend some time together."

"Oh, great," Amanda mumbled, sarcastically. "Just what I was hoping for."

"What was that?" William asked innocently.

"Oh, nothing." Amanda made a point of taking Daniel's hand and squeezing it in front of William. "Just looking forward to spending time with my dear old cousin."

"Good," William answered, handing the tickets to Daniel. "I'll be back before you know it."

As William left, Amanda could feel all hope leaving with him. How was this happening? Was she the unluckiest person in the world? All the excitement she'd felt hours before was gone. What was she supposed to do now? Was she really supposed to entertain the Neanderthal for an hour while waiting for William? Something told her Daniel didn't have anything better to do or he would have left. Clearly, he didn't have a real job or a boss to get back to, or he would have taken the moment to exit as well.

Amanda thought about leaving, but if she did, she wouldn't get a chance to sit next to William at the game and catch a baseball in his presence. Besides, it was too early in their relationship to look difficult just because of a little inconvenience. Still, what was she going to do about Daniel? She'd have to entertain him, and that was not even remotely something she wanted to think about. Well, there was one thing she definitely could do, she decided, and if she was forced to sit here with Neanderthal man, she wanted to get started with it right away. Drink. "I'll have another," Amanda exclaimed the second the waitress dropped off their drink order. "And keep them coming." Thankfully she'd ordered a martini, and she had William's order to fall back on, so she didn't have to wait to get started. Taking the straw out, Amanda put the glass to her mouth and started chugging. Amanda was halfway through her martini when she noticed Daniel didn't look any more comfortable than she did. They'd sat in awkward silence feeling each other out since their drinks arrived. It wasn't until Daniel had finished his own drink that he turned to Amanda, hoping to break the ice.

"You going to wear that all day?" Daniel asked, referring to Amanda's baseball glove, which she still hadn't taken off.

"Maybe," she responded defiantly.

Daniel raised an eyebrow. Surely she wasn't serious.

"I hope you're not eating lobster then." It was a feeble attempt at a joke, Daniel knew, but he had to say something.

Amanda scowled, gulping down more of her martini.

"You know, you don't have to be so angry," Daniel said. "It isn't that bad."

"Speak for yourself," Amanda hissed. "I thought I was going to lunch with William, and I ended up with you."

"I see," Daniel said, standing. It was time for him to leave. He hadn't wanted to come in the first place with

William there, a man she was clearly interested in, and he had overstayed. "Enjoy your day." Daniel set money on the table for the drinks and started to leave.

"Wait!" Amanda called out. She would probably regret it, but she was already feeling bad. "I'm sorry. I just have a lot of things going on right now." Amanda thought of the busted engagement, the Starlight wedding she would probably never have, and the impending call from Mayberry, and her eyes began to well. "I was just hoping for a good day finally."

Daniel stopped, temporarily immobilized at seeing Amanda vulnerable. It was the first time something other than anger had transpired between them, at least on her end.

"Ever since my broken engagement, things haven't gone according to plan."

"I see," Daniel responded. "Do you want to talk about it?"

"I don't know. Maybe after a drink," she joked. Though she wasn't serious, there was truth to it. Things were still a little raw, despite her attempts at moving forward.

"Then let's have one," Daniel said matter-of-factly.

"What?"

"Another drink. Look, I know it's not an ideal situation," Daniel explained. "For either of us. I'm not stupid. But we're here. We could still have a good time. And then I'll go just as soon as he returns."

"As friends?" Amanda asked.

"If that's what you want," Daniel accepted. "Friends, cousins...whatever it is we're supposed to be."

"And you won't try anything? You won't try and kiss me?" Amanda was starting to feel more relaxed, but she wanted to make things clear.

Daniel held up two fingers in response. "Scouts honor. Let's just have a good time, and then I'll ride off into the sunset, and you can be with your perfect doctor and have your two point whatever babies."

"One," Amanda clarified. "Two point one."

"Of course," Daniel accepted. "Two point one."

Amanda considered it a moment. It wasn't a horrible plan. At least she'd have someone to sit with until William came, as long as Daniel was a perfect gentleman.

"Alright."

"Alright?"

"Yes. All right. But you better not try anything," Amanda warned.

"I told you, you have my word," Daniel promised. "From here on out, I won't kiss you unless you kiss me first."

"Which isn't going to happen."

"If you say so," Daniel said, less convinced.

"It won't," Amanda stressed, her head already swimming from the back and forth exchange, or maybe it was the martini. Either way, she had no plans to get intimate with the paperboy, or delivery boy, or whatever it was he was supposed to be.

Just then, the waitress appeared, interrupting the exchange. "Are you ready to order or would you like more time?" she asked.

"I think we're ready," Amanda answered. "Daniel?"

"I don't know," Daniel responded, taking a long look

at the menu. "How's the lobster?"

Amanda shook her head and smirked. "Fine. I'll take the glove off. But only while we eat!" At least the Neanderthal was passably funny, she accepted, removing her glove, but she still wasn't going to kiss him.

***

The stadium was surprisingly packed for an afternoon game, Amanda noted as she sat in her chair. William had still not shown, so Amanda found herself alone with Daniel once again. Well, him and forty thousand people. Luckily their lunch together hadn't been horrible. Daniel had actually been quite charming and surprisingly funny and knew how to hold a conversation. They'd even managed to talk about a number of things before they realized they'd better get moving or they would be late for the game. Still, Amanda kept checking her phone for signs of William. Where was he? He was taking forever. How was she supposed to catch a ball next to him if he never arrived? They were playing the Mets, and she hated the idea that he wasn't sitting right next to her, cheering alongside her. Well, at least she had someone to high-five and yell obscenities with, not to mention the people around them who all appeared to be diehard Yankees fans. At least Daniel was good for something.

"What do you think?" Daniel asked from somewhere behind her. He had gone off to get sodas and had returned just in time for the game to start.

"About what?" she'd responded, turning to the aisle where he stood grinning, holding two Pepsis in hand. At first, Amanda wasn't sure what he was referring to. And then she saw it. He was wearing a Mets hat, and worse, he seemed to be proud of it.

"What are you doing?"

"Just supporting my team," he responded proudly.

"No! Absolutely not," she said flatly. "You are not sitting next to me wearing a Mets hat!" Amanda moved to block Daniel from getting in the aisle, but he just laughed and squeezed on through.

"But I have to support my team."

"Tell me they are not your team." Amanda could feel her blood boiling.

"Of course they are," Daniel said. "Who doesn't like the Mets?"

"Uh, no one!" she demanded.

"Come on, what's the matter?" he asked, offering her a drink. "You said you liked baseball."

She couldn't even look at him.

"What? Don't you want your Pepsi?" he said mockingly, waving the drink in front of her.

"Not from you."

"Okay... It'll just go to waste," Daniel said, making a big show of getting rid of it.

"Fine," Amanda said, grabbing the Pepsi. "Give me that! But don't even think about looking at me with that hat on!"

Daniel laughed. As much as they'd had a nice conversation at lunch, there was something fun about getting a rise out of her. It made him feel alive. This was going to be fun, he thought.

Amanda didn't talk to him during the national anthem. She didn't even look at him. In fact, she didn't make any sort of movement until the first batter for the Yankees stood at home plate. Then it was as if she immediately sprang to life. Unable to control her emotions, Amanda stood and began cheering for the batter. "Come on, Ellsbury! Hit it out of the park! You can do it! Take us home!"

Daniel looked at Amanda, amazed and slightly scared by her enthusiasm. Not to be outdone, he stood and began cheering, too. "Come on, Neise! Strike him out! He can't hit! He's washed up!"

Amanda turned to Daniel, livid. "Would you shut up?"

"What?" Daniel replied. "I'm just cheering for my team."

"The visiting team!"

"My team."

"Ugh! You are such a Neanderthal!"

Amanda turned back to the field, too angry to look at him, as Ellsbury swung and missed.

"Steeeee-rike one!" Daniel yelled, making Amanda's skin crawl.

"Stop it!" Amanda demanded. "You're in Yankee stadium! At least have some class!"

"Why can't I cheer for my team?" Daniel asked.

"You can. Just not here. And not around me!" Amanda said. "I've been coming to this stadium ever since I was a child, and I don't want to sit here and be embarrassed by some fruit loop Mets fan who doesn't know the first thing about etiquette, or courtesy, or human decency, or..."

Amanda was so wound up by her rant she never heard the crack of the bat or the fans yelling in excitement as the ball came tumbling their way. It wasn't until the last second that Amanda even saw the ball heading straight for her head. Before she knew it, it was there. She had no time to think. She had no time to react. One second she was telling off Daniel and the next thing she knew, he was lunging in front of her trying to block her from the incoming assault. For a moment, time stopped. Sound stopped. Nothing seemed to matter except the ball she suddenly saw careening straight at her at what seemed a million miles an hour. But it was too late. There was nothing she could do. It was going to hit her, and it was going to hit her hard. Amanda was mid-sentence when it hit her head, knocking her back. It all happened in an instant. Before she knew it, the ball had bounced off her head and landed with an anticlimactic thud into her glove. To Amanda, it was over before it started. Stunned, she looked down at the ball and immediately felt lightheaded and knew she would pass out. She'd done that before and knew exactly what it felt like, just like she knew she'd eventually be okay. Yet as the world began disappearing into a black void of nothingness around her, she had a moment to realize her dream had come true. She had finally caught a baseball. She was no longer a stadium virgin. She had become a stadium woman, if there even was such a thing. Elation filled her senses as the satisfaction pushed out the pain, briefly filling every bit of her until she realized who she was with. It wasn't the doctor or Carl or the faceless man in her dreams. It was the Neanderthal. She'd finally caught a ball and it was with the one person she didn't want to be with. As the realization crashed through her euphoria, the last thing she would see before hitting the cement was Daniel watching her fall. The last thing she would hear was the sound of her own voice screaming "NOOOOOO!!!" as everything went black.

***

Amanda woke to complete silence. Gone were the lights, the stadium of fans, the organ music, and the vendors with their peanuts, hot dogs, and drinks. Gone was everything you'd expect to find at a baseball game. Amanda knew she was lying down; that was certain, and she knew she was comfortable. Her head rested comfortably on a pillow, and she could feel sheets wrapped around her, keeping her warm. After taking a moment to get her bearings, Amanda opened her eyes. She was in someone's bed, and her head ached something fierce, but it wasn't unbearable. Amanda could still feel the pounding where the ball had struck. She'd be fine, eventually. She knew that. Not to mention, she was fully clothed except for her shoes, and wasn't in a hospital gown, which was a relief. At least the person who had brought her here felt she was well enough to not have to go to the hospital. Or had she gone already and just didn't remember? The truth was she didn't remember anything after the hit.

Whoever had brought her here had clearly gone out of their way to make sure she was okay. But then where were they? Why had they left her all alone? Amanda looked around the room for clues as to where she was. She could tell she was in a loft by the high ceilings. And it was clearly someone's bedroom. There was a nightstand

and a lamp with an alarm clock, but she couldn't see any photographs giving any indication of who it belonged to. Instead of photographs, there was a cup of tea, still warm enough that it was leaving a trail of hot steam above it. Next to that stood a bottle of aspirin, a glass of water, and a hastily scrawled note from someone saying they'd be right back.

Feeling a dull pain where the ball had struck, Amanda reached for the aspirin. Taking two, she popped her head back and downed them with the water. She must have been thirsty, she decided, because she nearly drank the entire thing. Setting the glass back on the nightstand, Amanda stopped and listened for signs of movement. "Hello?" Amanda called out, seeing if anyone would answer. "Is anyone there?" Getting no response, Amanda reached for her head again. Yelling sent an unbearable stab of pain through her skull. She made a mental note not to try that again as she gently swung her legs over the side of the bed. She knew she should rest, but she wanted to see where she was. Of course, standing took some doing. The rush of blood to her legs only made her more lightheaded. To keep from passing out, Amanda braced her hand against the wall and took slow, measured steps forward as she worked her way to the door. It was open, and she could already see out enough to know she was looking at an artist's loft.

Amanda stood at the door taking it all in. It was quite a space. She'd kill to have this much room in her apartment. It was clearly a working loft, and whoever occupied it was really good at what they did. She imagined it must be Daniel's. He hadn't mentioned anything about being an artist, but then again, she didn't know much about him. Amanda stepped into the room and saw an easel with a white sheet over it, hiding a painting below. Behind it, more paintings stood lined against the wall. She knew she'd have to move slowly if she wanted to see them, but now that she'd committed, she was determined to make it across. Stopping to brace herself on the easel, Amanda took a breath and then continued forward to the paintings. She was just about to look through them when she saw something out of the corner of her eye. It was a sculpture of an angel. The kind you'd see displayed at a church or synagogue with giant wings spread behind it. Even from a distance, she could tell it was special. Leaving the paintings, Amanda walked to the sculpture. It seemed the closer she got the more intricate it became. And there was something familiar, something intimate and personal about it like the artist had made it for her. Amanda looked over every inch of it, starting at the base of the feet, and worked her way up, taking in every detail. Moving past the legs to the torso, she continued her visual journey, marveling at the chest and wings with their intricate feathers, the strong neck and arms, until reaching the face. That's when she realized it. She was looking at herself. Every inch of her face had been captured in stone. The expression wasn't what she was used to or what people around her had ever seen. It was the person beneath. The one she always hid. He'd captured a part of her no one ever saw. Amanda stepped back, overwhelmed. Her mind raced, trying to piece it all together. Why was it here? And why had they used her face? It must have been Daniel. Her mind always came back to Daniel. She didn't know whether to be thankful or angry. In truth, she didn't know what to think. There was a giant beautiful statue with her face on it. A statue she hadn't known existed. Her head swimming from all the stimuli, she needed to sit down. She needed to take a moment. Moving back toward the bedroom, Amanda grabbed the easel, steadying herself as she took another breath, unable to take her eyes off the statue. Confused, she just wanted to hide under the white sheet until she could figure it all out. That's when she remembered it:

The white sheet...

Amanda needed to see what was under it. There was something underneath, and she knew she had to see it. Amanda desperately pulled at the sheet, sliding it away, revealing the painting below. Her breath caught when she saw it. It was like all the wind had been knocked out of her. It was a painting of her mother, so real it was like she was standing there in front of her. In the painting, her mother had a smile and a glow of happiness. The Starlight Comet twinkled behind her, glowing just like her. Amanda stared at the image in awe. Daniel had painted her mother exactly as she remembered her, so real Amanda wanted to reach out and touch her. Tears stung her eyes. All she wanted was to look at the painting forever, to somehow crawl up inside of it and feel the security and love she remembered from being with her parents. Minutes passed, yet still Amanda remained, silently staring at the painting until a latch clicked, and the door swung open behind her.

It was Daniel. He had a bag in his hand from the pharmacy and another from the supermarket with God knows what inside. He took a step into the room but froze the second he saw her. Amanda turned, briefly registering him, but then immediately swung back. Daniel's heart raced at seeing Amanda in front of the painting. She wasn't supposed to have found it. She wasn't even supposed to be here. He had brought her to his loft out of necessity after taking her to the stadium medical room. They had told him to walk her home and let her rest, but when she hadn't been able to remember her own address, he had decided to bring her here. Amanda was showing classic concussion symptoms, something he knew from his football days, and needed to lie down. After giving her his room, he'd run out to get the recommended medicine and something to eat, then ran back so as not to leave her alone for too long. He knew that was important. Daniel thought he'd only be gone five minutes, but the pharmacy had taken longer than he'd expected. Of course, he was shocked to find her awake, even more so to find her in front of the painting he'd quickly covered up when they'd come inside. Now he'd have to explain where he'd gotten the image. He'd have to explain a lot of things, but that would be later. First he needed to make sure she was okay.

Not knowing what to say, Daniel set the bags on the ground and moved closer to Amanda. Standing beside her, he could feel his heart pounding inside of him. To his surprise, she didn't move, speak, or do anything. She just stood there staring at the painting.

"It's my mother," she said finally, simply.

"Yes." He didn't know what else to say. "I found some photos. They dropped out of your purse on accident."

Daniel stopped upon seeing a fresh tear roll down Amanda's cheek.

"I'm sorry," he continued. "It was a mistake. I didn't mean for you to find it."

Daniel paused, not sure what else to say, when Amanda suddenly turned and looked at him like she had at the hospital. It was that connection again. He wasn't sure if it was the painting, but he knew he had to kiss her—so he did. Daniel stepped forward and kissed her on the lips, despite his promise.

At first she accepted it, but then she suddenly jerked away.

"No! Stop! Gross!" she said, shaking her head.

"Gross?"

"Yes! Gross. You can't do that. You can't just..." But then she'd lunged forward, devouring his lips with her own. Shocked, Daniel stood there, his body frozen except for his mouth, enjoying every bit of it until, after the longest time, she pulled away.

"Still gross?" he asked.

"Yes," she responded, but then lunged forward kissing him again, pushing him back to the wall as she did it. It was raw and passionate and animalistic, and despite hating herself for it, she didn't want it to end. It had felt so right after the painting and everything, even though her mind was screaming for her to stop. Warning lights flashed through Amanda's mind, but her emotions overcame them. It must be the concussion, she told herself, or the hit on the head, she reasoned. Yet the more she kissed Daniel, the more she wanted him, the more her insides screamed with desire. She knew she had to stop. She knew she would regret it in the morning. She told herself she had to get a hold of her emotions—that she didn't want Daniel, she wanted William. It was a fact, and she knew it. But every time she attempted to pull away or break free, Daniel kissed her again and it was over. She knew she had lost. Her future might be with William, but for one crazy, stupid, fleeting night—she belonged to Daniel.

CHAPTER NINE

AMANDA AWOKE IN PANIC at the sound of her phone going off somewhere below the bed. What had she done? Had she really just gone to bed with Daniel? Neanderthal Daniel? No, she told herself, it couldn't have been real. It was just a dream, or worse, a nightmare. That's it, she believed, it was a nightmare. She knew she wouldn't have been so stupid. The hit on her head must've just put her into a really deep sleep. But then why was she in Daniel's bedroom? Reaching over the side, Amanda slipped her hand into her purse and pulled out her phone. There were a dozen missed calls, all from William, including the one she'd just heard. She knew he'd understand why she hadn't called him back once she explained about the baseball hitting her head. As long as she hadn't done anything with Daniel, everything would be all right. She'd awoken on her side, facing the door, and hadn't checked to see if someone was beside her yet. If she was lucky, she would just roll over and Daniel wouldn't be there and everything would be all right. William would understand, and they could go back to their storybook romance like she'd imagined. Closing her eyes and praying in fear, Amanda slowly turned to see behind her.

"Please don't be there... Please don't be there..." she repeated as she turned. If she were lucky, she would open her eyes and find herself alone. It could happen, she told herself. Strange things happened after a blow to the head. She was sure it was just a very vivid dream. Having rolled over, Amanda mentally prepared herself for what she was about to see. She'd give herself the count of three, and then she'd open her eyes. With enough luck, this whole thing would be a funny bedtime story she'd soon quickly forget.

"One...two..."

On the count of three, Amanda opened her eyes to find an amused Daniel staring back at her. "Good morning," he said with a smile.

It was at that moment she realized it wasn't a dream. It was at that moment she realized her future was over.

"No!" Amanda protested, falling back on the pillow and covering her eyes with her hands. There was no avoiding it. It wasn't a dream. It was a nightmare, yes, but in reality. "What have I done?" she cried, seeing her future life as a spinster now assuredly on its way to becoming a reality.

Daniel rolled over and kissed her before returning to his old position. "Nothing too terrible, I hope."

Had he really just said that? Her life was ruined, and all he could say was that he hoped it wasn't too terrible? He had a lot of nerve, especially because he was the one responsible for all of it.

"You did this!" she immediately accused.

"Did what?"

"Took advantage of me! You knew I hit my head and wasn't thinking straight!"

"What?" Daniel couldn't believe what he was hearing. It was her who had attacked him.

"And you did it after a baseball game and a fancy lunch, all of which was planned by William!" Amanda knew she wasn't making much sense, but she wasn't about to stop. "You know how women like those kinds of things!"

Daniel looked at her, genuinely confused. "What things?"

"Sit down meals and planned activities! You let William plan it, and then you took advantage! It's practically fraud!"

"Fraud?"

"That's right. Fraud. You should go to jail."

"Thank God you're not a jury," Daniel said, wounded.

"Well I am!" Amanda responded, jumping out of bed and gathering her clothes. "Judge, jury, and prosecutor! And I find you guilty!" Okay, she thought. If she hadn't gone too far before, now she definitely had reached the limit.

"Guilty?" Daniel hopped out of bed to try and calm her. "Whoa, whoa, whoa...calm down. Everything is going to be okay. Just take a deep breath."

"I don't want a deep breath! I want my clothes, and my baseball, and my life with William," Amanda demanded.

"Fine," Daniel responded.

"Fine!" Amanda agreed.

Just then, the doorbell rang in the other room.

"Who's that?" Amanda questioned.

"Who do you think?"

"William?" Amanda's eyes shot open. She couldn't believe it. This could not be any worse.

"I called him when I went out," Daniel explained. "I used your phone. I thought you'd want him to know where you were."

"Well you thought wrong!"

"I'm sorry! I didn't know you were going to..."

"What?" Amanda glared, daring him to say it.

"Nothing."

"Say it," she demanded.

"I didn't know you were going to attack me."

In hindsight, Daniel realized it probably wasn't the best thing to say. If anything, it only pushed Amanda over the edge. Grabbing her purse, Amanda proceeded to hit Daniel with it, making her point.

"I didn't attack you! I kissed you! There's a difference! And I shouldn't have done it anyway! I don't like you! I. Don't. Like. You. Get it through your head!"

Amanda would have kept going. In fact, she could have probably gone all evening if she hadn't heard William's voice in the other room.

"Hello? Amanda? Daniel? Is anyone here?"

William had clearly made his way up to the apartment and let himself in. Within moments, he would find them, and it would be the end of everything Amanda had hoped for.

"Put your clothes on!" Amanda ordered Daniel.

"Put yours on!" he'd responded.

"I am!" Amanda yelled as she struggled to pull her jeans on. She was tugging with all her might, trying to get her leg all the way through when she fell. Stupid skinny jeans, she thought, as she lay sprawled on the ground. They'd be the death of her and William. Standing, she tried again, pulling with all her might, and finally succeeded.

Grabbing her blouse off the floor, Amanda threw it over her head as William's footsteps got nearer.

"Get in bed!" Daniel called out to Amanda from across the room.

"No way!" He must be crazy, she thought, if he believed she was making that mistake again, but he insisted. "Get in bed! You hit your head, remember?" he reasoned. "You're supposed to be in bed!"

He was right. She had hit her head. It was only natural she'd be lying down. Fastening her blouse in place, Amanda dove in bed, slipping her legs under the covers just as William entered.

"There you are," William said upon entering.

"Here I am," Amanda responded with forced cheerfulness.

William looked the room over before turning to Daniel. "How's the patient?" he asked, genuinely concerned. "Is everything alright?"

"Fine," Daniel insisted. "The patient is fine." Daniel shot a look to Amanda, not sure what else to say. "But you're the doctor. Why don't you have a look?"

It didn't take long for William to determine that what Amanda most needed was rest. She'd been through an ordeal, but since only a minimal amount of swelling had occurred, he felt sure she'd be okay without further intervention.

"And you're sure she'll be fine?" Daniel had asked.

"More than fine," William answered. "In a few days, she'll be good as new."

Eager to reconnect with William and establish her relationship in front of Daniel, Amanda took William's hand. "Thank you for coming. You took so long I was beginning to worry."

"I'm sorry about that," William answered. "I'm afraid it was a bigger emergency than I thought. But all is well. I'll just have to make it up to you another time. Perhaps we'll get box seats next time to protect you from falling balls."

Amanda gave him her best smile, eager to forget about Daniel. "That sounds lovely."

"Great," William said. "Now why don't I take you home?"

William put out a hand and helped Amanda from the bed. As he did, Daniel couldn't help but feel jealous. He had met her before William, yet despite what had happened, she was clearly set on being with William.

In fact, since his arrival, Amanda hadn't even looked in his direction. Defeated, Daniel reached for Amanda's shoes. "I'll just get your things."

As William and Amanda left the room, Daniel walked behind them. William had his arm around Amanda, helping her stay upright. When they reached the front door, William turned, offering a hand in thanks, making Daniel feel guilty.

"Thank you for looking out for her. And for filling in for me," William said.

"Anytime." It was the only thing Daniel could think of. He knew if William knew the truth of what had happened, he wouldn't be saying that. In fact, he might be throwing punches.

But he didn't know and it appeared Amanda would soon forget it. William squeezed Daniel's hand in genuine friendship, making Daniel feel worse. "I'll make sure she gets home alright. Don't worry about a thing."

"Thank you," Daniel said as William turned back to Amanda and led her out. She had her head leaned against his shoulder and didn't even look back as she walked through the door. Daniel watched as they made their way down the hall to the elevator. He watched the elevator doors open and close with them inside. As the elevator descended, he walked to the window and watched William and Amanda exit the building and get into the back of a waiting taxi. There she goes, Daniel bemoaned. There she goes, and there's nothing I can do about it.

***

"You did what?" Margot exclaimed, stopping her constant pacing back and forth in Amanda's living room. She was looking straight at Amanda with her mouth open, completely shocked at what she was hearing, as Amanda sat on the couch holding an ice bag to her head per William's instructions. William had a left a few minutes before, and now it was just Margot and Amanda.

"I may have kissed him," Amanda admitted.

"William or Daniel?" Margot asked, confused.

"Daniel."

"But you were with both of them?"

"Yes. But then William left to go to the hospital," Amanda explained.

"So you kissed Daniel?"

"No! I didn't just kiss him! I…slipped."

"You slipped?" Margot gave Amanda a look telling her she wasn't buying it.

"I don't know. My head hurt. I was confused," Amanda pleaded.

"That's not an excuse." Margot couldn't believe what she was hearing. "So what else happened?"

"Nothing!" Amanda promised. She was already going to hell ten times over. Might as well add a little more fuel to the eternal fire.

"Nothing?"

"Nothing!" Amanda wanted to stop there. She wanted to stop the conversation and have it end right there. But she knew she wouldn't be able to hold out on her best friend. "Except…"

"I'm listening." Margot put her hand on her hip again, waiting for what was about to come.

"Except," Amanda began, "I may have slept with him." Amanda winced the second she'd said it, knowing what was about to come.

"You slept with him?"

"Maybe."

"Daniel?" Margot clarified. "You slept with Daniel? The one you call Neanderthal?"

"He's still a Neanderthal! I just…" Amanda was trying to think of some excuse, but in truth, she really didn't have one. "I hit my head, and then there was this sculpture, and a painting of my mother."

"He had a painting of your mother? Okay, that's officially weird."

"No, it was nice," Amanda admitted. "But then I was vulnerable and with the head thing and the full moon…"

"It was the middle of the day!"

"The full sun then!" In truth, Amanda didn't have any sort of reason unless temporary insanity counted, which she was pretty sure it didn't. She'd kissed the Neanderthal, slept with him, and now everything with William would be ruined and there was nothing she could say to change that.

Margot stopped pacing midway and now stood there, shaking her head. "You certainly keep things interesting."

"Thanks?"

"That wasn't a compliment. You realize your life would be much easier if you actually did the right thing every once in a while."

"I know!" Amanda had to admit it was true.

Margot let out a deep breath. "So what did William say when you told him?" Margot waited but when Amanda looked away after the question, Margot realized she hadn't told him.

"You didn't tell him?"

Looking for any kind of distraction, Amanda picked up the remote and turned on the TV.

"Amanda?" Not to be outdone by electronics, Margot walked over to the TV and pulled its plug from the socket. "Amanda? What did he say?"

"Nothing."

"He said nothing?"

"No, because…" Amanda shrank as she said it. "Because I'm not going to tell him."

"You're not? Ever?"

Amanda sat up, ready to defend herself, causing a slight stab of pain to register under the ice. "Why would I tell a guy I want to marry I slept with someone else? He'd break up with me in two seconds!"

"I don't know. Honesty?"

"Okay. There's that? But what about trust? He'd never trust me if I told him, and if I want to marry him in a matter of months, he needs to trust me sooner rather than later."

"Sounds like you've thought this out," Margot said sarcastically.

"Oh, believe me, I have," Amanda responded, not registering Margot's sarcasm. "And this is definitely the best way."

Margot shook her head, grabbed the ice from Amanda, and put it against her own forehead, then collapsed onto a chair next to Amanda.

"Amanda Jones, you are definitely going to hell."

"I know."

***

Mayberry was asleep in his chair when the knock at the door woke him. Once again, it had been another sleepless night. It was the third in a row, and he was starting to feel like he'd never sleep again. Spent Kleenex cluttered his desk and wastebasket. His nose was puffy and red. How much longer was this thing going to last, he wondered? His nose had been running nonstop for days, and it had only now started drying up. It still looked terrible. He'd rubbed it so raw people were actually moving out of the way when they saw him, thinking he must have contracted some odd, horrible illness. An old lady on the subway had gone so far as to tell him he had no business leaving the house in his condition, and if she got sick, it would entirely be his fault. Mayberry shook his head just thinking about it. Even now, safe in his office, he felt ashamed. He wished he could go home, but he had used up all of his vacation days and wouldn't have another one for months. Oh well, he thought. This thing had to end sometime. He'd just have to accept the fact that he'd be miserable until it did.

The knock was from Father Browner's secretary, Sarah. He wanted to see Mayberry right away in his office. It must be important, Mayberry decided, or he wouldn't have sent her to fetch him personally. He'd only been to Browner's office a handful of times, and each visit always brought bad news. There was the time they'd lost Father Henry over the holidays, then the time they'd had the flooding in the rectory, not to mention Mayberry's performance review a few years earlier, which he'd like to forget most of all. It had been during a time when it seemed like every bride was canceling at the last minute during the recession, and he'd lost a number of accounts.

Despite capturing the brides' deposits, Mayberry's naivety in trusting hopeful brides that their wedding was still going to happen when it clearly wasn't had cost the church plenty and nearly put him out of a job. Churches are founded on religion, Browner told him, but they still require money to keep the lights on. From that point on, Mayberry followed the rule that brides aren't to be trusted. They're too emotional. They're too hopeful. And they need to be watched at all times. It was New York, after all. There weren't enough churches to go around. He had no excuse for leaving one of the city's premiere churches empty on a perfectly good day due to some delusional, romantic bride.

Reaching the door to Browner's office, Mayberry knocked and took a deep breath. Here goes, he thought. With any luck, it'd be nothing. Perhaps Browner had called him in to catch up after his two weeks away. He knew that was unlikely, but he could hope nonetheless. After wiping his nose one last time, Mayberry listened for the go ahead to go in. When it came, Mayberry stepped inside and was surprised to find that Browner was not alone. He was sitting with two people. The first was an older woman and the other a girl who looked barely out of high school. Upon recognizing the older one, Mayberry knew immediately his hopes for a pleasant meeting would be disappointed. It was Madeline Helmslow, one of the richest women in Manhattan and the church's biggest benefactor. To say she was difficult was an understatement. She was the kind of woman people avoided. If it weren't for her late husband's money and her ability to use it to her advantage, he doubted she would have any friends.

Unfortunately for Mayberry and the rest of the congregation, she had made St. Patrick's her home, so until that glorious day when she went on to be with the Lord, they would be stuck dealing with her. Mayberry had never seen the young woman sitting next to her, but by the look of her, she was as unhappy to be there as he was.

Browner didn't waste time getting started.

"Mayberry, have a seat," he began, introducing the women immediately. "This is Mrs. Helmslow, as I'm sure you're aware. And this is Caroline, her granddaughter."

"How do you do?" Mayberry replied, still standing, not sure if he was expected to bow or do something respectful in their presence. "I'm sorry; I'm a little under the weather, so forgive my appearance."

"You look dreadful," Helmslow responded crustily. "You shouldn't be working."

"Yes, I'm sorry about that," Mayberry said, sitting. He didn't know what else to say. He fully agreed, but unless she was willing to convince Father Browner to pay for his days off, there was really nothing he could do. This was already starting poorly, Mayberry determined, exactly as he thought it would.

Eager to move things along, Browner got straight to the point. "The reason I brought you in here, Donald, is we have a bit of a situation."

"Caroline has gotten herself into a situation," Helmslow clarified. "And we need your help to get her out of it."

"It's not a situation, Grandma!" the young girl protested. "I'm fine. It's the twenty-first century!"

"You're not fine. You'll be fine when I say you are," Helmslow demanded. The elder Helmslow was clearly upset about something, Mayberry surmised, and if he was here, he had a good idea what it was.

"The fact of the matter," Helmslow began, "is that Caroline has gotten herself pregnant by some vagabond..."

"I did not get myself pregnant! And he is not some vagabond!" Caroline responded, upset. "He's my boyfriend!"

"Regardless," Helmslow continued, "as we all know, it is improper. And it's a sin."

"It's not a sin. He loves me," Caroline protested.

"It's a sin if you're not married," Helmslow demanded. "And Father Browner will back me up on that."

By the look on Browner's face, Mayberry concluded the man would say just about anything to get the meeting over with.

"We don't need to be married," Caroline pleaded fruitlessly.

"You do in this family! And that's all there is to it. Now stopping making this difficult or you won't be in this family any longer."

It was clearly the final word, as Caroline immediately turned and folded her arms, sulking.

"So you see, Mr. Mayberry," Helmslow continued, directing her look to Mayberry. "We need you to find us a wedding day and do it immediately." Helmslow reached into her purse and pulled out a piece of paper and handed it to Mayberry.

Mayberry looked at the paper. On it were a few dates only a few months out. Mayberry could already feel his insides tightening.

"These are the dates that are acceptable," Helmslow continued. "It can't be too far out for obvious reasons, and I'll be out of town just before and after, so the wedding must fall on one of those few weekends. Let me know which works better for you and we'll get started."

Mayberry could feel his throat going dry. Did she really expect him to have something available in a matter of months? He barely had an opening in the next two years.

"I'm sorry," Mayberry began as kindly as he could manage. "But I don't think that's possible. It would be impossible for me to find something at this late a date."

"Excuse me?" Helmslow responded, sitting up in her chair. She was clearly not used to being told no, and this was no exception. Helmslow turned, directing a leveled gaze at Browner. "Father Browner?"

Browner shifted uncomfortably. This was not going well and could turn into a disaster if allowed to continue. The last thing he wanted was to upset his biggest benefactor. It would be disastrous for their budget. "What he means, Mrs. Helmslow, I believe...is that it will be difficult. But I have full faith in Mr. Mayberry that he can find one of those dates for you, and everything will work out. Isn't that right, Donald?"

The words were a directive, not a question. It was little matter to anyone that a written contract had been signed with other prospective brides. It was little matter that his life just got a lot more complicated. Mayberry would appease the Helmslows, or there would be hell to pay, and he had no doubt he would be the one paying it.

Browner stared at Mayberry until he was sure he'd gotten the point. "I said, isn't that right, Donald?"

Mayberry crouched in his chair, wishing he could just disappear right there. What they were asking was impossible, and everyone in the room knew it, but of course that didn't matter. All that mattered was that Helmslow got her way. Defeated, Mayberry dropped his head to his chest with nothing more to say. "Of course, sir. I'll do my best." To which Helmslow smiled, pleased to have gotten her way.

"See, Caroline? It's just as I told you. That wasn't so hard," she said proudly. Then, satisfied, she got up to leave.

Back in his office, Mayberry collapsed into his chair and opened the appointment calendar on his computer. He didn't know how he was going to do the impossible and find an open slot that didn't exist, and he didn't want to start. He just wanted to magically disappear and reappear back in his own bedroom. His cold wasn't going away, and now he had a headache after dealing with the likes of Helmslow. He knew it would be bad the second he saw her, and she had lived up to his worst expectations. Just a quick glance at the appointment book told Mayberry everything he needed to know. The month in question, in fact the entire summer and fall, was blocked off with weddings. Unless someone canceled at the last minute, he saw no way to give Miss Helmslow what she wanted without causing problems. Mayberry typed in the two weekends Helmslow had given him, hoping for a miracle. Unfortunately, twin brides Fergie and Felicity, who had convinced their respective fiancés to have a double wedding extravaganza, had booked the first weekend and paid the entire thing in advance. Mayberry wasn't so sure about the extravaganza part, but unless they both came down with an illness, there was little chance of them backing out. Disappointed, Mayberry clicked to the following weekend and immediately sat up. It was Amanda Jones. Surely, if anyone was a sure thing to cancel, it was her. He'd called her recently after his trip, but she'd yet to call him back. Surely she was avoiding him. She must have been mistaken on her fiancé's proposal. With any luck, she would still be without a fiancé, and he could replace her with Helmslow's granddaughter without fear of legal ramifications. All he needed was proof she was lying. But how would he get that? Mayberry leaned back in his chair searching for a solution. He had nearly fallen asleep when it hit him. He'd have her come in with her fiancé and meet him personally. When she didn't show or made up excuses, he'd drop her and replace her with Helmslow.

Happy for the first time in weeks, Mayberry picked up his phone and dialed Amanda's number.

***

Daniel was lying in bed going over everything that had happened and didn't know what to make of any of it. On the one hand, he was glad he'd gotten to spend time with Amanda and had broken through some of her walls, not to mention being intimate, but on the other, he couldn't dismiss the fact that she still acted like she couldn't stand him. She was in such a hurry to marry some fictional dream man, that she hadn't stopped to look at what was in front of her, and the few times she had, it had been short lived. No sooner had she opened up than she'd panic and revert back to her dismissive ways. There must be a reason, he thought. There must be something she wasn't telling him. It probably had something to do with her parents' deaths. Or maybe it was that scrapbook she seemed to always have with her. Whatever it was, he was just wishing he could figure it out, when the phone rang.

It took Daniel a moment to realize the phone wasn't his. He'd picked it up from the other side of the bed and answered it without thinking, his mind too caught up in his daydreams to notice. It was only after the caller had asked for Amanda that he'd actually realized it was hers. It must have dropped out of her pocket sometime after she'd jumped in bed when William had come in. The caller identified himself as someone named Mayberry.

By the tone of his voice, Daniel could tell he was really eager to speak with her.

"I'm sorry," Daniel began, "this is Amanda's phone, but she's not here right now."

"Not there?" Mayberry responded, disappointed. It must be Amanda's fiancé, he determined, if he was answering the phone for her. Mayberry wondered if it was the elusive Carl. Perhaps if he played it right he could find out all he needed to know without even speaking with Amanda. At the very least, he could find out if they were engaged, and if they weren't, he could dump them and replace them with Helmslow's granddaughter. Mayberry decided to start with an easy one. "This is Donald from St. Patrick's. You must be Carl."

"Carl?" Daniel replied. He had never heard the name before. William he'd heard of, but Carl? Daniel was starting to wonder how many guys Amanda actually had. No wonder she didn't have time for him.

"Her fiancé," Mayberry clarified.

"Fiancé?" Daniel couldn't even pretend to mask the surprise in his voice.

On his end, Mayberry already tasted victory. If this was Carl, which he doubted, it was clear he hadn't proposed like she'd planned, and if that was the case, he would certainly know nothing about St. Patrick's. It was time to go for the jugular. "Yes," Mayberry continued. "I'm calling about your and Amanda's wedding." Mayberry practically laughed at the silence coming from the other end of the phone. Whoever this guy was, he was clearly confused. Mayberry almost felt bad. If it weren't for Helmslow breathing down his neck, he certainly would have felt sorry for the guy.

"My and Amanda's wedding?" Daniel didn't really know what was going on, but as much as this had all come as a shock, he needed to remember this wasn't his phone and he shouldn't have answered it in the first place. But he still wanted to know who Carl was and exactly how he had gone this long without hearing about him. Left with no choice, he decided to play along and just hope Amanda never found out.

"Of course, our wedding," Daniel pretended to suddenly remember. "We're really looking forward to it."

It was Mayberry's turn to be confused. "So you know about it, the wedding at St. Patrick's?"

"Of course," Daniel lied as confidently as he could.

"But remind me again, what date was it? I keep getting the dates mixed up. I don't have my calendar in front of me."

"September twenty-fourth," Mayberry answered. "The day of that Starflight or Starbright Comet thingy." Mayberry couldn't believe he'd forgotten the name after how much Amanda had droned on about it in their first meeting. She'd given him so many useless details about its arrival he could practically track its movements around the universe by memory.

"Right. The comet." It was starting to come together for Daniel. But he still didn't know who Carl was or why Amanda would pretend to be getting married when she clearly wasn't. The whole thing didn't make sense. He needed to know more. And to know more, he'd have to get more out of Donald. "Oh, so you know about the comet?" Daniel asked as innocuously as possible. "I didn't realize she'd told you."

"Are you kidding?" Mayberry practically choked with laughter. "It's all I heard about for two hours! How special the day was, how her mother and grandmother got married on the same day, how it only comes once every thirty years, how she'd always dreamed of having her own Starlight wedding at St. Patrick's. I was skeptical of a bride who wanted to book so far in advance, especially without being engaged, but she was determined. I guess she found her groom to go along with it." Though he'd said it, Mayberry still didn't believe it.

What he needed was a plan to make sure the person he was talking to really was Amanda's fiancé. For all he knew, he was a friend covering up for her. And Mayberry certainly wasn't giving up until he knew for sure this guy was who he said he was. Mayberry had never met Carl, but it was way past time for him to do so. It was time to put his plan into action. It was time to force them to come to his office. And when they didn't show up he'd know none of it was real. Then Helmslow would get her wedding, and he could keep his job.

"Well, if there's nothing else..." Daniel began, trying to get off the phone, "I'll tell Amanda you called."

"Actually, there is one small detail," Mayberry said. "It's customary to have a final pre-wedding meeting at the cathedral with our brides and grooms. It's just a formality, of course, but I'm sure you can appreciate how important it is for us to get to know our couples and make sure we're on the same page with all of the arrangements. How does the morning of the twenty-first sound? Say, eleven?"

"Uhhh..." Daniel didn't know what to say. When Amanda found out he not only answered her phone, but also ruined her last hopes of having her Starlight wedding, she'd go ballistic. "Maybe I should have you speak with Amanda," Daniel responded desperately. "That way she can look at her calendar."

Nice try, Mayberry thought. He wasn't falling for that one. It was time for him to be firm. "I'll tell you what, I'll pencil it in for the twenty-first, and if she has a problem, she can call me. See you then." And with that, he hung up.

Daniel stared at the phone for a full minute. Had Mayberry really just hung up on him? What was he supposed to do now? Tell Amanda? That did not sound appealing. He could just imagine her reaction. Maybe he should just pretend it never happened or throw the phone in the Hudson and plead ignorance. Daniel groaned and fell back onto the bed and shook his head. Why did these things always happen to him?

***

As Daniel lay in bed, he thought about the phone call. So that was it. Amanda wanted to be married on the same day as her mother and grandmother. And she must've made up this Carl guy to save her wedding, unless... Daniel closed his eyes as the realization hit. She had been engaged. Carl was real, but their relationship must have ended. No wonder she was so emotionally erratic. It was what she alluded to during lunch before the baseball game. She'd not only lost her boyfriend, or fiancé, or whatever he was, she'd also lost the wedding she'd been planning for God knows how long.

Daniel couldn't help but feel sorry for her. That must be why she'd responded so much to the painting of her mother and why she kept pushing him away. She was on a deadline, and he was getting in the way. Grabbing his phone, Daniel pulled up a browser and did a quick search for the Starlight Comet. After a few missteps, he found what he was looking for on Wikipedia. The Starlight Comet would appear on September the twenty-fourth and then wouldn't appear again for another thirty years. Thirty years? Daniel couldn't believe it. Like it or not, if Amanda didn't marry this year, she would never get her Starlight wedding.

CHAPTER TEN

AMANDA SLID INTO THE PRIVATE Starlight Wedding's bathroom, closed the door behind her, and collapsed into it. With the rush of summer weddings nearing their peak, the place was packed. How was it possible there were so many brides this time of year in the city? There couldn't possibly be enough churches to accommodate them all. That was something she of all people should know. They'd swarmed the shop the second it had opened, and every hour there seemed to be a new wave of brides clamoring for her attention, and now her head was hurting something fierce. Popping an aspirin, Amanda held her forearm to her head, thankful the day would be over soon. At least she had dinner to look forward to. William had promised to make up for his absence the day before by taking her somewhere romantic. With her head still hurting, she had been tempted to postpone, but time was of the essence. If she didn't get a proposal soon, it'd be over for her Starlight wedding. Taking her makeup bag from the drawer where she'd stowed it, Amanda pulled out a bottle of eyeliner and leaned over the sink to put it on over her existing makeup. Smokey eyes were a plus for a hot date, but they didn't exactly work in a bridal shop. William would be here any minute, and she wanted to be ready. It wasn't the most ideal circumstance to go on a date after work, but she certainly wasn't complaining. With any luck, she'd be married soon, and then perhaps she'd hire another person to help around the shop. Amanda paused and smiled just thinking about it. Everything was going perfectly. Well, almost everything. There was still Daniel. Amanda's smile dissipated. Why had she been intimate with him? Just thinking about it made her skin crawl. It had to be the hit in the head, she convinced herself. Regardless, it was one time, and it would never happen again. She was not about to be Mrs. Deliveryman. The next time he showed up unannounced, she was going to tell him to get lost once and for all. Little did she know it wouldn't take long for that to happen.

"Amanda?" a voice asked after a knock on the door. It was Daniel. What was he doing here? He clearly didn't appreciate boundaries or the fact that this was a place of business. At least now it was her chance to get rid of him.

"What?" she yelled through the door, her annoyance clearly apparent.

"It's Daniel."

"Yes, I know! Now go away once and for all!" Amanda smiled at herself, proud that she had actually said it. Of course, she knew he wouldn't listen.

"Really?" he responded, hurt.

God, he sounded like a wounded animal, she thought. Stupid pansy. Grow up. Groaning, Amanda turned the handle and opened the restroom door.

"What do you want?" she asked.

"Good to see you too," he answered, taking out her phone and waving it in front of her. "You left your phone in my bedroom." Handing it over, Daniel waited for a reaction but nothing came. "Well?"

"Well, what?" Amanda responded coldly.

"That's it?"

"What's it?

"You're just going to pretend like nothing happened?"

"Nothing did happen. At least nothing I want to remember."

"So you don't want to talk about it?"

"Nope." She knew exactly what he was referring too, and the sooner both of them forgot about it, the better.

"Fine." Daniel turned to leave, but then, thinking about it, he swung back around. There was something he needed to say. "You know, you pretend to hate me, but I think you're just afraid you might actually like me."

"Is that right?" she answered.

"Yes. And I think you're going to regret it when you have time to think about it, which you will when you're seemingly perfect doctor is at work twenty-four-hours a day."

"Thanks for the insight. Is that all?" Amanda turned away and went back to putting on makeup, hoping he'd get the hint. She didn't have time for this. She had a date to get ready for.

Daniel wanted to walk away. He wanted to leave her

in the mess of her own doing, but he knew he had more to say. "No. It isn't. I know about your Starlight wedding and your reservations at the church. I know what you're trying to do. I'm sorry it didn't work out with Carl, but if you think getting the doctor to fall in love with you in time, just to have a great wedding, will somehow make the rest of your life better, you're going to regret it."

Amanda could feel herself getting flushed. How did he know all of this? And why did he think it was any of his business? Turning back to him, she pointed a finger warningly. "Listen, you may think you know what you're talking about but you don't. You don't know anything. You just met me. You know nothing about me, or Carl, or anything that could make me happy. And as the future is concerned, the only thing I know is that you won't be in it!"

"Fine," Daniel answered. "You win. I'm leaving. You're welcome about your phone, by the way, even though you weren't kind enough to thank me. And for the record, St. Patrick's called."

"What?" She hadn't expected this.

"That's right. You and your fiancé, Carl, have a meeting with Mayberry on the twenty-first about your engagement. Good luck with that. I hope it all works out for both of you!" With that, Daniel turned and walked off.

"Wait!" Amanda chased after Daniel. Grabbing his arm, she spun him around. "Who did you talk to?"

"Someone named Mayberry. He seemed very eager to hear about you and Carl. Hey, I have an idea. Why don't you take William with you as well? I'm sure Mr. Mayberry would be very excited to meet him, too. Maybe you can marry both of them. It could be a double Starlight wedding. Or do you have another fake fiancé you're planning to use?"

Amanda wanted to say something witty to blast Daniel into another orbit, but just as she was about to speak, William walked up stopping her midway.

"Hey, you two. How's everyone doing today?" William asked innocently, leaning in to give Amanda a kiss.

"I was just leaving," Daniel responded icily. "Enjoy your night. Ask her about her plans for the future. I'm sure it'll be very illuminating."

With that, Daniel stormed off.

"What's wrong with him?" William asked, watching Daniel leave.

Amanda shook her head. "Who knows? He probably lost a dry cleaning order."

Amanda rolled her eyes and hooked her arm around William's, pretending not to care.

"So, where are we going to dinner, Doctor?"

***

The dinner with William had been wonderful, in fact near perfect, Amanda thought. Except for the part where she had been thinking about how much she wanted to kill Daniel. How did he know about St. Patrick's? Had he really answered her phone? That was so disrespectful. Who did he think he was?

"Is everything alright?" William asked from across the table, catching Amanda looking off into space.

"Yes, fine." The truth was even without worrying

about Daniel, she still had the matter of the church to deal with. If she didn't show up with Carl for her appointment with Mayberry, she'd lose all hope, no matter how slight it was, of having her Starlight wedding. "I just have a problem, and I'm having trouble figuring out how to solve it."

"Something at work?" William asked.

Amanda questioned whether she should continue. Tread carefully she told herself, or you'll blow this relationship out of the water before it begins. Amanda shook her head, "No, it's something else," she began. "Somewhere I need to be, and I need someone to go with me, but the person I'm supposed to go with is unable to attend."

"Is it something I can help you with?" William asked innocently, hoping to help.

"I wish." Amanda almost laughed at the idea. Talk about pressure. Inviting a guy you had just started dating to a church where you were hoping to marry him a few months later and had already set a date to marry someone else would be so desperate it would be comical.

To William's credit, he let it drop. Reaching across the table, he took Amanda's hand and looked at her with his most comforting gaze. "Well, let me know if there's anything I can do."

See, this is how it's supposed to be, Amanda thought. Screw Daniel. And screw Carl and everyone else like them. They could all go to you know where. She had a real man who happened to be a doctor. And by the way he was looking at her, he was just as happy to have her as she was to have him.

STARLIGHT WEDDING

"Thank you," Amanda answered, and she meant it. Still, for the rest of dinner Amanda was only half there. The other part of her was thinking about Mayberry and St. Patrick's. If things continued to progress this quickly with William, she could possibly be engaged in time to get her wedding, but it would all be for nothing if she lost her booking at St. Patrick's. She'd have to come up with a plan and to do so she needed Margot. Amanda smiled at William as she took a bite of pasta. As soon as she got home, Operation Save Starlight Wedding would begin.

***

"Operation what?" Margot asked as she made her way around the island in Amanda's kitchen with a cup of freshly brewed coffee.

"Operation Save Starlight Wedding!" Amanda exclaimed. "What do you think?"

"I've heard worse," Margot admitted, pouring a mountain of sugar in her cup before taking a sip. "But what does it entail? We're not doing anything illegal are we?"

"Of course not!" Amanda answered, though in all honesty it took a moment to think about it. "Actually, I don't know. I haven't come up with the plan yet. That's why you're here. We're going to come up with it together."

"You want me to come up with a plan to save a wedding that isn't real with a groom that doesn't exist so you can replace him with a man that's not your boyfriend?"

"Exactly!" Amanda answered. "See, you get me."

Margot shook her head again. "Sometimes I wish I didn't."

"So, are you in?"

Margot pretended to think on it. "Oh, alright, of course I'm in. Does it look like I have anything better to do? Don't answer that."

"Fine," Amanda agreed.

"So where do we start?" Margot asked after a long sip of coffee.

"Well, we need a way to make St. Patrick's believe I have a fiancé."

"Which you don't."

"And that he loves me."

"Which is impossible."

"Who knows we're getting married."

"Which you aren't."

"Right. So what do we do?"

Margot didn't know how to answer. "I have no idea," she said, sliding onto a stool at the counter.

"Oh, come on! I need you to help me through this!" Amanda pleaded.

"Alright." Margot accepted, thinking. "Well, first you need a groom."

"That's what I thought."

"What about William?"

"Definitely not! He can't know."

"Daniel?"

"No way."

Margot thought on it a moment. This wasn't going to be easy. "Well you need someone quick, and you don't have many options. Do you know anyone else?"

Amanda racked her brain. "I don't think so."

"What about Eduardo?" Margot asked.

"He'll be out of town."

"Too bad. It needs to be someone who knows you well enough he could pass for a fiancé." Margot paused and then got an idea.

"What?" Amanda questioned, seeing the look on her face.

"There is one person. He's not the most ideal candidate, mind you, and would require a little clean up...but I know for a fact he's available," Margot reasoned.

"Who? Tell me!" Amanda begged.

"Alright, but you're not going to like it," Margot cautioned, then leaned in and whispered a name in Amanda's ear.

"No way," Amanda said immediately.

"He's the only one who knows you," Margot explained.

"You want me to take Henry? The homeless guy?" Amanda asked doubtfully. "How? It would never work."

Margot had come up with a lot of crazy ideas over the years, but transforming Henry into her fiancé for her meeting with Mayberry had to be one of the most ridiculous things Amanda had ever heard.

"Come on," Margot implored. "Never say never."

"That's a James Bond movie."

"Well, at this moment, James Bond is all we got. Who else are you going to get?"

Amanda hated to admit it, but Margot was right. Everyone else she knew worked during the week and would be unavailable. And truth be told, though a bit older, a cleaned up Henry would make quite the specimen.

"Well?" Margot asked. "What do you think?"

"I still think you're crazy..."

"But?"

"But since we have no choice..." Amanda shook her head at what she was about to say. "I say we go to the alley and find our new Carl."

***

Amanda and Margot waited nervously outside the Starlight dressing room for Henry to exit. It had been almost five minutes since he'd gone inside with the wardrobe Amanda had bought for him, and neither could wait to see what he'd look like with it on. Of course the idea to use Henry was bold and reckless, Amanda knew, but desperation left her little choice. Though a few years older, and yes, currently housing challenged, Henry could at least hold a conversation. Sure, it was a gamble, but she didn't really have another choice. She'd have to show up with someone Thursday, and Henry seemed to know as much about her as anyone and she trusted him. So what if he was homeless? He wasn't a drunk or in trouble with the law, he just didn't care to live by other's rules. What was wrong with that, she wondered? Of course, now that it was time to put her crazy plan to action, Amanda was starting to have second thoughts. Amanda was still thinking about the madness of it all, when the changing room door opened, and a dapper looking Henry stepped out.

"Well, what do you think, my dears?" Henry asked as he spun in place in front of Margot and Amanda. "Do I look official?"

Margot and Amanda looked at each other with surprise before turning back to Henry.

"Wow, you really do," Amanda commented enthusiastically.

"Yeah, you should dress like this more often, Henry," Margot agreed. "You look great!"

Henry snorted. "And have to get a job and bow to the man? No way. I like my freedom exactly how it is, thank you very much." With that, he turned to Amanda.

"I'm doing this for you and then I'm going back to my life off the grid."

"Fine," Amanda consented as Henry returned to the dressing room to change back into his original clothes. The truth was Amanda knew Henry received disability from the government, so he wasn't destitute, but she still worried about him living on the street, especially when it was cold.

"So now that that's done," Henry said upon exiting the dressing room in his street clothes, "what's next?"

"Next we teach you about Amanda," Margot responded.

"That's right," Amanda agreed. "We need to make our relationship fully believable."

"You mean like…?" Henry made a gesture indicating intimacy, causing the girls to double over in laughter.

"No!" Margot responded. "You just need to know everything about her for Mayberry's questions."

"Oh, that's not so bad," Henry acknowledged. "So

where do we begin?"

"Well, I figured we'd start with Amanda's childhood and work our way up," Margot explained, ushering Henry and Amanda to the couch and chairs. "If that's alright with you guys."

"Fine with me," Henry agreed.

"I'm okay with it," Amanda seconded.

"Great," Margot said, sitting. "Then if we're all in agreement, let's get started with Amanda one-o-one."

CHAPTER ELEVEN

DANIEL STOOD IN FRONT OF THE BLANK canvas, staring at it like he'd done the last hour. It had been days since he'd last seen Amanda, and it seemed all of his creativity had disappeared with her. In typical muse fashion, she had callously taken his creativity and left him with nothing. He couldn't sculpt. He couldn't paint. He couldn't do anything creative, no matter how hard he tried. Everything in the apartment reminded him of her. He'd left the painting of her mother uncovered, trying to master his emotions, but each glance in its direction sent a flood of memories rushing through his mind. Daniel's heart raced just thinking about the kiss as he turned to the painting of her mother, unable to keep himself from looking away. That's where he'd found her. That's where he kissed her, despite telling her he wouldn't. He had promised to hold back but had failed miserably after seeing that look in her eyes. It was a look she was now giving someone else. William. The doctor. The guy she'd convinced herself was better for her.

Daniel shook his head thinking about it. It was ironic, of course. He could be that guy if he wanted to. With a phone call, he could work for his father and be given all the money he needed. He could take her to Paris. He could sweep her off her feet. But it would come at a price. His happiness. He'd been that guy in high school and college, getting his way by throwing money around. He'd romanced girls with fancy cars and dinners and whirlwind vacations. He knew as long as the money flowed, they were content. But it was ultimately not satisfying. In the end, they were never the type of girl he was looking for. And something was always missing because it wasn't who he was. He was an artist. He was creative. He loved passion and desire and spontaneity. Yet where had that gotten him, Daniel mused bitterly, looking at the painting of Amanda's mom. His muse had left him. His muse had cared more for aligning her wedding with the Starlight Comet in the painting than finding true love. Of course, in a few hours, she was going to meet with Mayberry, and that dream would be crushed, but she'd still be with William. Daniel looked at the clock on the wall and registered the time. It was still early. He had planned to spend the day lost in the netherworld of creativity, but without his muse, there was nothing he could do. Without inspiration, he would more than likely stand in front of the canvas all day and end up empty just like Amanda would be empty when she met with Mayberry. Daniel was sure, when Mayberry found out Amanda was lying, it would be the end of her Starlight fantasies. Good, Daniel thought. At least she won't keep deluding herself with dreams of what would never happen. Perhaps then she wouldn't rush down the aisle with William just to live out a foolish dream to be like her mother. Regardless, it was none of his business, and that was the truth of it. Daniel looked at the time. The day was passing, and he was completing nothing. He needed to do something. More importantly, he needed to stop thinking about Amanda.

***

Mayberry called Amanda at noon to verify the appointment. Too nervous to speak with him, Amanda let it go to voicemail. The appointment was still on, though; that was for sure. At least he hadn't canceled. She'd get through this as best she could with Henry, and it'd be smooth sailing after that—at least until she switched grooms at the last minute. But Mayberry didn't need to know that detail yet. It's not like he would be at the wedding himself anyway. He just cared that it was booked. Amanda smiled as she poured herself a midday coffee. It was all going according to plan. Henry had learned everything necessary in a short amount of time and would definitely pass as her future husband. There was one thing, however, that still worried her. Henry had sneezed a few times on the way out before he left. It was probably nothing, she knew, but she should check on him nonetheless. Grabbing a piece of his favorite cake from the counter, Amanda headed outside.

Reaching the alley, Amanda looked around but didn't see him. That's odd, she thought. He wasn't in his usual spot. She told herself not to worry. It's not like he was a statue. People moved about all the time. Besides, it was a beautiful day. He was probably taking a walk through the park or something. She was starting to feel better about the whole thing when she found him alone, leaning against a wall with his eyes closed. His entire face was wet with perspiration.

"Henry?" Amanda asked. "Are you okay?"

Henry's eyes fought their way open. "Amanda? What are you doing here?"

"I came to check up on you. What's wrong?"

"Nothing," Henry promised. "Just a little under the weather."

Amanda put her hand to Henry's forehead. "Henry! You're burning up. You need to come inside."

"Oh, I don't want to put you out."

"Nonsense," Amanda said, putting her arm around him and helping him to his feet. "We need to get you taken care of."

Dumping the unused cake in a trashcan, Amanda used her arms to steady Henry as she led him through the back door. "Here, have a seat," she said, dropping him off on a couch in the back room. "I'll get you some water." It was a couch he had been on before but only in the dead of winter when it was too cold to sleep outside. Amanda had insisted he stay there as long as he needed. But sure enough he'd gone back to his normal arrangement outside the next night when it warmed up a few degrees, claiming he didn't want to go soft. Fat chance, Amanda thought. He seemed to be immune to the cold weather that made her run for cover no matter how many coats she wore.

Pouring water into a cup, Amanda tried not to think

about what this meant for her meeting with Mayberry. If Henry were too sick to leave, she'd have to go alone. And if she did, she was sure Mayberry would drop her reservation, destroying any slim chance she had at having her wedding. Of course now was not the time to think about it. She needed Henry to get better. That was the most important thing. He was like family, and she hated seeing him suffer. It was for times like these Amanda had plans and backup plans so this type of thing wouldn't happen. But in this instance, there was nothing more she could do. If he didn't get better, it was over. Turning the faucet off, Amanda returned to the room where Henry lay with his eyes closed and put a hand on his shoulder.

"I brought you water, Henry," Amanda said, offering him the cup.

"Thank you, dear," Henry responded, taking a sip.

Amanda looked at her watch. There were less than twenty-four hours remaining. If he didn't get better soon, her last chance for her Starlight wedding would be over.

***

Amanda picked up the pace as she hurried past pedestrians on her way to St. Patrick's. For a Thursday morning, the New York streets were extra empty, she thought, and any other day it would have made her glad to be out among her Manhattan brethren without the normal overcrowding one was used to putting up with in the city. But today was different. Today would be the last day for her Starlight wedding dreams. She was going to meet Mayberry and would have to admit she didn't have a fiancé. He wouldn't care to hear excuses. He wouldn't care that she felt certain William would propose. He would just cancel her reservation and give it to someone else, and there was nothing she could do about it. Not to mention she was late and looked terrible. She'd stayed up most of the night watching over Henry until his fever broke. She would have rushed him to the hospital if he didn't have such an aversion to establishments and hospitals in particular. Thank goodness William had at least assured her over the phone that there was little more they could do for him there, over what they were doing. It was best for Henry to just take an over-the-counter fever reducer and wait it out: the same thing he would have recommended at the hospital. So far he seemed to be right. At least Henry looked a bit better this morning. His fever had come down. He had insisted on still coming with her to St. Patrick's, but Amanda knew he was in too much pain, so when Margot showed up in the morning to take over, Amanda slipped out the back door alone. Now here she was on her way to what was sure to be an unpleasant meeting to tell Mayberry she was lying all along, well at least since Carl had unceremoniously dumped her on his way to marrying someone else. Stupid Carl.

Crossing the street, Amanda saw St. Patrick's in the distance and felt a twinge of sadness. This was it—the end of her dream. She would never marry at St. Patrick's on the same night as her mother and grandmother. She would never have her Starlight wedding. Feeling her eyes growing moist, Amanda attempted to wipe away any potential tears before they could form. She didn't have time for crying. She was late and once the tears began, there would be no stopping them. As it was, Mayberry was probably wondering where she was. Or worse, was already on the phone to whatever bride he had already promised to give her day to. The way he was constantly pressuring her, she was certain he must have been receiving a kickback. There was no way he'd be such a jerk on his own. If that were the case, St. Patrick's would have never hired him. They were still technically a church, after all.

Reaching the door to the church, Amanda stopped to gather herself for the unpleasantness that was about to come. Her heart racing after the brisk walk through town, Amanda caught her breath, knowing heartbreak was on the other side of the door. She could do this she told herself. Once it was over, she would do her best to move on and never think about it again. That's all she could do.

Somewhat believing that, Amanda took a deep breath and walked through the door.

***

Daniel woke from his nap with a vision of Amanda showing up at St. Patrick's empty handed. There would be no shining knight to save her, no savior to make the impossible possible. The only hero she considered real would be in surgery oblivious to it all and would have no idea the event had even occurred. Amanda's father was dead, too, and even if he was still alive, what could he do? He couldn't change the fact that there was no Carl. A pang of sympathy shot through Daniel's heart. No wonder she felt alone. She was alone. She'd lost her father and her mother on the same day. Every Christmas, every holiday had been changed forever. She had no backup. She had no one to pick up the pieces when things fell apart. She had to go through life alone. As Daniel looked over the painting, a tide of guilt overcame him. He was the only one who could help her. He could be Carl. He could show up and give her more time. In the end, she would marry William faster, so ultimately it would lead to his demise. Yet it was within his power to save her dream.

Or was it, Daniel asked himself? Amanda had strictly told him to stay away, and that was exactly what he should do. If you want your precious doctor, then let him save you, his mind reasoned. I need to get on with my life. Daniel knew in order to do that he needed to forget about Amanda. But then what was he going to do with the painting of Amanda's mother constantly staring back at him? He'd have to sell it. That's all there was to it. He'd get rid of the painting, forget about Amanda, and move on to better things. Determined, Daniel ripped the top sheet off his bed and dragged it to the other room. It's time to move on, he decided, and then flipped the sheet over the painting, hiding it from sight. "Now, let's get back to work." Proud of himself, Daniel strode back to the easel and the blank canvas he'd prepared, dipped his brush in paint, and determinately made a line across it. Ecstatic to be working again, Daniel worked feverishly, happy to have overcome his roadblock. He was an artist again. Inspiration had taken hold, and his hands were doing the work for him. He didn't need Amanda. He didn't need anyone. He was moving on.

***

Proud of himself, Daniel stepped back to look at the beginning of what was sure to someday be a great masterpiece. With overwhelming pride, Daniel stared at the canvas and smiled until he realized what he'd done. His traitorous fingers had created no new masterpiece or fresh idea or otherworldly creation. They'd painted the Starlight Comet. It was then he knew what he needed to do, whether it was the right thing or not. Taking a quick look at the time, Daniel rushed to his closet and grabbed the first button down shirt he came across and threw a tie over his shoulder. He'd have to hurry if he wanted to be on time, but he knew exactly where he had to go.

CHAPTER TWELVE

MAYBERRY LEANED BACK in his chair, exhausted. He'd been there since seven and not by choice. Father Browner had scheduled a meeting with Miss Helmslow about his progress in procuring a date for her granddaughter's wedding at her insistence, and with no good news to report, it had not gone well. The best hope he could give them were his suspicions about prospective bride Amanda's lack of a fiancé and his hope that, after today's meeting, he would be able to put the younger Miss Helmslow in her spot. Of course, he didn't remind them that if he were wrong and there was a Carl, there wasn't much he could do. There were only so many dates Helmslow considered acceptable in her limited time frame, and they were already booked up. Not that Browner cared to hear excuses. Once again, it was made very clear his job depended on it. Browner wanted a new wing for a children's daycare center, and he wasn't letting anything come between his dreams and Helmslow's money.

STARLIGHT WEDDING

Mayberry glanced at the tiny bottle of sand he'd brought back from his now seemingly distant vacation and sighed. Oh, how he'd love to be back there, soaking in the sun, away from all of this. If only he could snap his fingers and never have to see another bride again. Maybe if he got Helmslow her wedding she would give him a gift in thanks. Fat chance, he thought. He'd be lucky to keep his job. Speaking of which, it was five past eleven. Amanda and the infamous Carl had yet to show. Maybe they weren't coming, he thought. Maybe he could breathe easy after all. It might not put him in the Caribbean, but it would keep him off the breadline. Mayberry was beginning to feel a sense of hope until he heard the knock at the door. Disappointed, he got up to answer it. Even more disappointment flooded over him as he opened it and found a man standing on the other side.

"Good afternoon," the man said, offering a hand. "My name is Carl."

***

By the time Amanda reached Mayberry's office, she was fifteen minutes late and exhausted. It didn't help that his office was on the third floor. They really need to install an elevator here, she determined. Not that she was going to give her opinion on the subject to Mayberry. He wouldn't really care what she thought; especially after he heard all she had to tell him about her lack of a fiancé and the fact that she'd been lying to him since the infamous dumping. He'd probably yell at her and throw her out or call security. She'd be banned from the church, banned from heaven, and excommunicated.

Amanda felt a knot in the pit of her stomach. This was not going to be fun. But as she stood in front of the door, she decided it was long past time to do what was right. It was time to tell the truth. She didn't have a choice anyway, but she couldn't keep lying. Here goes, she thought, then knocked on the door and waited for Mayberry to answer.

When the door opened and Mayberry stood there with his forced smile, Amanda nearly turned and ran away.

"Good morning, Miss Jones," he said, none too happily. "Do come in."

"I'm so sorry for being late," Amanda began, following him into the room. "Something came up. I didn't mean to make you wait."

"Nothing too urgent, I hope," Mayberry responded, clearly disinterested, while moving around his desk to his chair. "Please, have a seat."

Amanda sat and took a moment to gather her thoughts. It was time to come clean. Mayberry probably already knew she didn't have a fiancé anyway, she told herself. Heck, he'd probably had her followed or hired a private investigator to verify her story. All that was left was to trap her in the lie. There were probably cops waiting in an adjoining room to bust her for marriage fraud and take her to jail. Or maybe he'd just throw her from the third story window to be done with her, she imagined, as her fears got away from her.

"The truth is, Mr. Mayberry, I have some explaining to do." Amanda began.

"I imagine you do," he replied.

What does that mean, she wondered? He was acting

strange, and she wished she knew why. "First, let me apologize," Amanda got out.

"Apologize?" Mayberry answered, sounding genuinely surprised. "Actually I believe it is me who owes you an apology, much to my chagrin."

"You?" Amanda responded, confused. "What for?"

Mayberry shifted in his seat. "Well, for starters, for doubting you." The way he said it made Amanda feel worse. "Believe me, it gives me great pains to say that, for reasons you could only imagine."

The conversation wasn't going anywhere like Amanda had intended. Why was he acting so strange? She hadn't yet told him what she needed to, but he was so completely different than when she'd spoken to him on the phone she wasn't sure how to continue.

"No, Mr. Mayberry, the truth is you were right," Amanda interrupted. Amanda had wanted to let it all out, but it was getting increasingly hard due to the way he was looking at her. She was starting to feel like a mouse waiting for the cat to pounce and it made her uneasy.

"I was right?" he answered, confused.

"Yes. The truth is I don't have a fiancé, and there is no Carl," Amanda admitted. "Well there is, but he's a jerk. I pretended he was my fiancé because I wanted so badly to be married. As you know it's a special day for me, and I really wanted to be married here at St. Patrick's. But I lied." Amanda paused to gauge Mayberry's reaction. "The truth is Carl left me, and I was stalling in the hopes of finding someone else. So you were right. I'm sorry."

Having let it all out, Amanda felt a sense of relief. There was something about being honest that made her feel better despite the inevitable consequences. Dropping her head in her hands, Amanda apologized one last time. "I'm so sorry."

Amanda braced for the onslaught of rage that was about to come from the other side of the desk. She waited for the flying objects, for tables to be overturned, and for contracts to be burned, but instead of screaming and yelling and tirades, she only heard silence.

"I had a feeling you were going to say that. But are you sure that's all true?" Mayberry asked, unconvinced.

"Yes," Amanda promised. "Believe me, I don't have a fiancé, and there is no Carl. There's a William, maybe. But certainly no Carl."

Mayberry nodded for what seemed like an eternity before responding. "He told me you would say that," Mayberry finally said, standing, motioning behind her.

"Who?" Amanda questioned. "Mr. Mayberry, I assure you I don't know what's going on, but I truly don't have a fiancé."

That's when she turned and saw Daniel. He must have stepped in or been hiding when she'd come in. He was dressed to perfection and had clearly gotten here ahead of her and talked to Mayberry before she'd arrived. About what she had no idea. Well, she had an idea, but she couldn't believe he would do that or understand why.

"Would you like to speak, Carl?" Mayberry asked Daniel.

"Carl?" Amanda exclaimed. "Him?"

To his credit, Daniel stepped up quickly without missing a beat and put a hand on Amanda's shoulder. "Yes, dear." Kneeling beside her, Daniel put his hand on

Amanda's leg. "Honey bear, I'm sorry I made you angry. I didn't mean to upset you. But don't act like I don't exist and ruin our wedding because of a minor disagreement. I love you too much for that." When Mayberry looked away, Daniel winked at Amanda before turning to Mayberry apologetically. "I'm sorry we had to involve you in all of this. The truth is, she's been upset the last few days, and it's all my fault." Daniel turned back to Amanda. "Haven't you, dear?"

Amanda wished someone had taken a picture of her face at that moment because she knew it would be priceless. Her jaw was most definitely on the floor. Was Daniel really helping her save her Starlight wedding by pretending to be Carl? Why? How could it possibly help him? It wasn't like she was going to marry him instead. "Uh, I guess so." It was all she could think to say.

"Look at her. She's speechless," Daniel commented to Mayberry before turning back to Amanda with his most apologetic face. "So, do you forgive me, honey? I promise not to stay out late with my friends again." Daniel turned to Mayberry giving him his best guilty frown. "I'm always doing that."

Amanda almost laughed, ruining the moment. In fact, if the situation weren't so serious, she would have laughed herself out of her chair right then and there. Daniel, Mr. Neanderthal, had just apologized to her for staying out late as Carl with his or Carl's or whoever's friends in order to save her wedding. Well, she had to admit, he certainly had balls.

"So is that a yes, dear?" Daniel asked as convincingly as possible, so much so even Mayberry seemed on the edge of his seat waiting for the answer. "Will you forgive me so we can go home?"

Now it was her turn to put on a show, Amanda thought. She'd been confused this entire time and hadn't contributed much to the conversation due to shock, but it was time she start doing so if she wanted to save her wedding. It was time to lay it on thick. She'd ask God's forgiveness later.

"Oh, honey," Amanda began, putting her hand on Carl's or Daniel's or whoever's hand it was as convincingly as possible, "I was just so angry. The way you left me at home and were looking at other girls, I just didn't know what to do. But I don't know what I would do without you. You're so big and strong and you take care of me with your real job..." Amanda couldn't help putting a dig in at Daniel occupation. "I will forgive you. I'll always forgive you. Now let's go home and restart our lives."

"Shouldn't we kiss and make up first?" Daniel said with a smirk.

"Carl!" Amanda responded, her face growing red. "Not in front of Mr. Mayberry! This is a church."

"Oh, it's alright," Mayberry interjected a little too acceptingly for a man who worked in God's house, Amanda thought.

Not surprisingly, Daniel didn't let up. "Please?" he begged. At this point, Amanda couldn't tell whether it was in character or not, but she had her suspicions it wasn't considering his track record at weaseling kisses.

"We'll talk about it at home, dear," Amanda responded, smiling through her teeth.

"That's all I can ask," Daniel answered, pulling his hand away from her viselike grip.

Helping Amanda out of her chair, Daniel put his arms around her and, despite her objections, gave Amanda a kiss. Hey, he might as well get something for all of his hard work, Daniel thought. He was certain Carl would have gone for it, too, and he was supposed to be the jerk, after all. Besides, he had to be convincing, and it wasn't like she was going to protest in front of Mayberry. And she didn't. To her credit, she kissed him back hard, making it look real.

She really wants this wedding, Daniel thought, going along as long as she'd let him. When it was over, Daniel stared at her in wonder. "Wow, honey, I don't remember you being so passionate. Maybe we should have another?"

"Nice try," Amanda said, stopping him from continuing, "Remember, you're still on probation." She'd said it as sweetly as she could, batting her eyelids. "How about we wait until we get home, sugar plum? I'm sure Mr. Mayberry has seen enough."

Daniel doubted it. By the look on Mayberry's face, he probably would have filmed it and watched it later if he could.

The matter settled, Amanda turned to Mayberry and gave him her sweetest fake smile. "Thank you for being so understanding, Mr. Mayberry. You've saved our wedding and our love." Taking Daniel's hand, Amanda quickly led him out of the room and closed the door before Mayberry could ask any more questions.

Mayberry watched in stunned silence as the door

closed behind them. Had that really just happened? Had he just helped save a wedding he wanted more than anything to cancel.

"What did I do?" Mayberry asked himself, collapsing into his chair. He'd just helped the one engagement he needed to fail, guaranteeing he'd be out of a job. Father Browner and Helmslow would be irate. More importantly, he would be fired, and worse—it would entirely be his own fault.

***

Amanda held Daniel's hand all the way down the hall in case Mayberry suddenly appeared out of nowhere. As they walked, Daniel glanced at Amanda. Despite a few looks in his direction, he wasn't exactly sure what she was thinking. She was clearly smiling on the outside, but he knew it was a facade. Underneath, something was definitely brewing, and he was certain once they reached the stairs it would come out. To her credit, Amanda managed to make it down a full flight of stairs before she yanked her hand away and pushed him against the wall in anger.

"What were you doing showing up like that?" she demanded. "You could have ruined everything!"

"You mean for your fake wedding?"

"Yes, my fake wedding, which is none of your business!"

"I just wanted to help," Daniel responded innocently.

"By pretending to be Carl?"

"Yes, pretending to be Carl. I knew it was the only way."

"Well, it's unacceptable!" she railed, wanting to bite his head off. "It could have been a disaster."

"But it wasn't."

"But it could have been!"

Daniel held up his hands, relenting. "You're right. I'm sorry. I wasn't thinking. I just wanted to help, and it was all I could think of. It was rash and stupid and it won't happen again."

"It was rash! And it was stupid!" Amanda roared before softening. "But…" Amanda shook her head at what she was about to say. "I can't believe you did that. You saved my wedding. At least my chance for the wedding, however minuscule it is. So…thank you."

Daniel couldn't believe what he'd just heard. "Did you just thank me?"

"No," she lied.

"You did. You just said something nice to me."

"I did not."

"Yes, you did. You thanked me."

"Well, you'd better forget it before I throw you down these stairs!"

Amanda wanted to move on, but with the way Daniel kept looking at her, she didn't know what else to say. "What? Why are you looking at me like that?" she asked.

"Because…you were nice to me. I'm not used to that."

"Ha-ha." Amanda rolled her eyes as she continued moving. Yet as they descended the stairs, something was eating away at her. There was a question she needed to be answered.

"Why did you do it?"

"What?"

"Why did you help me? You knew it wouldn't help you. It can only help William, if anyone, and even that's probably impossible."

It was crazy. Daniel knew that. He also knew he had to. "I don't know," he began. "I knew it would make you happy. That's all I thought about."

"Why?"

"Because…" Daniel remembered back to when he had found Amanda in the apartment looking vulnerable in front of the painting of her mother. "I saw the way you looked at that painting, and I saw the photos and her obituary. Right or wrong, this wedding means everything to you."

"What do you mean right or wrong?"

"I just mean as a point of emphasis. To me, a wedding is only as good as the couple taking part in it. Without the right person, it wouldn't matter when or where you got married and vice versa. If you really did have the right person, you'd be happy getting married in the deli, just like my grandparents."

"Fair enough. But how does helping me help you?"

"It doesn't."

"Then why did you do it?"

They had reached the bottom of the stairs and were on their way out when Daniel stopped and turned to Amanda in all seriousness. "Because I care about you, and that's what you do for someone you care about, even if it means sacrificing yourself in the process."

"But you just met me. You don't even know me," Amanda answered, incredulously.

"I know enough."

Amanda didn't know how to respond. "But I practically hate you."

"No, you don't," Daniel responded. "Not practically. Fully? Yes. But not practically," he said with a smirk.

Amanda laughed. He was funny she had to admit. Maybe the Neanderthal wasn't so bad after all. I mean, he did save her wedding. And now he promised to disappear, though she didn't know whether or not she believed him. "Well, you did get a kiss out of it."

Daniel smiled thinking about it. "Yes I did."

"Something you always seem to come away with," Amanda accused.

"I choose my moments."

"That you do."

They reached the curb. A taxi would be along any minute, and this time Amanda knew they would part indefinitely.

"You know, it wasn't that terrible," she finally admitted.

"What?"

"The kiss. And, well...everything else."

"Really?"

"Yes. But don't quote me or I'll deny it," she said with a smile. Hey, if she wasn't going to see him again, she might as well admit it. "And did you see the look on Mayberry's face?" she continued. "It was priceless."

"His heart was beating so fast I thought he might have a heart attack," Daniel agreed.

Amanda was laughing when the taxi neared, putting a stop to the conversation.

"Well, I guess that's it," Amanda commented.

"I guess so," he agreed. Stepping onto the street, Daniel politely opened the door for Amanda and waited for her to get in.

"Thank you again," she said.

"You're welcome," he replied. "Good luck."

"You too."

Amanda shook Daniel's hand for a brief moment, and it felt surprisingly good. It was that connection again. The same connection she'd felt before she'd lost herself in front of the painting—which meant it was time for her to go. It was time to get back to her life with William and the shop and away from Daniel. Her future was elsewhere, she told herself. She was sure of it. Besides, she had a doctor waiting. The decision made, Amanda released Daniel's hand and stepped into the car and closed the door behind her, giving Daniel one last look as the taxi pulled away. Relieved, she settled into her seat and gave the driver her address, confident she was on her way to something better, yet in the back of her mind she had to admit, there was a small part of her that wanted to stay.

CHAPTER THIRTEEN

"HE DID WHAT?" Margot exclaimed only a few feet from a sleeping Henry in the Starlight back room.

"He pretended to be Carl!" Amanda responded. "Do you believe that?"

"And you never asked him to? Not once? It never came up in conversation?"

"No. He just showed up. One minute I was asking Mayberry to forgive me for lying, and the next thing I know Daniel's professing his undying love for me as Carl."

"And you went with it?"

"Of course went with it. It was weird at first, but then it kind of came naturally."

"Really?" Margot asked, intrigued. "How interesting."

"Not like that! He was just a good Carl," Amanda clarified.

"I'll bet. So you and Daniel?" Margot pressed.

"No, me and Carl. Daniel was Carl and I was me,"

Amanda reiterated.

"Sounds confusing."

"It is."

"And Mayberry believed you?"

"I think so." Amanda thought about it a moment. "At least he seemed to. Daniel was very convincing."

"At pretending to be your boyfriend? How is that surprising? It's his superpower."

"That's not true," Amanda hissed. "Regardless, one minute everything was off, and the next it was suddenly on again."

"Unbelievable." Margot shook her head as she took another bite of some cake she'd brought in the room. "You have all the luck, and sadly, more fake boyfriends than I have real ones."

"It's not my fault. They won't go away! Well, except Carl. I guess he found a way."

"Yeah, and you replaced him with two more," Margot said.

"I know. It's ridiculous!" Amanda agreed.

"Clearly. But why did Daniel do it? I understand you doing it to save your wedding but why Daniel? It's not like it helped him at all."

"Maybe he was just being nice."

"Or maybe he really is crazy and delusional."

"He's not delusional," Amanda objected. Wow, was she really defending the Neanderthal? "The truth is it was actually kind of sweet," Amanda admitted.

"Like stalker sweet?"

"No."

"Jeffry Dahmer sweet?"

"No! Like...I don't know, *sweet* sweet. He said he just wanted to help save my wedding, no strings attached. And when it was over, he said goodbye and let me leave."

"And he didn't try and kiss you?"

"No. Okay, once. Maybe twice."

"Twice?" Margot laughed, giving Amanda her most doubtful stare. "No strings attached indeed."

"Okay, I see what you're thinking, but it was only to play the part," Amanda said, attempting to clarify. "And I only let him kiss me once."

"Yeah, you're a real pillar of strength. A real example to us all," Margot said sarcastically.

"I'm serious," Amanda demanded. "It was only for Mayberry. After that, he was quite the gentleman," Amanda explained, stealing a bite of cake off Margot's plate.

"Maybe I should send him a gift or a thank you card or a toaster."

Margot smirked. "Because nothing says thank you like a toaster."

"What else could I do?" Amanda asked, stumped.

"You could invite him to the wedding."

"There's an idea."

"I was kidding."

"I'm serious," Amanda said.

"So am I," Margot replied.

"Well, I've got to do something to thank him."

"The Neanderthal?"

"The...whatever he is."

"So he's no longer a Neanderthal? He's evolved?"

"No, he's just one of the later ones, like a Cro-Magnon

man or someone from Brooklyn." Amanda thought about what she'd just said. Had he really evolved?

Maybe she was just finally seeing him for who he really was?

Margot watched as Amanda fought the battle in her head, trying to gauge Amanda's direction. "Well, do what you want," Margot said, taking another bite of cake, "but it sounds like he made out okay already with the kiss."

"He did, didn't he?" Amanda agreed.

"Unless you go around kissing men for favors, which, considering my current state of singleness, does not sound all that bad."

"You're right," Amanda quickly agreed with Margot. "He doesn't need anything more. He was just being nice."

Margot stared at Amanda, who was trying to figure it all out. There was something going on in her head, Margot guessed, and as Amanda's friend, it was her job to get it out. It's what best friends were for. It only took a minute to hit her. "Oh my God."

"What?"

"Oh. My. God," she repeated.

"What?"

"You like him!"

"Who?"

"Daniel."

"No, I don't." Amanda shook her head vehemently denying it.

"Yes, you do!"

"I do not!"

"That's why you're making excuses," Margot continued. "That's why you're not completely disgusted by the kiss! You have feelings for him!"

"I do not! I do not like the Neanderthal!"

"Oh, so he's a Neanderthal again?"

"No! I just don't hate him as much," Amanda made clear.

"Okay, whatever you say."

"Don't say it like that!" Amanda demanded. "It's William! I like William!"

"Fine."

"Fine."

"Fine!"

"Fine!"

The two sat in awkward silence a moment before Margot finally turned to Amanda as lovingly as she could. "You know, it wouldn't be all that bad if you did like him. In fact, it would actually be kind of sweet."

"But I don't!" Amanda said throwing up her arms. And she didn't, she told herself. Yet despite her objections, she could feel the doubt suddenly creeping back in, refusing to let go. It was accompanied by a question too scary to entertain: What if she did?

***

It wasn't more than a few hours after Amanda had convinced herself she didn't like Daniel again before everything was suddenly right with the world again. William had called and asked her to dinner the following night, Henry had miraculously gotten over his sickness, and most importantly, Amanda had fully convinced herself Daniel wasn't the one for her. Satisfied she'd come to her senses, Amanda breathed a little easier; confident that order had once again been restored. As for Henry, he had insisted on going back outside where he could breathe the fresh air and live his life under the stars without restriction in what he described as the sanctuary of God's creation. Though New York probably had more man made creations than God's, Amanda didn't argue and just smiled and let him go. She made sure to make him a special plate of food and then sent him on his way. Her talk with William had been refreshing as well. She had been so concerned about her meeting with Mayberry the last few days she had neglected poor William, yet now that it had been settled, she would finally be able to give him the attention he deserved. Of course, William had made it easy. He had promised to take her some place special the following evening where they could be alone and really enjoy each other's company. He even hinted that there was something he wanted to ask her and he thought she might like it. She had no idea what it could be, but with his creativity in planning the lunch and baseball date Daniel had usurped, she was sure it must be good. Everything was working out perfectly. So why was she still thinking about Daniel? It's not like she liked him. Of that she was sure. She had spent the first few hours since she'd returned going through every detail of her emotions, but after a plus and minus chart, an Excel spreadsheet, and a small PowerPoint presentation she'd created detailing his shortcomings, she had fully convinced herself she was not only not in love with him, but she also didn't care if she ever saw him again. So why did he keep popping up in her mind?

Amanda racked her brain, searching for the answer.

After a quick Google search yielded nothing, Amanda banged her head on the desk trying to shake something loose. Finally, when she couldn't take it anymore, it hit her: She had never properly thanked him. It wasn't her love for Daniel that was annoying; it was her lack of kindness. Her parents had always taught her to repay kindness, and if she did that, she was sure to feel better. That had to be it, she convinced herself. She just needed to get Daniel something to acknowledge what he did for her, and then she could be on her way to wedded bliss with William. Impressed by her brilliance, Amanda restarted her computer, searched under the heading Thank You Gifts, and looked at everything that came up. Finding nothing, Amanda decided to stick with her original toaster idea. Satisfied it was the right choice; Amanda closed her laptop, grabbed her purse, and headed to the nearest mall.

***

Daniel had just finished lunch when he heard the knock at the door. Certain he wasn't due to receive any packages or hadn't ordered anything online; he had no idea who it might be. Unbolting the lock, Daniel opened the door and saw the last person he ever expected to see. It was Amanda. She was standing there holding something and staring at him with the oddest face he had ever seen. Was it a smile? A frown? Daniel's mind raced at the possibilities as he looked at her not knowing what to say.

"Amanda?" he finally got out.

"Hi," she responded with a wave.

For a moment, both stood there staring at each other until Amanda awkwardly thrust the package into Daniel's hands saying, "This is for you," and quickly turned to leave.

"Wait!" Daniel said, stopping her. As she reluctantly turned around, Daniel looked at the package. Was it a gift? A bomb? At this point, both seemed equally probable. "What is it?"

"A gift."

"You got me a gift?"

"Yes, I got you a gift," Amanda said belligerently. "Now goodbye." Amanda turned to leave again.

"Wait!" Daniel said, stopping her again. "At least let me open it."

"You want me to wait while you open it?" Amanda hated the very thought of it.

"Yes."

"Do I have to?"

"Yes."

"Fine," Amanda consented, rolling her eyes. Why did he have to make this so difficult? She was trying to get rid of him, not keep him around.

Once he was satisfied she wouldn't leave, Daniel ripped open the package and paused. "You got me a toaster?"

"It's a thank you gift," Amanda said proudly.

"You got me a thank you toaster?"

"It's a Cuisinart Hybrid Four Slice Toaster," she explained. "It has six settings. You can warm up to four pieces of toast and they'll never burn. And it's got this great catch drawer for crumbs."

"That's great," Daniel replied, not knowing what else to say. "Uh...thank you?"

"You're welcome. Now we're even. Now I don't owe you anything."

"For what?"

"For helping me with St. Patrick's."

"You didn't owe me anything to begin with," Daniel explained, wanting to be clear. "I wanted to help. I wasn't looking for anything, and you certainly didn't need to get me this."

"So you don't want your toaster?" Amanda asked, taking it back.

"No, I love the toaster," Daniel promised, snatching it back again. "It's great."

"You're sure?"

"Yes," Daniel responded. "But you didn't have to buy it. I really am happy for you, Amanda."

"Thanks. I'm happy for you too." Though she said it, she had no idea why. There certainly was nothing for him to be happy about. "Well, I should go," she continued awkwardly.

"Okay," Daniel agreed. "But Amanda, I really meant what I said about the wedding. You don't need a doctor or St. Patrick's or a Starlight Comet for a perfect wedding. As long as you're with the one you love, you'll have an amazing wedding. And it'll be even better than any picture in that book of yours."

"Says the guy who wants to get married in a sandwich shop and will probably smash cake in his bride's face at the reception?"

"Says the guy who could get married in a sandwich

shop and will probably smash cake in his bride's face," Daniel modified. "Just so long as it is the right woman. If it were me, I'd want to know it was me you wanted to marry, not some idea of perfection you cooked up in childhood."

"Then it's a good thing it's not."

"I guess so," Daniel agreed.

Amanda looked over her shoulder awkwardly, wishing she could disappear. "Well, I should go," she said. Yet before she could move, Daniel reached out a hand, stopping her.

"Amanda, why did you come?"

"I told you. The toaster."

"Why else?"

"There is nothing else. Why would there be something else?"

"I guess there wouldn't," Daniel said, disappointed. "Thank you for the toaster. I'll think of you every time I make toast."

"And waffles!" Amanda added.

"And waffles," Daniel agreed.

"Well, bye," Amanda said awkwardly turning to leave.

"Yeah, bye," Daniel responded, watching her go. Daniel watched her walk all the way down the hall, then looked at his toaster completely confused.

***

Amanda took the subway to the office on the way home. She'd given Daniel the toaster, and that should have been the end of it. Right? So why was she still thinking about him? She'd said thank you. She'd said her goodbyes, and now it was time to get on with her life. So why was she still uncertain? Why did his words keep going through her mind, driving her mad? She knew she didn't need a doctor or St. Patrick's to make her happy. Those were just things she wanted, same as everyone else. Not to mention she was in the wedding business. It was normal to want such things. She could give them up at any time if she wanted to. And if she did happen to get them, she could enjoy them as things she'd accomplished, and there was nothing wrong with that. It was none of his business, anyway. And she was not some trashy bride who would laugh off getting cake smashed into her face, on the most important night of her life, for that matter, either. Daniel needed to stop focusing on her and start focusing on himself for a change. He could start by getting a better job or moving to a different part of the city. No, she thought, as the subway car stopped at her station. In all fairness, Daniel really was a great artist. If she were honest with herself, she of all people understood the importance of finding work doing something you love. She'd slaved away at bridal shops for years before opening her own and loved every minute of it. She would have done it for free because it made her happy. Daniel was the same. He was a good artist. She couldn't deny that. His angel sculpture had sent shivers up her spine, not to mention the painting of her mother. Maybe he was more like her than she originally believed. All this time, she had focused on the negatives of him being an artist, when really she wasn't much different. He was a sculptor and painter, and she was a wedding artist. The only difference was her canvases were engagements, chapels, and hopeful brides; her colors the unlimited possibilities of what to do with them. His art wasn't much different. But instead of flowers and gowns and bridesmaid dresses, he used color and light and shading, and he was really good at it, she had to admit. His work had moved her. It made her feel safe. It was the reason she couldn't help but be with him that day. Amanda remembered that afternoon. It was the first time she'd been intimate with someone since Carl. Daniel had found her standing in front of her mother's painting and had kissed her. He had been gentle and kind and passionate. Amanda blushed thinking about it as she opened the door to her office and found William standing in front of her desk looking down at her scrapbook.

"William!" Amanda exclaimed, hoping he didn't notice her blushing cheeks. "What are you doing here?"

"Margot, let me in," William answered guiltily, raising the flowers in his hand. "I wanted to leave you these."

"More flowers?" Amanda asked, still red.

"I hope it's okay."

"Of course. Why wouldn't it be?" Amanda took the flowers and looked them over. "They're beautiful."

"I didn't want to overdo it, but I had a few minutes in between patients, and I thought I'd surprise you," William explained.

"Oh, you did," Amanda replied, taken aback. "You definitely did."

"I was concerned it'd be too much but," William paused to glance at the open scrapbook, "apparently you like flowers."

STARLIGHT WEDDING

Amanda groaned. He had found the book and, worse, probably his picture. Now he'd know for sure she'd stalked him. Maybe it was for the best, Amanda decided. Maybe it was time for her to give up her stupid fantasy.

"About that…"

"Don't worry, I didn't look," William reassured. "Okay, maybe a little. I was just so surprised to see my picture I had to see what more was in there."

"Let me explain," Amanda pleaded.

"You don't have to. It's fine."

"You're not mad?"

"How could I be mad? The woman I care for has my picture in a scrapbook. It's flattering."

Amanda relaxed. He saw the scrapbook, and he wasn't running away. Maybe she would get through this after all.

"There is one thing," William began. "Something I'm confused about."

Amanda tensed as William flipped through the pages. Amanda's heart sank, hoping he wasn't turning to the page that would scare him off for good. Amanda could feel her heart beating a million times a second as William's hand stopped on the one page she hoped he hadn't seen.

"This," he said, pointing.

It was her Starlight wedding page. On the top the date was written in. Amanda knew it would be hard to ignore in a scrapbook like this, especially because it was so close. This was it, she thought. He had found her secret.

"I can explain," she said.

"Please do," he responded, intrigued.

"The truth is…" Amanda started but didn't know how

to continue. She knew she had to be honest. Hopefully he wouldn't laugh too hard before he ran off. "The truth is it's the day I want to get married. It's the day my mother was married and my grandmother before that. It's the day of the Starlight Comet, and it only comes once every thirty years. When I saw your picture, I made up an excuse to meet you in the hopes we might..."

"Fall in love?" William asked.

Amanda nodded. "And get married. It's stupid, I know."

"Wow," William responded, floored. "It's not stupid..."

"But?" Amanda asked.

"It's just a lot to think about. It's certainly not what I expected."

Amanda shook her head, ashamed. "I know."

William's phone beeped causing an even bigger delay in the conversation than she expected as William lifted it out of his pocket to see who it was from. "It's the hospital. Perfect timing as ever," he commented, sliding it back in his pocket. "It appears I have to go."

"Okay. Will I still see you tomorrow?" Amanda asked nervously.

William hesitated, clearly distracted. "Of course. And about that thing..." William pointed to Amanda's book. "Don't worry, it's fine. Everything's fine."

"You sure?" Amanda asked.

"Yes," he said, casually flipping the scrapbook closed. "Enjoy the flowers."

"Thanks. Good luck at the hospital."

"Will do," William said automatically and then

walked out.

Amanda watched William go. If anything was certain it was that nothing was fine. How could it be? She looked like a stalker. No, she was a stalker. And now he knew it. He probably wouldn't show up for dinner. He'd probably move out of the country or file a restraining order. Amanda collapsed into her chair and dropped her head in her hands. Why did this always happen to her? As her mind churned through every horrendous possibility, Amanda flipped through her scrapbook, sure she'd never see him again.

CHAPTER FOURTEEN

AS MAYBERRY SAT IN BROWNER'S OFFICE he looked at the calendar on his phone for what seemed like the millionth time before his meeting with Browner began. Yet no matter how many times he looked at it, the outcome was the same: With Amanda's wedding an apparent go, there was nothing he could do for the formidable Mrs. Helmslow without a miracle from St. Patrick himself. So unless Helmslow had special powers he didn't know about that could bend time to accommodate two weddings at the same time, her granddaughter would have to find somewhere else to get married. It meant he would probably be without a job, but he didn't see any other option. He'd called every bride with a date within a four-month radius and even some of St. Patrick's sister churches to see if they had any openings and came up empty. They'd all said what he already knew. There was just no way to move the time and place of a wedding once the invitations were sent. Everyone knew that.

Some brides had even laughed at him for suggesting it, to which he had responded that he agreed with them before hanging up ashamed. And now here he was waiting for Browner and Helmslow to come in and make him feel like an idiot for not doing the impossible.

Mayberry took a breath as the door opened behind him and Father Browner and Helmslow entered. They were laughing about something, which was odd, Mayberry noted, as he'd rarely seen Browner laugh and was certain Helmslow hadn't cracked a smile in years. Good thing, Mayberry thought, as they were about to get news that would send both raging in anger when he told them he'd failed to carry out their wishes.

"Donald, so good to see you," Browner expressed upon seeing Mayberry, much to Mayberry's surprise. "Tell us the good news." After which Browner turned to Helmslow, offering a chair. "Please, take a seat, Mrs. Helmslow. Let's get down to business."

Mayberry found the words discomforting. His time of having any sort of business was coming to an end, and he felt no need to speed up the process.

Mayberry watched as Browner sat in his chair, opened his calendar, and turned to him expecting good news. "Well, Donald, exactly what date is it going to be? I'm sure our guest is eager to get busy and not a moment too soon. Isn't that right, Mrs. Helmslow?"

"My thoughts exactly," Helmslow agreed crustily. "The sooner we get this little nuisance behind us, the sooner we can get on to planning the details."

I'll bet, Mayberry thought. She'd barely have enough time to plan a dinner party in this amount of time, let alone a wedding. Too bad neither were going to happen.

"So," Browner continued, turning to Mayberry. "When is the lucky day? When can we look forward to joining the young Miss Helmslow in matrimony?"

Mayberry looked at the floor, then the ceiling, and then the wall, searching for an answer he knew would never come. "It's a funny thing, sir," he finally spit out.

"What do you mean funny?" Browner responded, not the least bit amused.

"I mean unfortunate," Mayberry replied, to which Helmslow sat up in her chair.

"Excuse me?" she asked, suddenly serious. "Exactly what do you find unfortunate?"

Mayberry squirmed in his seat. Here goes. "The thing is..." he began. "You asked me to do the impossible. There's just no bride willing to give up her day so near the actual wedding date."

"Then offer them money," Helmslow demanded.

Of course it was her answer to everything, Mayberry thought. But it wasn't going to work this time, not with weddings and arrangements that had been planned for months and years in advance.

"I'm afraid it's not that simple," Mayberry explained. "Of course I tried, but no one would budge. The average wedding is planned years in advance. There's just no space for a..." Mayberry stopped before saying it.

"For a what?" Browner asked.

"Yes, for a what?" Helmslow demanded.

Mayberry shrunk in his chair. He'd really stepped in it now.

"Donald?" Browner insisted, leaning forward onto his

desk. "Tell us what you were going to say."

"Yes, sir. But I meant no harm."

"Say it," Helmslow insisted.

"Fine. What I was going to say was that there's just no space at St. Patrick's for a shotgun wedding," Donald muttered, knowing the reaction he would incite.

"A what?" Helmslow looked at Mayberry like she could kill him, and then turned to Browner, irate. "Are you listening to this, Father?"

"I'm afraid I am," Browner answered.

It was time to explain, or at least ask for forgiveness, Mayberry thought. But how do you reason with someone as unreasonable as Helmslow?

"I did everything I could!" Mayberry pleaded. "I know that's not what either of you want to hear, but it's the truth. We've been booked for over a year, and no amount of money can change that. I'm sorry, Father."

Helmslow stood from her chair, incensed. "That is unacceptable! You will get me that wedding!"

"It is impossible," Mayberry pleaded. "I've tried everything."

"Clearly you haven't," Helmslow barked, before turning her attention to Browner. "Let me remind you of my generosity, Father. Generosity, which will find its way to another parish if this failure of a man continues."

Browner face was beginning to turn red. "Now, Miss Helmslow, let's not jump to conclusions. I'm sure if St. Patrick's were given a little more time…"

"There is no time!" she insisted. "I want a date, and I want it now, or there will be no new children's wing because there will be no new donations. Do I make myself clear?"

"Yes, Mrs. Helmslow," Browner squeaked as Helmslow turned her venomous attention to Mayberry. "As for this gentleman, I don't ever wish to see or listen to him and his incompetence again, and I think we both know what I mean by that." With that, she stormed out of the room, slamming the door behind her.

Both Mayberry and Browner sat in stunned silence.

It was Mayberry who was the first to speak. "I'm sorry, Father," he said apologetically.

"I'm sorry, too, Donald."

Here it comes, Mayberry thought. There was no use pleading, no use begging for forgiveness. He was finished. Helmslow had all but demanded it. All that was left was for Browner to say the words, and he'd be gone. To his credit, Browner didn't waste any time.

"I'm afraid I'm going to have to let you go," Browner stated.

"Of course, Father," Mayberry answered, disappointed.

"Good luck, Donald."

"Good luck to you, sir."

That finished, Mayberry stood and walked to the door, shell-shocked and disappointed, taking in the room for the last time. Despite his complaints and constant grumbling, he was sure going to miss this place.

***

Amanda stood in front of the mirror of the Starlight bathroom getting ready as Margot watched beside her.

"Do you think he'll show?" Amanda asked, pinning

the final earring in her ear. She was due to meet William in a few hours, and she was still nervous he wouldn't show after their last conversation. Of course, needing to leave from work again due to the busy wedding season didn't help. Amanda couldn't believe she was getting ready in the store bathroom again. She was starting to think she should just go ahead and move her stuff there, as it was starting to be a normal part of her routine. Oh well, she thought, at least she had a date and Margot for support, not to mention no Daniel showing up at the last minute to make her feel uncomfortable. Of course, as she thought it, Amanda's mind wandered to Daniel for what seemed the hundredth time. Stop it, she told herself. Each and every time she tried not to think of him, he somehow squeezed his way back into her mind. Shaking free of him once again, Amanda forced her mind to William.

"Well, do you?" Amanda asked again, looking at Margot who was now preoccupied, holding a pair of Amanda's earrings up to her own ears. "Margot? Do you or do you not think he will show?"

"Oh, sorry," Margot apologized, setting the earrings down and picking up another pair. "Of course he'll show. Why wouldn't he?"

"Because I'm crazy," Amanda answered.

"Well, there is that," Margot responded. "But I think he already knew that."

"Thanks," Amanda smirked. "But I'm serious. He seemed really weird when he left."

"You mean after he found out the girl he'd been seeing only a few weeks had his picture in a wedding scrapbook between pages of flowers and doilies and their future wedding, which was already planned?"

"Something like that."

"He's fine. Just cut him some slack," Margot reassured. "No one likes to be pressured. I know this as someone who can't help but pressure men." Margot turned to Amanda and put her hand on her shoulder. "William is different. He just needed a little time to process everything."

Amanda hoped Margot was right. If not, it was sure to be a short dinner even if William did show.

"Maybe I should call him and make sure he's coming," Amanda wondered aloud.

"Why?" Margot asked.

"Because he hasn't called."

"Because he's busy saving people's lives," Margot reassured.

"I guess you're right," Amanda agreed. "How about a text?"

"No."

"Tweet?"

"No."

"Email?"

"No!"

"Fine. I'll just show up and hope he's there."

"Which he will be," Margot reassured.

"And if he's not, I'll just take a detour on the way home and throw myself in the Central Park lagoon," Amanda exaggerated.

"Stop worrying," Margot demanded. "He'll be there! Now go! Get out there and get your man while I sit here planning the rest of my life as a spinster."

"Fine. And you're not a spinster. Not yet anyway. You've got at least another six months."

"Thanks," Margot replied sarcastically. "Now go or you'll end up like me."

"Okay." Amanda threw up her hands in defeat, gazing at her hair one last time in the mirror. "Wish me luck!"

"Good luck!" Margot replied.

And with that, Amanda was out the door.

***

As Amanda sat at the table waiting for William, she couldn't help but notice more and more couples entering. Perfect, Amanda thought. All the more people to watch her get stood up. And of course she had arrived early, so even if William did arrive on time, she'd still have to sit alone for what seemed like forever waiting for him to show.

Rearranging the silverware for what seemed the thousandth time, Amanda's mind drifted to Daniel. She wondered if he'd used his new toaster. She wondered if he was enjoying it. She wondered if the next time he had company he'd use all four slots to toast with. She wondered if his company would be a woman and felt a sudden twinge of jealousy.

"What am I doing?" Amanda asked herself. What was wrong with her? Daniel was over and done with. He technically hadn't even begun. It was time to get on with her real life with William. The William she wanted to be with, she told herself, the William who may or may not be showing up in the next few minutes to meet her for dinner. The same William she would be having two point whatever doctor babies with if all went well.

When William did finally arrive, Amanda relaxed. He was dressed nicely, she thought, even more so than usual, if that was possible, and he was smiling as he neared. That had to be a good sign.

"Sorry I'm late," he said apologetically. "I had an emergency appendectomy and we just finished up. I hope you weren't waiting long."

"Not at all," Amanda lied. "Besides, all that matters is you're here now."

"That I am," William smiled, picking up his menu.

"And you're not mad?" Amanda asked nervously.

William set the menu down and gazed at Amanda. "Of course not," he replied. "But I'd be lying if I said we didn't need to talk."

"Really?" Amanda didn't like the sound of that.

"Yes. Seeing your plans and all that work you put into your scrapbook has definitely made me think."

"Bad think or good think?" Amanda asked nervously.

"We'll talk about it," William responded vaguely, picking up his menu again.

What does that mean? Amanda wondered. She hated to be kept in suspense. He was probably going to break up with her, she reasoned, which is why he was hiding behind his menu. And he would do it in that emotionless doctor way where they drop a bomb on you and pretend like nothing happened. Amanda couldn't believe this was happening again. Why did she keep meeting men for dinner? She was practically asking to be abandoned. From here on out, she determined, she was eating alone in the comfort of her own home and was never going to dinner again.

"Is everything alright?" William asked.

They'd ordered dinner, and now that there was nothing to take over Amanda's attention, she'd resorted to fidgeting nervously and twirling her hair.

"I'm great," Amanda responded.

"Good," William said, taking a quick sip of wine before continuing. "Then why don't we get to it?"

Get to it? Amanda's heart sank. Here goes, she thought. It would be the beginning of the end.

It didn't help that William started off exactly like Carl had.

"First of all, Amanda, you're amazing," he began.

"Thank you," she responded warily.

"And any guy would be lucky to have you," William continued.

Amanda shrunk in her chair. Does every guy follow the same script, she thought, because it certainly seemed like it.

William paused before continuing. "Amanda, with my profession, I don't have a lot of time to waste, so if I know a relationship's not working, I end things quickly."

"I understand," Amanda whispered.

"That said, when I discovered your book it was clear that there are certain things you want and certain ideas you have for achieving them, and I wouldn't want you to waste your time either. I don't want to cause uncertainty. That wouldn't be fair to you or to me."

"Of course." Amanda was starting to feel sick to her stomach. Maybe she would pass out again. At least that would temporarily take her out of her misery.

"Having said that..." William continued.

Amanda wanted him to stop. She wanted him to just quit and walk away. More than anything, she wanted to disappear. Why couldn't she disappear, Amanda thought, as William began backing up his chair? He was going to leave. He was going to walk out on her just like Carl had. Amanda couldn't watch. Burying her face in her hands, Amanda attempted to gather her senses. Why did this keep happening to her? Why did she keep getting broken up with at restaurants?

"Amanda?" William asked from somewhere beyond her fingers. "Amanda?" he repeated, causing her to look up from behind her hands. It was at that moment Amanda realized William wasn't walking away or breaking up with her. She knew because when she pulled her hands away, she saw that William was still right in front of her, he was on one knee, and he was holding a ring out to her.

"Will you marry me?" he asked.

"What?" Amanda responded in complete shock.

"Will you marry me?" William repeated. "I know it's sudden, but that's what both of us want. Marry me and let's have your Starlight wedding."

Amanda wanted to respond. She wanted to jump up and run around the restaurant waving her arms in victory like the winner of the New York Marathon. But with so many emotions running through her head, and even Daniel's face popping up in there, too, Amanda felt herself getting lightheaded. It was happening again. She was going to pass out. One second, she was looking at William and the ring, and the next she was staring at the black void of darkness trying to overtake her. Amanda never felt herself slip from her chair. She never felt herself land with a thud on the carpet. It was only after she came around again and saw William and what seemed like the entire restaurant looking down at her that she knew it had already happened. Yet there he was, still on one knee, still holding the ring and, miraculously, still waiting for an answer. Amanda felt herself get lightheaded again. She felt herself floating away. But this time, before losing herself to unconsciousness, she reached out, grabbed the ring, and screamed, "Yes!" before everything went black.

CHAPTER FIFTEEN

MARGOT STARED AT THE RING in disbelief. This couldn't be happening. She was sure of it. It had to be a figment of her imagination. Yet there it was on Amanda's finger as real as could be, which meant Amanda was getting married. Amanda was going to have her Starlight wedding. "You said yes?" she repeated for the tenth time since Amanda had shown her.

"Of course I said yes!" Amanda responded, as she walked around the desk in her office. "I'm wearing it, aren't I?

"True."

In truth, Margot had seen the ring a million times since Amanda had stopped by her apartment the night before, but Margot still couldn't believe it. "You got engaged!"

"I did!" Amanda hopped in place in celebration. "But why are you acting so surprised?" Amanda asked, suddenly self-conscious.

"I don't know," Margot answered. "It's just, you usually do the wrong thing."

"Thanks," Amanda replied sarcastically.

"That's not what I mean," Margot tried to explain. "I just mean I'm not used to you doing that. There's usually a good story to tell. You know, like someone falling off a cliff or a car chase or something."

"I did pass out," Amanda responded matter-of-factly.

"Good point," Margot admitted before adding, "Wait, what about Daniel?"

"What about him?" Amanda was doing her best not to think of him. She hoped he'd be happy cuddling up to his toaster in the mornings.

"I don't know. It seemed like you were warming up to him. You're not having second thoughts? You're not wishing he were the one?" Margot asked.

"Of course not!" Amanda denied it a little too forcefully. "I'm happy for him—and his toaster."

"Good. So you haven't thought of him once since the proposal?"

"Not once," Amanda lied. "Because I don't want Daniel. I want William."

"Really?" As her best friend, Margot could tell when Amanda was lying. Putting her hand on her hip, Margot gave Amanda her classic stare.

"I mean not like that," Amanda promised.

"Then like what? You did get him a toaster, remember?" Margot reminded.

"A goodbye toaster!" Amanda assured.

"Whatever. As long as you're sure."

"A hundred percent. He's a Neanderthal, remember?" Amanda added somewhat desperately.

"A cute Neanderthal," Margot pointed out.

"Fine. He's cute. Now can we focus on the ring and the proposal and William?" Amanda pleaded.

"It is a pretty ring," Margot said, gazing at the ring again. "And big!"

"It is isn't it? I think it's two carats," Amanda boasted.

"That's exactly what you wanted!"

"See? William gets me!" Amanda agreed. "Not that I wouldn't have said yes otherwise. But it doesn't hurt."

"No, it doesn't. He could have had me for one and a half," Margot said. "And you guys haven't even done it yet."

"Margot!"

"Well..." Margot raised her hands in defense. "I'm just saying! Speaking of which, are you going to save yourself for the wedding?"

"Of course."

"Really?"

"I don't know. I hadn't thought of it."

"I have," Margot replied. "I mean not like that. I just find it interesting that the only one you've been with since you met William is Daniel, not William."

"Don't remind me."

"Was it that bad? I thought you were warming up to him."

"I was. And no it wasn't," Amanda said truthfully. Amanda shook her head trying to get rid of the image in her mind. "But no more talking about Daniel!"

"You're right. Sorry. No more Daniel," Margot promised. "Daniel has been stricken from memory. There will be no more Daniel."

"Good," Amanda relaxed. "So what was it you came

to tell me?"

"Nothing. Just..." Margot shrugged guiltily, then handed Amanda a note she'd carried in from the other room. "Daniel called. He said he had a question about the toaster."

After Margot left, Amanda crumpled the post it and threw it in the trash. So what if Daniel had questions about the toaster? He could figure it out on his own. It's not like she owed him anything. She had a wedding to plan: a real wedding in a real venue. Besides, she was going to be William's now, and she didn't have time to waste on Daniel or his toaster. Amanda knew he was calling because he'd heard about her engagement. No, it had just been last night, so unless he had been at the restaurant, there'd be no way he could know. It's not like William would have told him. Besides, it wasn't his business anyway. He could figure it out on his own or not. Amanda looked at her ring and had to admit it felt oddly bittersweet and wondered if it had something to do with Daniel. No, it was probably just nerves she told herself. Once again confident she'd made the right decision, Amanda picked up the phone to begin doing the thing she'd waited so long to do—make her wedding arrangements.

***

Daniel sat silently at the kitchen table reading the paper while Amanda's toaster heated up behind him. As far as morning news was concerned, it was much the same—war in the Middle East and politicians arguing about everything. Nothing new there.

The latest rift was over an oil pipeline, not that Daniel could remember anything about it. He had read at least a half-dozen articles so far but couldn't remember a single one. Despite his determination to move on, all he could think about was Amanda. It had been days since he'd heard from her, and seeing how she hadn't called him back after he'd left her a half a dozen messages, he wasn't sure if he'd ever hear from her again. Of course, none of it made sense. He had accepted her wishes to be alone after helping her with Mayberry but then she'd shown up at his door with the toaster acting all strange. Why give someone a gift, he reasoned, especially an odd one like a toaster, if you wanted them out of your life? Daniel knew Amanda was trying to convince herself she didn't want him. He had to admit, women were a mystery, and Amanda was the biggest mystery of them all.

Flipping the newspaper page, Daniel found himself at the announcements section and laughed at the irony. Typical, he thought, hearing his toast pop in the toaster behind him. The world had good timing, as usual. Getting up, Daniel grabbed his bread from the toaster, the jam from the fridge, and brought them back to the table. He was just about to sit down when he saw Amanda's picture. It was in the center of the page under wedding announcements. William's photo was next to hers in a separate photo. Both sat below a caption announcing their engagement. Daniel looked at the photos, stunned. She'd done it. She'd actually gotten engaged. Of course her photo looked amazing, as expected, as did William's, he had to admit. Daniel assumed they were in separate pictures due to time. Clearly, the toaster had been a goodbye gift after all, Daniel sadly realized. And clearly, his help with Mayberry had worked because she was now engaged to William with a wedding date set. Lucky them. Once again, the fancy doctors of the world had won, and the seemingly poor artist had proved no match.

Daniel thought of the irony of it all. If he had just told her he was wealthy, if he had shown her there was more to him than that of a struggling artist, maybe things would have been different. But then she would have been like every other woman hanging around for the wrong reasons. Not to mention, he would have had to actually take his father up on his offer, join the corporate world, and give up on his dreams.

No, it was a no-win situation, and Daniel knew it. Amanda wanted William, was going to be wed to William, and there was nothing he could do about it.

***

As Mayberry finished packing up the last box of items from his office, he couldn't help wondering what had gotten him to this moment of uncertainty. Just weeks ago, he had come back from vacation, tan and relaxed, with his job secure, knowing he had nearly every weekend of the Cathedral booked for the next two years. He'd worked hard, done his job, and should have been able to relax until his next vacation. Now that would never happen. In one meeting with that spinster Helmslow and her expecting granddaughter, everything had changed. She had demanded the impossible, and when he hadn't been able to deliver, he had been fired and would now have to find a job elsewhere. It would probably mean moving. It would probably mean being out of work for an extended period of time. How in demand were people like him? He didn't know. He might never again get to spend time relaxing on the beach, and if he did, it would probably not be for a long time. Mayberry picked up the jar of sand he'd brought back from vacation and frowned. Why did life have to be so complicated? Why did it have to be so hard for everyone but the Helmslows of the world, who seemed to get everything they wanted? Well, not this time, Mayberry realized. She hadn't gotten what she'd wanted, which was why he was let go. Unfortunately, she'd taken him down with her, and there was nothing he could do to stop it.

Mayberry sighed as he set the sand garden he'd brought back from vacation in the box and wished things had gone differently. If only there had been some way to give the old bat what she wanted to save himself from her wrath. Then he could have gone on his way and forgotten her unpleasantness with his job still intact. Who knows, after time she might have grown fond of him, offering a wave or a hint of a smile when she saw him in Sunday service instead of demanding he lose his job. Not that he really cared or expected any pleasantries. He just wanted his job back. As annoying as working with brides was, he had to admit he was going to miss them. They were all a pain, but they were his pain, and the truth was he was going to miss their crazy demands. Well, all but one. Mayberry grew bitter thinking about the one bride who was responsible for his predicament more than any other:

Amanda Jones. If it weren't for her and her precious Carl, none of this would have happened. He was certain there was still something under the surface she was hiding, but that didn't matter now. Picking up the St. Patrick's calendar book off his desk, Mayberry flipped through it one last time, taking note of all the names he'd worked with over the last few years. He was just about to toss it aside when he heard the knock at his door. What now, Mayberry wondered? Who could possibly need anything from him now?

"Go away!" Mayberry grumbled but moved to the door nonetheless. Even though he'd been fired, he couldn't very well ignore everyone who showed up, despite the fact that he'd like to. "What do you want?" he said grumpily, swinging the door open.

On the other side of the door, a man stood waiting with a young lady. Both smiled hesitantly back.

"Nothing. We were just hoping to get married at St. Patrick's, and we were told you were the one to talk to," the man said reluctantly.

"Not anymore," Mayberry complained.

"Oh, sorry." The two looked at each other awkwardly. "Then I guess we'll come back," the man continued, apologetically.

"Good," Mayberry barked and then started to close the door.

"Wait," the woman said, stopping him. "Can we at least leave our number for someone to call?"

Mayberry sighed. This is what his life had come to. He was now errand boy for his replacement. "I suppose," he said, moving out of the way for them to enter. "Name?"

he asked, walking over to his desk. After grabbing a notepad and pen off his desk, Mayberry waited for them to answer.

"Well, my name is Carl Firestone, and this is my fiancée, Rachel," the man began. "And we'd like to get married…"

"What did you say?" Mayberry interrupted him.

"I said my name is Carl Firestone," the man repeated, "and this is my fiancée, Rachel."

"Your fiancée? And you're Carl? Carl Firestone?" Mayberry reconfirmed.

"That's right."

Mayberry shook his head in wonder. What were the odds of two Carl Firestones looking to get married around the same time? Even in New York.

"Why? Is everything all right?" the man asked, seeing the look on Mayberry's face.

"Yes. Oh, yes," Mayberry responded, suddenly hopeful. He wasn't sure what was going on, but he had a feeling he was going to enjoy the conversation very much.

"Everything is more than all right," Mayberry assured, smiling a little too broadly. "Why don't you two have a seat?" Offering chairs for the two to sit on, Mayberry walked around and took a seat behind his desk. "I believe we have a lot to talk about."

***

Daniel stood outside his friend Sheila's art gallery too conflicted to go inside. After an hour of nerve-wracked pacing back and forth at the loft, he had decided that to move on from Amanda, he'd need to get rid of all reminders of her once and for all. He'd already taken the statue with Amanda's face to the church a week ago. Now it was time to get rid of the other, more painful reminder—the painting of Amanda's mother. In order to do that, he'd have to get Sheila to put it up for sale. It should have been easy, but now that he was here standing outside the gallery, the idea of parting with his last reminder of Amanda was proving far more difficult than he'd originally imagined. Yet as much as he hated to get rid of it, he knew it would continue to remind him of her as long as he had it. Luckily, since Sheila owned the gallery and would take it on consignment, he could make the best of a difficult situation. He could earn a little money, get it out of his sight, and know it had gone to someone who'd appreciate it. Satisfied he'd made the right decision, Daniel grabbed the painting and headed inside.

***

"Are you sure about this?" Sheila asked, looking over the painting as Daniel stood nearby. "Are you sure you want to sell it?" Even in the light, she could see nothing wrong with it. "It has no sentimental value?"

"Of course not," Daniel responded. "Why do you ask?"

"Because you've never brought anything here before."

"So?"

"So I know you, Daniel, remember? We went to art school together. I know you wouldn't bring it here if it didn't mean something to you."

"That doesn't make sense," Daniel argued. "This is a

gallery."

"But it's true, isn't it? Otherwise you'd paint over it. So who's the woman?" Sheila asked. "Someone special?"

"No," Daniel lied.

Sheila didn't believe him. "I'm not selling it until you tell me."

"Fine," Daniel consented. "It is someone special, but not to me. She's special to someone I care about. And I don't want to look at it any longer. Now will you take it?"

Sheila reluctantly took the painting and leaned it against the counter. "If you're sure. Because once it sells, I can't get it back. It'll be gone for good."

"I'm sure," Daniel affirmed.

"Okay," Sheila agreed. "Then I'll call you when it sells."

"Thank you," Daniel said relieved, watching her carry it to the back room.

Yet even as the painting disappeared around the corner, Daniel realized he still didn't feel better. He wasn't foolish enough to think his feelings for Amanda would magically disappear, but getting rid of the painting had done nothing for him. In fact, he felt worse. The painting was his last physical connection to Amanda, and now it was gone.

Even worse, he had no idea who it was going to or where it would end up. It was like breaking up with someone all over again, which was ironic, Daniel realized, because not once in this whole time had he actually ever really been with Amanda. Yet even now, something was eating him up inside and had been ever since Amanda had shown up on his doorstep—the fact that she had come to him. She had made an excuse and come to him. It wasn't something he had planned or maneuvered.

It was her meeting him halfway. But why? As Daniel exited the gallery, he looked up and saw a perfume advertisement and finally figured it out. In the ad, a caption read, "The heart wants what it wants," and it suddenly clicked for him. That's why she'd come. Amanda's head might be telling her one thing, but her heart was saying something else. She was in love with him even if she didn't want to admit it, and she was about to make a mistake by marrying William instead of following her heart and marrying him. But what could he do? It's not like she would listen to him. She had made her decision. Showing up now would amount to nothing. Passing a subway tunnel, Daniel realized it was time make a decision. Go straight and forget about her once and for all or take the train to her and face certain rejection. Daniel's legs wavered back and forth. Straight, Daniel decided. He should go straight. He had caused enough trouble. It was time to move on. But no sooner had Daniel taken his first step than he knew he couldn't continue. His heart wouldn't allow it. He had to give it one more chance. His decision made, Daniel turned and raced down the stairs into the subway tunnel.

***

Exiting the station by Amanda's shop, Daniel saw the sign for Starlight Weddings. With any luck, Amanda would be there and he'd—well he didn't know what he'd do, he just knew he needed to see her as soon as possible and tell her she was making a mistake. After that, it would be up in the air. More than likely there'd be yelling, objects thrown, and she'd force him onto the street, but he knew he couldn't let that stop him. He had to say something—for both of them. Reaching the front entrance, Daniel flung the door open and barged inside, but Amanda was nowhere to be seen. In fact, other than shop girl, Chloe, there was no one in the store. He'd missed her again. According to Chloe, Amanda had just left and was headed for Central Park. If he left quickly, he might be able to catch her.

Thanking Chloe, Daniel raced outside and down the street, passing shop after shop to no avail. With so many people in New York, it was doubtful he'd get within a thousand feet of her. Daniel told himself he needed to move faster. Picking up speed, Daniel entered the park and ran up the first path he came upon. Thinking Amanda might be more inclined for solitude, Daniel decided to check the northern trails first and stay away from the touristy southern section, but aside from the occasional picnicking couple and jogger, he didn't see anyone, let alone Amanda. Exhausted, Daniel stopped on the bridge overlooking the lagoon to catch his breath—and that's when she saw him.

"Daniel?"

She had come up behind and was looking at him in disbelief.

"Amanda...you're here."

"I'm here," Amanda responded, confused. "What are you doing here?"

Daniel saw she was holding the scrapbook in her hand as she moved closer.

STARLIGHT WEDDING

"I need to talk to you."

"Why?"

"Because..."

Daniel took a deep breath. It was now or never. It was time to say what he came to say before he went away forever. "Amanda, you can't marry William. I know you want to, or think you want to, but you can't."

"Why?" Amanda looked back sharply.

"Because you have to marry me. You love me, Amanda. I know you do." Daniel felt relief just saying it. "There's something between us. I've felt it ever since I met you. I know you feel it, too. That's why you came to the apartment. That's why you gave me a toaster. You have feelings for me. I know you do."

"I don't!" Amanda promised. This was not what she wanted to talk about. Not here. Not anywhere. "I love William. The toaster was just me being nice."

"And the other stuff?"

"What other stuff?"

"In the apartment…"

"That was a mistake!" Amanda said adamantly.

"It wasn't," Daniel responded. "I can feel it every time I kiss you."

"Then stop kissing me!"

"I will," Daniel promised, "if you can kiss me one time and tell me it doesn't mean anything."

"I'm not doing that."

"Because you can't."

"Because I don't want to."

"Because you can't."

"Because I don't want to!" Amanda said firmly. "And

I don't have to. I'm a grown woman, and I choose not to."

"Chicken."

"What did you say?"

"I said, chicken."

"Fine. Whatever. I'm a chicken. I'm still not kissing you."

"Then I'm kissing you." With that, Daniel lunged forward and kissed her. There it was. The connection. He'd felt it. He was sure she felt it, too.

"Stop it!" Amanda said, pushing him away.

"Why? Because you liked it?"

"No, because I didn't," Amanda lied. "I don't want to kiss you. I want to kiss William!"

"Mr. Perfect?"

"Yes, Mr. Perfect. Not Mr. Delivery boy." It was a low blow, but he deserved it, Amanda thought. "Is that good enough for you?"

"So you're a snob."

"Fine, I'm a snob," Amanda said proudly. "I like nice things—things that people with plans have. Crazy things like food and shelter and, oh, here's a wild one…paying bills on time! Things I didn't have after my parents died."

"But what about passion?"

"I have passion," Amanda insisted. "Just as much passion as you do."

"Really? Then prove it. Show me it somewhere in this book of yours," Daniel asked, grabbing the scrapbook and flipping it open.

"No! Give it back!" Amanda commanded.

"I will but…"

"Give it back right now!"

"Just prove it."

"No!" Amanda lunged for the book, accidentally knocking it from Daniel's grasp. As both watched, the book went flying. Daniel reached for it. So did Amanda, but it was too late. The book flew over the edge and dropped into the water below.

Amanda stared at the water in disbelief. "My scrapbook!" she screamed. All she wanted was to jump in and save it, but it was too late. It was gone.

Daniel's heart sunk. "Amanda, I'm sorry. I'm so sorry," Daniel pleaded as the book sank below the surface.

But Amanda couldn't hear. Every bit of her was concentrated on the water where the book she'd spent a lifetime creating had disappeared. "It's gone."

"I'm sorry," Daniel repeated, reaching out to comfort her. "If I had…"

"Stop! Get away from me!" Amanda screamed, pushing him away. "It's too late. It's all too late!" With that, Amanda took off as fast as she could to get away from him.

As Amanda raced through the park, she couldn't help but feel like she'd lost her most important possession. The scrapbook was a symbol of everything she held dear. She had started it as a child. She had worked on it as a teenager. She had spent countless hours with her mother pouring over it and improving it—and now she would never see it again. Amanda slowed to a stop letting the emotion overwhelm her. Just a few hours before she had been in complete control, and once again, Daniel had ruined it. Now she would have to finish planning her wedding without the use of the scrapbook that held all of her and her mother's ideas. Every part of her wanted to cry. Every part of her wished it were a bad dream—yet when she believed it couldn't get any worse, she felt her phone vibrate in her pocket.

"Hello," Amanda answered without looking.

"Miss Jones, this is Donald Mayberry." Amanda heard Mayberry say from the other end of the line.

Great, Amanda thought, just what I need. Mayberry was the last person she wanted to talk to. Why was he calling, and why now? Something must be wrong. He sounded strange, Amanda thought, even though he had only said a few words, and she sensed it would have been better had she not answered.

"How do you do, Mr. Mayberry?" Amanda asked warily. She didn't really care, but she felt she should start pleasantly.

"Funny you should ask, Miss Jones," Mayberry responded. "I was having the worst possible day..."

"I'm sorry," Amanda answered, though in truth she didn't know why he was telling her. "I hope it has gotten better."

"Oh, it has," Mayberry responded smugly. "It very much has. And do you know why?"

Amanda had no idea but was sure she was about to.

"It has gotten better," Mayberry proceeded, "because I just received a visit from someone you know."

Amanda stiffened. "Someone I know?" Crap, she thought. This really was getting worse. "Oh, really?" Amanda asked as nonchalantly as possible while her mind raced a million miles a minute. The suspense was killing her. Who could it be and why would it matter to her? "And who was that?" she finally asked.

The line went silent as Mayberry paused for effect. Each second that passed, Amanda could feel her insides twisting further into knots.

"Hello? Mr. Mayberry? Are you there?"

"Oh, I'm here," Mayberry answered. "And so is your fiancé, Carl. Well, I should say the real Carl. Not the one you brought. And guess who he brought? You'll never believe it. He brought his fiancé, Rachel."

Amanda gasped so loud she saw a few park goers turn around and stare at her. He brought Rachel? That could only mean one thing.

"I think you have some explaining to do, Miss Jones," Mayberry admonished. "But it's no matter. All is well."

Amanda didn't like the sound of that.

"It is?" Amanda asked skeptically. "But what about the wedding?"

"The wedding?" Mayberry asked, stringing it out for effect. "Oh, the wedding is off. At least your wedding. You may find a church to get married in, Miss Jones, but you will definitely, one hundred percent, not be getting married at St. Patrick's." And with that, he hung up.

CHAPTER SIXTEEN

DANIEL STARED DOWN AT THE WATER in shock. Had he really just done that? Had he really just destroyed Amanda's prized possession? How was that possible? Of course, he hadn't meant to ruin her scrapbook. He hadn't meant for any of it to happen. One minute he was trying to get Amanda to admit her feelings and the next her scrapbook was lost. Daniel felt a knot growing in the pit off his stomach. How could he have been so stupid? Now she'd surely never speak to him again. The scrapbook was ruined, and it was entirely his fault. Daniel moved to the railing and looked down at the spot where the scrapbook had disappeared. It was in there somewhere, sinking to the bottom. It was probably too late to save, but if there was a chance, he knew he'd have to act quickly; and to do that he'd have to go in. He'd have to dive into the water and go after it. Without a moment to lose, Daniel ripped off his shirt, took a deep breath, and dove into the lagoon.

STARLIGHT WEDDING

As Daniel hit the water, he felt a rush as the cold water overtook him. For a summer day, the water was surprisingly brisk. Of course, there wasn't much he could do about that now. He just needed to find the scrapbook and get out quickly. Desperate to get it over with, Daniel reached out blindly, feeling the water around him in hopes of finding it on the way down. The water was too murky to see clearly, but he was confident he was in the right area. He had to be, he told himself, or it would all be for nothing. Suddenly his feet hit bottom. Kneeling, Daniel swept the floor of the lagoon desperately, hoping to cover as much as possible before he had to return to the surface. Yet even now, Daniel could already feel his lungs burning. He wouldn't be able to last much longer. Out of air, he was just about to push off and head to the surface when he felt something hit him in the head. It was the scrapbook making its way down. Elated, Daniel grabbed it and made his way up. Breaking through the surface, Daniel gasped for air as he swam ashore. Of course he knew he didn't have much time. If he was going to save the scrapbook, he knew he'd need to get it in a freezer as soon as possible to begin the dehydration process, a trick he'd learned in art school. It wasn't foolproof, but it was his only chance. Luckily, any clippings inside the contact paper would be partially protected, which would help. Of course he wouldn't know for weeks if the attempt worked but he knew he had to try. It was the least he could do. So wet, shirtless, and clutching the book in his arms, Daniel took off for home.

***

Mayberry unpacked the last of the boxes. He'd done it. He'd gotten his job back. And all it had taken was a little luck, a little begging, and a little crushing of Amanda Jones's hopes. Poor girl—not that she didn't deserve it, he reminded himself. She'd lied to his face and, what's more, had brought in a fake fiancé. A fake fiancé! What would they come up with next, Mayberry wondered? After doing this for so many years, he thought he'd seen everything, but that one definitely took the prize for the most ridiculous thing he'd ever seen, which was saying a lot as far as brides were concerned. Not that he blamed her. He knew she was desperate and had her heart set on that day because of the comet thing he didn't really understand. Well, too bad. She'd cost him his job, which he was only fortunate to have gotten back through sheer luck, and now she wouldn't be getting married at St. Patrick's because of it. Taking his sand garden out of the box and returning it to his desk, Mayberry was just letting out a satisfied sigh as Browner's secretary poked her head into his office.

"Mr. Mayberry, do you have a minute?" she asked. "Father Browner has an emergency, and he'd like to see you in his office."

An emergency? That was certainly something Mayberry didn't hear every day.

"Of course. I'll be right there," Mayberry answered. As long as the emergency had nothing to do with him he didn't care. He'd go to Browner's office every hour if it meant keeping his job. Giving his office one last look, Mayberry put some sand in his pocket for good luck and followed Browner's secretary down the hall.

STARLIGHT WEDDING

***

Helmslow was waiting outside the door when Mayberry arrived. For a woman who'd just gotten her wish, Mayberry felt she could certainly appear more grateful. She had the look of someone doomed to the gallows, but he guessed she probably always looked that way no matter how she was doing. He certainly didn't expect a smile, that's for sure. She was on her cell phone and was pacing back and forth, and Mayberry could already tell what this meeting would be about—her. Oh well, he accepted. He had his job back, and that's all he could ask for. Whatever problems came now were secondary.

Hanging up, Helmslow followed Mayberry into Browner's office as if she had been waiting for him the whole time and his presence somehow allowed the meeting to begin. If that wasn't odd enough, even Browner stood upon Mayberry's entrance and greeted him immediately.

"Mr. Mayberry!" Browner began. "I'm glad you're here. We've had a bit of an emergency."

"So I heard," Mayberry answered, taking a glance over to Helmslow who had already taken a seat. "What seems to be the problem?"

"It's Miss Helmslow."

"My niece," Helmslow clarified. "She's gone missing."

"Missing?" Mayberry asked. "For how long?"

"Since this morning," Helmslow answered as seriously as could be imagined.

"She wasn't in her bed and didn't appear at breakfast."

Mayberry wondered what all the fuss was about.

Surely she'd just gone for a walk or to see her fiancé. That was hardly missing. Of course, with what few friends he had, Mayberry surmised he could be gone for an entire month before someone would notice, including his mother, and even then only because they needed something for their wedding, like keys to the cathedral.

"And you're sure she's gone?"

"She left a note saying not to go looking for her."

Mayberry did his best to act concerned. "I see."

As Mayberry thought about it, Browner stepped closer to address him personally. "We thought perhaps she might have contacted you."

"Me?"

"Yes. About the wedding," Helmslow added. "With it coming up so quickly, we thought perhaps she might have contacted you about arrangements."

"I'm afraid not," Mayberry answered, baffled he'd even registered in Helmslow's mind at all. It's not like they were exactly close. She had gotten him fired after all.

"Apparently she and Mrs. Helmslow had a bit of a disagreement yesterday," Browner expounded.

"She's been very difficult since the pregnancy. And the father of the child has always been disagreeable. I was just voicing my concerns about their future," Helmslow said almost apologetically.

Imagine that, Mayberry thought. Sounds like a match made in heaven. Together they could be one big disagreeable family.

"So what do you think?" Browner asked, directing his question to Mayberry.

"Me?" Mayberry hadn't the slightest clue what to say,

but with both eyes on him, he felt he had to say something. This was quite extraordinary indeed, he thought, considering he'd temporarily lost his job over the union in the first place and was persona non grata up until a few days ago. Mayberry paused to give the appropriate latitude to Helmslow's comments before speaking.

"I believe we should wait."

"Wait?" Helmslow guffawed.

"Yes, wait. The young Miss Helmslow is clearly having a bit of a crisis and doesn't want to be found," Mayberry began. "She is most likely expressing her free will, yet I believe it will be temporary. In fact, I'll bet she returns before sundown if she's not back already."

"Sundown?" Helmslow couldn't believe what she was hearing. "That might as well be ten years from now. We need the police!"

"Forgive me, but the police won't do anything. Not for a period of hours."

"He's right," Browner agreed. "Mayberry may not be perfect, but he's usually correct in his assumptions."

Helmslow took a moment to digest the suggestion. "Alright. But if you hear from her, I want you to let me know."

Both nodded in agreement.

"We'll do that, Mrs. Helmslow," Browner stated. "In the meantime, try not to worry. I'm sure she'll be back shortly, and everything, including the wedding, will be fine."

Helmslow stood with resolve. "It better be, or she will be cut off." Helmslow stood in emphasis.

"Now, now, Mrs. Helmslow..." Browner cautioned, standing to be on her level. "Let's not overreact. We will find her, and everything will go forward as planned. Isn't that right, Mr. Mayberry?"

"You have our word, Mrs. Helmslow. You have nothing to worry about," Mayberry lied. In truth, he had no idea what her poor niece was going through, and quite frankly, would have run away too if he had to deal with the likes of her on a daily basis. But if it were up to him, he'd never come back.

***

Daniel walked up the New York University steps faster than he'd anticipated. It had been a week since he'd emerged with the scrapbook, ran it twenty-two blocks to his apartment, and stuck it in the freezer to start the dehydration process, and less than a day since he'd taken it to the art department at his former school to use one of their commercial air dryers to speed the process. In just a few minutes, he'd know if everything he'd done had worked or if his efforts had been in vain. In a few moments, he'd know if the scrapbook was ruined indefinitely. Mack, his former chain-smoking art professor, hadn't offered any promises when he'd seen it the day before. It's not like air-drying scrapbooks was an exact science. He'd given Daniel reason to hope for the possibility of success, and that was about it. Then he'd asked if Daniel wanted a cigarette. Politely declining, Daniel had gone home reasonably assured. But that was yesterday, and today he was nervous.

Knocking on Professor Mack's door, Daniel couldn't

help feeling butterflies in the pit of his stomach. It was just nerves he told himself. It was exactly like how he'd felt before a big football game in high school. It would pass as soon as he saw the outcome, one way or another. Then he'd have to make decisions. Either throw the ruined scrapbook away or give it to Amanda in its new form, whatever that form might be. He hoped for the latter and hoped the scrapbook could be restored, but he knew it could go either way.

When the professor opened the door and saw Daniel, Daniel noticed he had a frown on his face, causing Daniel to panic.

"What is it? Is everything all right? How'd it go?" Daniel asked apprehensively.

After making a barely audible noise of frustration, the professor turned and waved for Daniel to follow. "You'd better see for yourself." Mack led Daniel to the back room where the now dry scrapbook sat resting by itself on a giant stainless steel table.

From a distance, it was hard to tell, yet as Daniel neared, he could already tell there was a large mark of discoloration on the front cover. Daniel's heart sank as the professor tried to explain what must have happened.

"More than likely the color bled as you were running home with it." The professor explained. "However, I went ahead and painted it, and once it dries, it won't even be noticeable."

The professor paused to gauge Daniel's reaction. "I know it's not ideal, but that's the worst of it. Now for the good part..." The professor flipped through the scrapbook, giving Daniel a look at each page. All seemed perfectly normal, as if nothing had happened. The drying process had worked. Aside from the damaged cover, the scrapbook was nearly perfect.

"It worked," Daniel said, relieved.

"It appears so," the professor answered.

"When can I take it?"

"You can take it now," the professor explained. "However, I personally would let it sit a couple more days before you do anything with it to give the paint ample time to dry. But I'm sure I don't have to tell you that."

Daniel felt relief as he looked down at the restored scrapbook. "No, you don't. Thank you, professor. I have a feeling this will make someone very happy."

***

Amanda was sitting in her office when it came. Closing her eyes after a long day, planning what seemed like a never-ending parade of wedding arrangements in between work appointments, Amanda had nearly dozed off to sleep when she heard the knock on her door.

"Come in," she replied, quickly straightening in her chair.

It was Margot. She had a look on her face like she'd just seen a ghost.

"What is it?" Amanda asked, concerned. "Is everything alright? Did something happen to Eduardo? Chloe?"

Margot shook her head. "I'm fine. The store's fine. Everyone is fine. It's this," Margot explained, holding out the package Amanda now saw she was carrying. "It's a package—from Daniel."

"Daniel?" Amanda hadn't heard from him in weeks. After the bridge incident, she wasn't sure she ever wanted to hear from him again. Not that she hadn't thought of him.

"I wonder what it is," Margot expressed, crossing over to hand the package to Amanda. "It's certainly heavy enough."

Amanda looked at the package like it was about to come alive. "Should I open it?"

"Up to you," Margot answered, shrugging her shoulders. "But if not…I certainly will."

Amanda immediately handed the package back. "Go ahead. Do it."

"Really?"

"Yes. I can't," Amanda promised.

Margot stared at the package, flipping it over and back to get a good look at it.

"Alright, here goes." Amanda watched nervously as Margot tore open the UPS package and looked inside. Upon seeing its contents, Margot's mouth dropped, causing Amanda to sit up in her chair.

"What is it?"

"Oh my God!" was all Margot could say.

"Well?" Amanda repeated, to which Margot shoved the half-open package to Amanda across the desk.

"It's…" Margot couldn't even get the words out. After hearing about the scrapbook incident over and over the last few weeks, it was the last thing she'd expected to see. As far as she knew, the scrapbook was still sitting at the bottom of the Central Park lagoon.

"My scrapbook," Amanda said incredulously upon

seeing it. "But how? That's impossible!"

Amanda pulled what should have been her ruined scrapbook from the package and stared at it in shock. Aside from a slight discoloration on the front cover, which she assumed Daniel must have painted to match the rest of the cover, it looked perfectly normal. Lifting the cover, Amanda turned to the first page, then another. To her surprise, they all looked undamaged. All of her years of hard work, all of that time spent with her mother, had been somehow saved. She was sure Daniel had ruined her book, but somehow he had also saved it.

"It looks amazing," Margot commented, taking the words out of Amanda's mouth. "But you said it dropped into the lake."

"It did," Amanda promised. "I saw it go in with my own eyes."

"He must have gone in after it."

Amanda pictured Daniel jumping into the water after the scrapbook. It didn't make sense. "But there's no damage. It should be ruined."

"But it's not," Margot responded. "You have your book back—and you have Daniel to thank for it."

"Which I'm not going to."

"What? Why?" Margot asked incredulously.

"I can't." Amanda began, speaking just as much to herself as to Margot. "This is it. It's my chance to break away. I have the book, I have William, and now I can break away cleanly. I have to."

Margot shook her head disapprovingly. "If you say so."

"I do. Trust me. It's for the best," Amanda explained.

"I really appreciate that he did this for me, but now's my chance to move on. Now if you'll excuse me, I have work to do," Amanda added hastily, knowing if she didn't get Margot out of the room and stop talking about it, it would blow up into some big thing.

Margot eyed Amanda warily. "If you say so. But..." Margot stopped herself before finishing.

"What?"

"Nothing."

"What?" Amanda insisted. "Margot, you're my best friend. Whatever it is you have to say I want to hear it."

"Truthfully?"

"Yes."

"Okay. Well, truthfully, I think you're making a mistake. I know you think you want to marry William, but there's something between you and Daniel. The man jumped into a river for you."

"It was a pond."

"It was a lagoon. And you're acting like he casually picked it up with his morning coffee. Then he did God knows what with it to get it looking like he did, all so you'd have your most cherished possession. I'd say that's pretty special. And if someone did that for me, I'd be pretty darn impressed."

"I am."

"But you're not going to do anything about it?"

"No."

"Really?"

"Yes. Now is that all?" Amanda asked.

"Yes."

"Good. Because I still have a fiancé. And I still have

work to do."

"Fine, I'll leave you to it. But I meant what I said. Don't do something you'll regret." Having said it, Margot turned and left Amanda alone.

Amanda flipped another page in the scrapbook. Again, the page looked exactly as it had before the bridge, and Amanda knew Daniel must have put a lot of work into making it happen.

"Damn you, Daniel," Amanda said aloud. "Why must you always make everything so difficult?"

"What was that?" a voice said from somewhere behind her.

Amanda looked up and saw William standing at the door. As usual, he was holding a giant bouquet of flowers like he was every time he came to see her.

"It was nothing," Amanda lied, trying to change the conversation. The truth was William was perfect, and she didn't want to somehow muddy the conversation by speaking of Daniel.

"Are those flowers?" she asked, referring to the bouquet. It was the fourth time in as many nights he'd brought her flowers, and her office was beginning to rival the florist's on the corner in sheer volume. Clearly he was ready to accelerate the relationship and was doing his best to warm her up by buying her flowers and taking her to dinner. And why shouldn't he want that? He was her fiancé for goodness sake. He deserved some acceleration. Heck, she deserved it too! It was beyond time. There was just something keeping her from opening up to him intimately. It seemed every time she was about to go there something came up that reminded her of Daniel. No sooner did she start kissing William than suddenly Daniel would pop into her mind, and that was definitely not what she wanted to think about.

"Amanda, are you all right?" William asked, sensing her drifting. "I brought lilies. I know they're your favorite."

Amanda sighed. See, this is what courting was supposed to be like.

"Yes. You are too perfect," Amanda replied, taking the flowers. Amanda searched for an empty place to put them. "I'm running out of room to put them all. Any more and you're going to win the fiancé of the year award."

"Then I guess I'll just have to bring more," William said with a smile.

That's it, Amanda decided. Tonight was the night, Daniel be damned. William was going to get some. And there wasn't anything stupid Daniel memories could do about it.

***

Having made her decision, Amanda did her best to show William a little extra affection at dinner. She'd held his hand, laughed extra loud at his jokes, and even whispered in his ear a few times when he was close. Not all of their conversations were the most romantic, of course. They still had to talk wedding logistics due to its rapidly approaching nature, and she informed him of her choices for venues, but she made it a point to let him know tonight was the night. And on their way out, when he'd offered to walk her home instead of calling her a cab, she'd responded with a smile and a not too subtle response telling him exactly how this night would end. After that, they'd walked the romantic path through the park to her apartment holding hands. It was a little out of the way, but the excitement of the night more than made up for it. Exiting the park, Amanda couldn't help but feel she was embarking on a new adventure. She was marrying William, and there wasn't anything anyone, including Daniel, could do about it.

As they turned the first corner and crossed the street after leaving the park, William turned to Amanda, taking stock of her emotions.

"What are you thinking about?" he asked.

"You," she's answered with a smile.

"Me?"

"Yes, you."

"What about me?"

Amanda leaned close, whispering something in his ear. Oh, yes, she was going to enjoy this very much. By his expression, William clearly hadn't expected her to say what had come out of her mouth, but had immediately nodded in agreement, causing Amanda to laugh out loud as they stepped up onto the sidewalk together.

Only a few blocks from her apartment, Amanda was already picturing them alone together, when she suddenly stopped, and all the blood drained from her face.

"What? What is it?" William asked, catching his balance from the break in his stride. Getting no response, William attempted to look where Amanda was looking to discover what had caused the interruption. Following her eyes, William found himself looking in the window of an art gallery at the painting of a bride standing under the sparkle of a night sky. Amanda seemed to be stuck in a daze and couldn't look away.

"Amanda?" William asked, touching her gently. "What is it?"

It was a lovely painting but nothing to cause such a reaction, William thought.

Yet Amanda continued to stare at the painting she knew from Daniel's apartment. What was it doing here? And why was it in the gallery, she wondered. The painting had sent her mind racing in a million directions. It was only after staring at it for some time Amanda found herself able to form words.

"It's a painting of my mother."

CHAPTER SEVENTEEN

THE REST OF THE WALK went in a blur. And when they finally reached Amanda's apartment, Amanda thanked William for the evening and said goodbye. Though clearly disappointed, William pretended to understand. After giving Amanda a hug and kiss, he walked away. He was so understanding, Amanda lamented as she watched him go, and he always did the right thing. In fact, everything about him was perfect. Every. Single. Thing. So why was she conflicted? Why wasn't she ravishing him in her apartment right now instead of standing there alone?

Amanda was still asking herself the same questions the next day as she tried on her wedding dress for Margot. At least that's what she told herself. In truth, she knew she was trying it on for herself. She had to see how it made her feel.

"Well, what do you think," Amanda asked, twirling on a step in front of Margot? "Does it still look fantastic?"

"Mostly," Margot responded unenthusiastically.

"Mostly?"

"Well, the dress is fine."

"But?"

Margot could see something was going on in Amanda's mind. "It's you that worries me."

"Thanks," Amanda shot back sarcastically.

"I just mean something's wrong," Margot said. "I can tell when you're not happy. Look at you. Here you are chasing some crazy fantasy, but none of it really matters if you're not happy."

"It's not a fantasy."

"So then what's wrong? Is it the church? William?"

Amanda stepped off the stool, finding herself face to face with Margot. "I saw Daniel's painting last night."

"What painting?"

"The one of my mother. It was hanging in a gallery window. William and I saw it on our way back from dinner."

"You mean the one from Daniel's loft? The one you were looking at before you—"

"Yes."

"Oh…" Margot exclaimed. "So that's why you didn't go through with it."

"Hey!"

"I'm just saying! But how? Why was it there?"

"I don't know. Daniel must have been trying to get rid of it. Maybe he's attempting to move on."

"And how does that make you feel?"

It was a good question, Margot thought. In truth, Amanda didn't know how to respond.

"I don't know."

"Are you having second thoughts?"

"No. I don't know. Maybe."

Margot thought about it a moment.

"Okay, it's time to figure this out. Close your eyes."

"What?"

"Close your eyes."

"Okay." Amanda skeptically closed one eye.

"Both," Margot demanded.

"Fine."

Amanda reluctantly closed her other eye and waited.

"Now clear your mind. Are you doing that?"

"I think so."

"Great. Now picture your wedding cake."

Amanda wasn't sure where this was going, but just to humor Margot, she pictured the multi-tiered masterpiece Margot had come up with years before. "Got it."

"Perfect. Now I want you to picture every detail of it, starting from the bottom. Think of the icing, the flowers and columns, the intricate designs... Are you doing that?"

"Yes."

"Now look at the bride and groom on the top."

"Got it."

Margot waited for the image to set in Amanda's mind before asking the final question.

"What color hair does he have?"

"Who?" Amanda asked, her eyes still closed.

"The groom," Margot insisted. "What color is his hair?"

"Amanda's eyes shot open as the look of panic registered on her face. It was brown. The color of the groom's hair was brown—the same as Daniel's. It wasn't blond, like William's. She had pictured a tiny replica of Daniel because deep down inside, despite her outward objections, she knew he was the one she wanted to be with. She could deny it all she wanted, but she knew she was supposed to be with Daniel. He was the one her heart wanted. What's more, she knew if she didn't end up with him, she'd regret it for the rest of her life.

"Well?" Margot asked. "Who was it?" She could already tell by Amanda's ashen face and shocked expression what the answer was, but she wanted to hear her say it.

"It was Daniel," Amanda whispered. "Oh, my God, it was Daniel." Amanda could hardly believe she'd said it. What's more, she could hardly believe it was true. She was engaged to the wrong man. She was in love with Daniel. All this time, he had known and had been begging her to see it, but she had been too blind and stubborn to admit it.

Amanda grabbed her purse and started for the door. "I have to find him. I have to tell him."

"Wait!" Margot said, stopping her. "What about William?"

Amanda realized Margot was right. She was engaged. She had a fiancé.

"I don't know." Amanda knew she'd have to figure out how to tell William, but for now, she didn't have a moment to lose. Daniel was out there somewhere wandering aimlessly because she had pushed him away, and now she had to find him and tell him, or she might lose him forever.

***

Daniel stood in the door of his apartment for what felt like the first time in years and gave it one last look around. It had been a crazy few weeks. First he'd lost Amanda, and then he'd gotten a call from his mother informing him that his father had relapsed. Wishing to help out, he'd temporarily moved to their apartment and taken over the family business despite not having the slightest idea what he was doing. And now it seemed like forever since he'd done anything creative.

Stepping into the hall, Daniel closed the door, taking one last look at the easel where he'd painted Amanda's mother, and wondered when he'd paint again. In just a few weeks' time he'd gone from part-time artist to full-time businessman and caretaker, spending most of his time helping his mother take care of his father, while simultaneously doing his best to run a family business he barely knew or cared anything about. As for his father, even the doctor's didn't know when he would recover. They told him to prepare for the worst. And with his father on so many medications and constantly in and out of consciousness, Daniel had been required to figure out all of the business stuff on his own. Setting the key in the lock, Daniel locked it for what felt like the last time and thought of Amanda. It had been weeks since he'd retrieved the scrapbook and mailed it to Amanda, and even longer since he'd heard from her. By now, her wedding arrangements were probably in full swing. He knew he shouldn't be thinking of her, but he couldn't help it. Daniel remembered how he'd watched her walk down the hall. She'd shown up unannounced with the strange toaster and had given him reason to hope before abruptly leaving, leaving him in confusion once again. As the door shut, Daniel knew it was beyond time to accept that it was over. He'd be a busy man and she'd be married. Besides, he didn't have time to waste on something that would never happen. He'd have other worries running the family business; plenty of them.

On the street, Daniel hailed a cab and gave the suitcase to the driver. Slipping into the backseat, Daniel gave the address for his parents' high rise on the Upper East Side. It was the home he'd grown up in with wealthy neighbors in every part of the building, with servants and butlers and city views. It was a life he didn't care much about and one that would once again take getting used to, not to mention the difficulty of seeing his father in such a weak and incapacitated state. In the hospital the first time, his father had been lucid and greater than it all, but this time was more serious. The medication was stronger, the situation direr, and even though he had been released to home care, it had only been after his mother agreed to constant supervision. Of course, with his mother in perpetual hysterics, it had fallen on Daniel to take care of everything, which was ironic, he knew, considering how little he and his father had talked after he'd essentially been cut off. Yet with his father's life at risk, it had created a need that superseded petty disagreements. Not that his father had apologized. As far as he was concerned, Daniel was doing his duty by taking over the family business. If anything, he should have done it sooner.

Reaching his parent's building, Daniel paid the driver

and wheeled his suitcase to the front door where Jarvis Jenkins, the doorman he'd known since childhood, greeted him with a warm hello and opened the door for him. After exchanging pleasantries, Daniel entered and made his way to the elevator where childhood friend Caroline Helmslow waited nervously in the lobby with a young man he'd never seen before. Owners of the penthouse floor, the Helmslows had been in the building since before Daniel was born, and despite their riches, Daniel couldn't imagine a more miserable family. It seemed poor Caroline always had a tough go of it and had rebelled at every turn. By the look of her current man's appearance and her expecting nature, it seemed she was still doing it. Whatever the case, she was clearly scared to get on the elevator, and Daniel would have given anything to know why. Of course with the crusty Mrs. Helmslow as her grandmother, she didn't need any other reason to steer clear of the penthouse, in his mind. If she were his grandmother, he'd stay in the lobby too. He'd spent many days in the lobby with Jarvis as a kid, and his father wasn't half as bad as the older Helmslow. Stepping onto the elevator, Daniel wished them both well as he waited for the doors to close. As they did, Daniel felt his phone vibrate. Retrieving the phone from his pocket, Daniel stared at the display. It was a blocked number. What in the world, Daniel thought. That made the third time in ten minutes. He was tempted to answer it and give the caller a piece of his mind, but he knew better. That would only encourage whoever it was. No, more than likely it was just another robocall trying to sell him something useless or the cable company reminding him of his bill. Daniel shook his head, sending it to voicemail, and stuffed the phone back in his pocket.

***

Amanda hung up in frustration. Once again she'd gotten Daniel's voicemail. Where was he, she asked herself as she raced down the street. That was the third time she'd tried, and he hadn't answered any of them. Why was it when she wanted to get rid of him he was everywhere, and now that she wanted to make things right he suddenly disappeared? Nearing the subway, Amanda bounded down the stairs and ran for the platform. It was there she first noticed people beginning to stare. She thought it was because she was running, but after catching a glimpse of herself in a window, she realized she was still in her wedding dress and must have looked crazy. Maybe she was, she thought, crossing the platform and hopping on the train just in time. She certainly felt crazy. She was chasing after a man who, minutes before, she had been convinced she didn't want, in a dress she'd planned on wearing in a wedding to a man she thought she did. It made her head spin just thinking about it.

"Nice dress," a woman commented, staring at her.

"Thanks," Amanda responded, not sure if the woman was kidding or if it was actually a compliment. Turning away, Amanda found herself face to face with a homeless guy.

"Rough day?"

"Something like that," Amanda admitted, suddenly wishing she had taken a cab. As much as she liked attention, this was not the kind she was hoping for. Yet everywhere she turned, more eyes were on her. Great, this was going to be a fun ride, she thought, wishing she'd changed before she left.

When the train finally arrived at its destination, Amanda was the first one out. Desperate to find Daniel and not be stopped by questioning New Yorkers, she ran the entire way to Daniel's building. From here on out, she was definitely paying the extra money to take a cab, she promised herself, if only to save her pride; not to mention, she really needed to change out of the dress. But she'd worry about that later. First she needed to find Daniel and tell him she'd made a mistake. Taking the elevator to Daniel's floor, Amanda ran to Daniel's door and knocked.

"Daniel, it's me, Amanda," she yelled impatiently and then waited for him to answer. Hearing nothing, Amanda pounded again. "Daniel?"

Suddenly a lock turned in the door behind her. The door opened and a neighbor's head poked out.

"If you're looking for Daniel, he's gone," the woman said. "He asked me to watch for packages."

This was news, Amanda thought. "Gone? Where?"

"Uptown. He's working for his father now."

"His father?"

"You know, the one who owns the Evelyn's."

She said it like it was common knowledge.

"Evelyn's cleaners?" Amanda asked.

"That's right."

Daniel's family owned Evelyn's? Really? That was news to her. It seems the former Neanderthal was full of surprises. "Well do you know when he'll be back?" Amanda asked.

The woman shook her head, unsure. "Nope. That's all he said."

"Okay. Thanks anyway," Amanda replied, disappointed. "Well, when you see him, can you tell him Amanda stopped by?"

"Amanda?"

"That's right. I'm..." Amanda hesitated, unsure exactly what she was to him. "...a friend."

The woman looked Amanda over. "Forgive me for asking, but do you know you're in a wedding dress?"

"Yes," Amanda answered, blushing. "I'm well aware."

"Okay. Just so long as you know. Good luck."

"Thanks."

With one last smile, the woman stepped back into her apartment and was gone.

"Evelyn's?" Amanda asked herself, turning from the door. She knew Daniel delivered laundry, but she didn't know it was because his family owned the entire chain. The more she thought about it, the more it made sense. But Evelyn's was in every part of the city, even out on Long Island. In fact, they were everywhere she'd been on vacation to, too. No wonder Daniel was able to be an artist. He was rich. Filthy rich. And here she'd given him a hard time for being a delivery boy, and he hadn't said anything. He hadn't denied it or tried to make himself look better, even when she was praising William and his seemingly wonderful career. Amanda suddenly felt sick to her stomach. How could she have been so shallow?

She, of all people, should have known that a person's circumstances were rarely dictated by their own. She must have looked like a fool for constantly belittling him for doing what he loved, exactly as she'd done after her parent's deaths. But why didn't he say anything? He'd just gone on as if everything she said were true. Maybe he didn't feel the need to correct her. Or he didn't want someone shallow hanging around for the wrong reasons. The more she thought about it, that's exactly what she'd been. She hadn't taken the time to find the truth out about Daniel because she'd immediately dismissed him because of what he did, yet even then he'd found a way to look past that. All of which meant the Neanderthal was a saint, which made her all the more determined to find him. Reaching the first floor, Amanda exited the elevator and walked out the front to the street where she scanned the busy intersection wondering where to go. Not knowing where to start, she decided to head to the one place she knew would have answers—Evelyn's.

***

As the elevator neared the top floor, Caroline Helmslow cast a nervous glance over to her fiancé, Teddy. She'd been holding his hand in silence the entire way, but it seemed with each floor they passed, she found her grip grow tighter in fear. In just a few floors, they'd be at her grandmother's floor, and the inevitable confrontation would begin. Being a Helmslow had never been easy, yet she and Teddy had waited in the lobby long enough, and now it was time to do what needed to be done. It was time to tell her grandmother the truth. She'd been gone a little over twenty-four hours, and her grandmother would be furious, but maybe with time she'd get over it. Of course she could be cut off. Caroline would be foolish to think otherwise. Her grandmother could be rash, mean-spirited, and spiteful, and that was on a good day. Mrs. Helmslow was from a different generation. One where children obeyed their grandparents and did exactly what they said without hesitation. But Caroline wasn't from that generation and had always bristled at the thought of growing up under such an oppressive yoke. Maybe that's why she was pregnant. Maybe that's why she'd done what she'd done. But she didn't regret any of it. She loved Teddy and if they had to live without her family's money, then that's what they would do. But that didn't help with telling her grandmother. That didn't help the conversation that was about to come.

Sensing her nervousness, Teddy looked over and squeezed Caroline's hand for extra support. "You okay?" he asked with genuine concern. "Everything is going to be okay. We have each other. That's all that matters."

Of course she knew that. It was all that mattered. Sometimes in life you go through things, she told herself. You just have to be strong. But as the elevator slowed to a stop on the top floor, Caroline couldn't help but notice the butterflies doing flips inside her stomach as she waited for the door to open.

Upon entering her grandmother's apartment, Caroline couldn't have been less prepared for what she would find. Her mother was there; police were there; even men in suits she didn't recognize were there. It seemed half of

New York was in her grandmother's apartment, running around like it was the end of the world. But that was nothing compared to their reactions upon seeing her. It seemed the entire world froze the second she walked in the door. Mouths dropped. Heads turned from every part of the room. Her mother gasped an ungodly sound she didn't know was possible. Everything came to an immediate halt as all eyes turned to her and Teddy, waiting for the inevitable explanation that was sure to come.

In the silence, her mother cried out, "Caroline!" and ran to greet her, practically stumbling over the couch along the way. Wrapping her arms around Caroline tighter than Caroline remembered her ever doing, her mother cried tears of joy as if she'd been abducted. "You're okay!" she'd said as if she hadn't seen her in months.

"I'm okay," Caroline answered, feeling foolishly responsible for the entire scene. As Caroline looked around, she nervously scanned the room for the person she most feared but didn't see her. All would be okay if somehow, miraculously, her grandmother wasn't there. They could tell her mother what they came to say and walk away feeling like they did what they needed to do, and everything would be all right.

But just as the impossibly pleasant thought crossed her mind, Caroline felt a disturbance in the room, a force entering from the hall leading to the back bedrooms.

Officers parted. Strangers stepped out of the way as her grandmother appeared—all five foot eight and two hundred and fifty pounds of her. And there she stood with her arm folded, scowling at Caroline with such disappointment it made Caroline want to drop Teddy's hand and run for the elevator.

"Where have you been?" the eldest Helmslow scowled, lashing out loud enough for everyone to hear. "Explain yourself!"

Caroline felt her heart drop into her stomach. She looked at Teddy for comfort, but his face was so red with fear she felt he might push her out of the way and run himself.

"Hi, Grandma," Caroline answered, at a loss for other words.

But Mrs. Helmslow was in no need to accept trifles. "Where have you been?" she repeated, stepping forward. With every step she took, Caroline could feel the world closing in around her. Maybe she'd made the wrong decision. Maybe she should have thought it out more. Once she came out with her answer, she would be cut off. She was doomed to be forced out, which meant this was the last time she'd see her mother. It would be the last time she stepped foot in this apartment and saw opulence on such a grand scale. It would be the end of her former life and the beginning of a much more frugal one.

"I said, where have you been?" Helmslow repeated, close enough to Caroline that she could smell the bitter lemon scent of her grandmother's perfume.

Caroline took a nervous look at Teddy for reassurance before turning back to her grandmother to say the words she knew her grandmother wouldn't want to hear. "Grandma, we eloped."

***

Amanda stepped inside Evelyn's with the bag of clothes she'd gotten at a nearby shop and asked to speak to a manager. When the manager, a slight Scandinavian named Ferdinand, arrived she told him a little of her predicament and asked where she could find Daniel. Ferdinand informed her that not only was Daniel the owner's son, but also he'd taken leave of his deliveries to run the global office, which was located on the twenty-third floor of a skyscraper uptown.

"Global office?" Amanda asked. "But I thought this was just a local dry cleaner."

Ferdinand laughed at the thought. "Evelyn's has over forty-three hundred stores operating in all parts of the country," he'd informed her. "We're the largest combined dry cleaners in the world."

"The world?" Amanda let that sink in a moment. Daniel's family owned the largest dry cleaning firm in the world, and he'd never said anything.

"Are you sure?"

"Oh yes ma'am," Ferdinand said proudly.

The thought was staggering. Daniel was much wealthier than she thought, and she'd treated him like a loser. It made her feel all the more foolish, and the need of finding him greater, if only to apologize.

"Ferdinand, can you tell me where the offices are?" Amanda asked. "I really need to find him. I keep calling, but he doesn't answer."

Ferdinand pulled a business card out from under the register and handed it over. "This is the address. All of the information can be found online as well."

"Thank you," Amanda said, relieved, as she looked over the card, which listed the global address as Rockefeller Center. "Rockefeller Center? Your global offices are located in Rockefeller Center?" Amanda asked, impressed.

"Oh, yes. This is not a small a corporation," he explained in his thick accent.

Amanda shook her head at her own stupidity. All those times she'd made fun of Daniel for his lack of ambition, and he was heir to a fortune large enough he didn't have to work a day in his life. It was the kind of life she could only dream about. No wonder he was so cavalier. She must have looked like such a fool, yet he'd never said anything. For that, he was a Neanderthal. For everything else, she was, but that was going to change. She was going to find him and tell him she'd made a mistake— just as soon as she got out of this dress.

***

"You did what?" Helmslow looked at Caroline like she was about to explode.

Even for Caroline, who'd seen her grandmother get angry more times than she could remember, this was by far the most upset she'd ever seen her. In fact, even with countless officers standing in between her and her grandmother, Caroline wasn't sure she'd make it out of the apartment alive.

"I said, we eloped," Caroline answered with little more than a whisper.

Feeling a sense of duty to contribute, Teddy stepped up beside Caroline and put his arm around her. "We love each other, Mrs. Helmslow, and we didn't want to wait. Surely you can see that."

Whatever his intentions, the words seemed to only incite Helmslow more.

"Is that so?" she scowled. "Because the only thing I see is a pregnant child too stupid to make her own decisions and the fool who disgraced her."

"Mother, please!" Caroline's mother begged. "There are strangers present."

"I don't care," Helmslow shouted, taking a cursory glance at the men and women around her. "I've pandered to your ungrateful offspring long enough, and I will not be made a laughingstock in front of the entire community while she decides to forgo all sense of decorum and marry her mistake of a child's father in the filth of the county courthouse."

"He is not a mistake!" Caroline rebutted. "He is my son, and he will be loved by two parents who love each other and are committed to putting the work in."

"With what money?" Helmslow questioned. "Or do you plan to get a job and support him on your own?"

"Teddy has a fine job. We won't live in high style, but we'll manage. All we want is your support, Grandma. That's all we ever wanted."

"It's true," Teddy added. "I'll take care of them, Mrs. Helmslow."

"Quiet! I've had just about enough of you!" Helmslow railed before turning her attention back to Caroline. "Now you listen here, young lady. You have disgraced this family for the last time. You will have your wedding, and you will get married in front of God and country like a responsible young lady and that's final."

"I won't."

"What did you say?"

"I said I wouldn't. We've made our decision and it's final."

Helmslow grew an extra shade of red, seething. "Then you are cut off," she barked. "And don't think you can just walk away from this." Helmslow pointed to the officers who were watching the drama unfold. "You'll be getting the full bill for the officers' time and the wedding, and you can pay for it from Teddy's supposedly fine job." With that, Helmslow turned and stomped off.

***

After a long twenty-minute cab ride uptown, Amanda stood across the street from Rockefeller Center in a daze. She had thought wearing something other than the wedding dress would make her feel less awkward, yet now that she was here in street clothes, she felt just as out of place. Most of the people going in and out of buildings near Rockefeller Center were in suits and dresses, and she looked like she had come from a picnic. Not that she was fully confident she could get in even if she wanted to. Rockefeller center would surely be closed to anyone who didn't work there, with guards and security ready to apprehend anyone who didn't belong before entering. Without an appointment, it'd be like trying to rob a bank, but it was her only chance to find Daniel.

Crossing the street, Amanda neared the front door where a foreboding doorman stood guard. Luckily, instead of blocking her way, he moved aside and opened the door. Well that was one problem solved. Buoyed with confidence, Amanda thanked him, then went inside and walked across the lobby to the elevators where a guard sat behind a desk, sipping coffee. Doing her best to act like she belonged, Amanda attempted to pass unnoticed when he suddenly stopped what he was doing and looked up.

"Good morning," he said warily. "Can I help you?"

Amanda immediately regretted her choice of outfits. There was no doubt a casual blouse and jeans were better than a wedding dress, but she knew she would stick out in a world of business suits and power lunches. The guard probably thought she was a tourist looking to take a quick ride on the famous building's elevator with no real need to be inside.

"No," she answered, hoping that would be the end of it. "I'm just heading up to…" Amanda took the business card out of her pocket and read the address again, "the twenty-third floor."

"Evelyn's floor," the guard said knowingly. "What time is your appointment?" The guard typed something into his computer and waited.

"Appointment? I'm afraid I don't have an appointment," Amanda answered nervously.

"You don't have an appointment?" the guard asked, looking up from his computer.

"Not exactly." Amanda blushed. "Actually, the person I'm seeing doesn't know I'm coming. It's a surprise." Amanda thought of all the times Daniel had come to see her unannounced and she had treated him like a leper. This must be some sort of cosmic payback, she figured.

"A surprise?" the guard mused, picking up the phone. "Well, we will need permission. Is there someone you'd like me to call?"

Amanda felt a knot growing in the pit of her stomach. Here she'd come all this way and hadn't thought it all through. This was a global office full of business people, not a small wedding shop, and she was showing up in clothes she might as well have bought at a thrift store. Not to mention she hadn't spoken to him in weeks. He could already be seeing someone. Or have gotten married! Besides, what did she expect would happen? Did she really believe she would show up at his office and tell him she'd made a mistake by saying she never wanted to see him again and everything would magically be okay? For the millionth time that day, Amanda realized what she was doing was crazy. The reality was that Daniel was busy running a multimillion-dollar enterprise. She should at least be in something remotely appropriate and know what she was going to say.

"Ma'am?" the guard reiterated, pulling Amanda from her thoughts. "Do you have a name? Someone I can call?"

As the guard waited, Amanda looked at the elevators with their marble facades and brass buttons and felt small and inconsequential. There was no way she could go through with it. Not here. Not today, especially in this outfit. She'd have to come back and try again some other time. The decision made, Amanda looked at the guard, feeling even more foolish than when she came in. "No. That's okay," Amanda responded, shaking her head in defeat. "I'll come back later." With that, she turned and walked off.

CHAPTER EIGHTEEN

"WHAT DO YOU MEAN you didn't go through with it?" Margot asked from across the desk. "How could you go all the way there and not go up?"

"I don't know!" Amanda responded. "I just couldn't."

"But you'd already changed outfits! You were in the lobby! All you had to do was let him call!"

"And say what? I'm sorry? Let me up so I can apologize in person for being shallow and petty and stupid?"

"Yes! Exactly!" Margot agreed, throwing her hands up. "That is exactly what you should have said."

"But I was wearing jeans!"

"It doesn't matter. This is Daniel we're talking about! He's a Neanderthal. He was probably not even wearing pants!"

"A rich Neanderthal."

"A rich Neanderthal who loves you. He dove into a lake to save your prized possession, not to mention spent

God knows how much time and money fixing it."

"That was before."

"Before what?"

"Before he was suddenly one of Forbes's richest."

"He's the same person, with the same feelings. He's probably thinking about you right now in his boring office."

"Or his private jet."

"Or his private jet," Margot conceded. "Where he's sitting without pants right now thinking of you."

"He's wearing pants!" Amanda rebutted. "And they probably have gold stitching sewn in by his butler."

Margot shook her head disapprovingly. "So that's it? You're just going to give up? You're just going to let him slip away?"

"Yes."

"Now you're being ridiculous," Margot accused.

"Fine, I'm being ridiculous," Amanda conceded. "It was stupid to think we could be together. We're nothing alike."

"You're more alike than you think. And I think you're now beginning to realize it."

"Are you finished?"

"No. I also think if you do nothing you're going to regret it for the rest of your life."

"Okay, Miss Melodramatic. Is that all?"

"No," Margot responded picking up Amanda's phone and holding it out to her. "There is one more thing. You also need to call William and call off your engagement."

"Now? But what do I say?" Fear shot through Amanda's nerves as she took the phone, dreading the call she knew she had to make.

"Tell him the truth," Margot replied. "Tell him you're in love with someone else."

***

As Amanda hung up with William, she felt relieved to at least gotten that over with. William had been nothing short of amazing, as usual, telling her he understood and wished her well. He was disappointed of course, but he had gotten a feeling after her reaction to seeing Daniel's painting in the window. She promised to return the ring, and he hurried off to take care of another patient. Great, Amanda thought, hanging up, now I've got no one. Her perfect doctor was gone, and Daniel had suddenly turned into a hard-to-reach millionaire, too busy to speak to her, and not to mention, the reality that her Starlight wedding was now impossible seeing as how she was alone and likely to be so forever. Once again, she was facing a future alone with a house full of cats she had yet to buy with no one to share it with. Putting her head on her hands, Amanda slumped to her desk and did a mindless Google search for the nearest cat shelter.

***

As Mayberry pressed the button for the top floor, he couldn't help but feel out of place. Talking with Helmslow in Browner's office was one thing. It was a place he knew, and he had Father Browner to take up any slack in the conversation. But now, here he was, riding up to Helmslow's penthouse alone, and it was making him uneasy. He had just finished unpacking and gotten settled after her last angry tirade had left him jobless. Surely she wouldn't have invited him if his job were in danger, he convinced himself. Of course, with Helmslow, anything was possible, and more than likely, it wasn't going to be good.

Wiping the sweat from his brow, Mayberry nervously watched the numbers climb as the elevator continued its ascent to the top floor. Perhaps she'd invited him for tea, Mayberry hoped, then laughed at the notion. More than likely it was something having to do with Helmslow's granddaughter. Mayberry had heard she'd been found, though he didn't know the details. Perhaps Helmslow wanted special accommodations for the wedding. If so, Mayberry wished Browner had come to deal with any fallout. Not that he'd object to any of Helmslow's demands. Browner had practically granted her sainthood and was relying on the wedding to reel in more money for his precious new children's wing. At this point, he wouldn't be surprised if Browner renamed the entire cathedral after Helmslow, just to keep the money flowing. But that was none of his business. Browner could do what he wished. All Mayberry cared about was keeping his job, and as long as that was safe, he'd continue dreaming of summer vacations and leave everything else to Browner.

Reaching the top floor, Mayberry stepped out of the elevator and froze at what he saw. The entire entrance hall was filled with stacks of boxes. Between them, workmen shuffled back and forth, loading more on top of the ones already there. That's odd, Mayberry thought. Browner hadn't mentioned anything about Helmslow moving. Maybe he'd gotten lucky, and she'd decided to leave the country. Fat chance, he thought, but at least he could dream.

"Excuse me," Mayberry spoke up, getting the attention of the first mover he came across, "is someone leaving?"

"Yeah, the youngest Helmslow," the mover responded. "She's been cut off."

"Cut off?" Mayberry didn't like the sound of that, especially now. For all he cared, she could fall into the ocean and disappear after the wedding, but before the wedding was another story. He needed everything to go smoothly, or he knew her problems would find their way into his life and make coordinating the wedding that much more difficult.

Moving further inside, Mayberry approached the mover in charge. "Excuse me…do you know where I can find Mrs. Helmslow?"

"In there," the mover said, pointing over his shoulder. "She's in the parlor. But be careful. She's in a mood."

"When is she not?" Mayberry responded under his breath before heading to the parlor. He'd be more surprised if she wasn't. Since he'd met her, Mayberry would wager on there ever being a time when Helmslow was not in a mood. Still, Mayberry followed the man's directions, wondering how all of this would affect the wedding. Who would he deal with? Caroline or Helmslow? If it were up to him, he'd prefer Caroline, but as long as Helmslow was still writing the checks, he assumed he'd have no choice.

Stepping into the parlor, Mayberry caught sight of Helmslow sitting in a chair all alone. Even from a distance, her scowl seemed more ferocious than usual.

Clearly she was not happy with something, and Mayberry was sure the details would somehow find their way into the conversation.

"Mrs. Helmslow," Mayberry began, getting her attention, "I got your message. How can I help you?"

"Get me that newspaper," Helmslow demanded, pointing to a newspaper a few yards away.

"Yes, ma'am." Mayberry obeyed, retrieving the paper and handing it over. "Anything else?"

Mayberry waited as Helmslow opened the paper and began reading it. How odd, he thought. For someone as socially conscious as she was, she should at least know how to carry a conversation.

"Mrs. Helmslow? Remember, you called me? Was there something else you wanted to say?" Mayberry repeated, forcing a smile.

"Oh, yes," Helmslow assured. "There most definitely is. I called you here to talk about my granddaughter's wedding."

"That's what I figured," Mayberry answered, feeling somewhat relieved. "And what exactly about the wedding is it you'd like to talk about?"

"All of it."

"All of it?" Mayberry asked, confused.

"That's right," Helmslow confirmed. "I called you here to tell you that the wedding is off!"

***

Daniel hung up the phone for what seemed the millionth time and leaned back in his father's office chair, exhausted. How did people do it, he wondered? How did they put up with boring office jobs on a daily basis? It wasn't that he was overly busy. Running a corporation he didn't know the first thing about certainly kept him occupied. That was expected. Yet it seemed like he was having the same mind-numbing conversations over and over again. At least with art, every day was a new day. Every piece was a new adventure ready to be taken. It was a world he missed. A world he couldn't wait to get back to. Of course all of that was behind him, at least temporarily until his father's recovery. Daniel shuddered at the thought of what would happen if his father somehow didn't recover or never recovered enough to return. The truth was his father had been right. Like it or not, he should have learned about the business long ago. It had paid his way. It had allowed him to focus on art and do the things he'd wanted to do. If he'd listened to his father, he wouldn't feel like a fish completely out of water. He'd spent so much time arguing with his father he hadn't allowed himself to listen to what his father was saying, and now he was paying the price. If and when his father recovered he'd have to do better. He'd have to learn enough to successfully manage the company to allow himself to do what he loved while keeping the business alive at least long enough to hire someone to take over.

Looking at his father's appointment book, Daniel realized he should call his father and check to see how he was doing. Since the relapse, Daniel had a lot of opportunities to speak with him, but since his father had been in and out of consciousness with the medication, the conversations had been stunted and random, but at least they'd broken the ice. Surprisingly, needing his father's advice on how to run things had allowed them to forge a bit of a bond since they now had something in common. Picking the phone up, Daniel was about to dial the number, when he heard a knock at the door.

"Come in," Daniel yelled, setting the phone down. He was relieved to have at least some interaction to break up the day. It was his former manager, Ferdinand, who poked his head in.

"Sir? Is that you?" Ferdinand asked.

"Ferdinand? What are you doing here?" Of all the people Daniel thought would walk through the door, as much as he liked him, Ferdinand was definitely not at the top of the list.

"I came to say hello," Ferdinand answered, crossing further into the room before continuing. "Wow, look at you, sir," Ferdinand said, getting a good look at Daniel behind the desk. "I hardly recognize you. You look so different in a suit."

"Don't remind me," Daniel insisted.

"No, it's good. You look very good, sir. Just not quite suitable for deliveries."

"Good!" Daniel laughed. "I'll take that as a compliment."

Ferdinand had always insisted on calling Daniel sir since he was the owner's son, despite Daniel's objections. He was a good manager, Daniel thought, and kindhearted, but nevertheless Daniel was surprised by the visit.

"Is everything alright?"

"Oh, yes, sir," Ferdinand responded. "I was just on my way back from a delivery, and I thought I'd see how you're doing. We've been short-staffed since you left, so I take a few deliveries on my way home and was in the area."

"I'm sorry," Daniel apologized. "I left so abruptly..."

"Oh, no, I wasn't complaining, sir," Ferdinand promised. "We are fine. I am very proud of you, and we have someone starting next week. There's no need for worry. Of course they won't be as good as you, sir."

Daniel laughed. "We both know that's not true, but thank you."

"Oh, you are too hard on yourself, sir. So how are you? Is everything okay?" Ferdinand asked.

"Everything's great," Daniel promised, doing his best to sound positive. "Though it's still a bit overwhelming."

"I'm sure you'll have the hang of it in no time," Ferdinand reassured. "Did you see your visitor?"

"What visitor?'

Daniel couldn't remember any visitor of note, certainly none of which Ferdinand would care to hear about.

"The woman."

"What woman?" Daniel sat up, intrigued.

"The one who said she needed to speak with you," Ferdinand replied matter-of-factly. "She said it was very important. She said she called you, but you didn't answer."

"Who?"

"The woman in the dress, sir."

"What dress?"

"The wedding dress?"

"Wedding dress?"

Daniel knew he was repeating everything Ferdinand

said, but he couldn't help it. The whole thing was confusing.

"Yes, sir. She said she'd made a mistake and needed to speak to you very badly, then she left the dress for cleaning and ran off to find you."

"Did she give a name?"

"Yes, I wrote it on her ticket. I have it right here." Ferdinand reached into his pocket and pulled out a receipt and read it. "Her name is Amanda."

"Amanda?" Amanda had come to see him?

"That's right. Does it sound familiar?"

"Amanda?" Daniel repeated.

"That's what I wrote, sir."

Daniel sat back, confused. Why had Amanda gone to his work? Even odder, why hadn't she just called? He would have answered, unless… Daniel grabbed his cell and looked at the missed calls. Someone had been trying to get a hold of him. It must have been her. But why was the number blocked? She must have called a dozen times, and he'd sent her to voicemail, not recognizing the number. She'd left messages, and he hadn't even bothered to listen to them.

"Sir?" Ferdinand asked, confused.

"One second." Daniel held up his hand as he flipped through Amanda's messages. As he listened to the first, Daniel could hear what sounded like desperation. Was it really Amanda? For the first time since the toaster incident, she actually sounded vulnerable. Then she'd said something about being foolish and needing to see him. Amanda had wanted to see him, and he'd sent her to voicemail. Well, it served her right, he thought. She'd ignored him for months. Maybe he didn't want to see her again. No, the more Daniel thought about it, the more he knew it wasn't true. He at least wanted to hear what she had to say.

"Ferdinand, is the dress still at the shop?" Daniel asked.

"Oh, no sir."

"No?" Daniel asked, disappointed.

"No, it's downstairs," Ferdinand informed him. "I was going to deliver it tonight."

"I'm coming to get it."

"You want the dress?"

"I want the dress."

As Daniel exited the office behind Ferdinand, he couldn't help but wonder what it all meant. Had Amanda had a change of heart? Why now? And why show up in a wedding dress? And where the heck was William? They were questions that needed answering. Daniel would find Amanda and talk with her, but to do that, he needed the dress because at least one thing was certain—he had one more delivery to make.

***

The package was on her desk when Amanda came back from lunch. There was no bow or card or even hastily scrawled note with it and no sign announcing who it was from. It was as if the package had been there all along. Amanda eyed the package warily. What was it? Who was it from? Where had it come from? A million questions swirled in Amanda's mind as she circled her desk and picked it up. Should she open it? Amanda was certain it was nothing or just something for the shop Margot or Chloe didn't know what to do with. Amanda knew, being the store owner, these kinds of things always found their way to her desk, but for some reason, this time seemed different. Something about the box told her it was different. Her curiosity piqued, Amanda slid the lid off to see what was inside and froze when she saw the dress. There it was—her wedding gown, folded perfectly inside, but how? And why was it here? She knew she hadn't asked for delivery.

"Chloe!" Amanda yelled, turning to the door. "Can you come in here?"

Within moments, Chloe arrived and poked her head in. "Did you call me?"

"Yes. Where did this package come from?"

Chloe took one look at the package and shook her head. "I don't know. I didn't see anyone come in."

"You didn't?"

"No. I was helping customers on the other end of the shop. I went into the storeroom a moment to get something. I asked Eduardo if he could watch the front. It must have come when I was back there. I hope that's okay."

"Yes, of course. Do you know where Eduardo is?"

"He's in front with a customer."

"Thank you," Amanda answered, starting for the door. Whatever the explanation, Amanda wanted to know the truth. It might be too much to hope for, but something told her this wasn't just a regular delivery.

Rounding the corner, Amanda found Eduardo giving samples of one of his creations to hungry customers.

Upon seeing her, his eyes lit up, and he quickly made his way over, giving the answer to her question before she could even ask.

"It was Daniel," he said.

"Daniel?" Amanda asked, stunned. "He was here?"

"In the flesh."

"But why? What did he say? Where did he go?" Amanda had more questions than Eduardo could answer at one time.

"He didn't say anything."

"Nothing?"

"Just that you knew where to find him if you needed him."

"That's it?" Amanda wasn't sure what Eduardo was talking about. Daniel could be anywhere in lower Manhattan for all she knew. There must be something he was forgetting.

"Think, Eduardo."

Eduardo shook his head. "That's everything." Eduardo thought back, visualizing the exchange. "He said you'd know where to find him if you wanted him, I asked him about the bread he was carrying, and then he left."

Amanda perked up. "Bread? What bread?"

"The bread in his hand. He said it was for the ducks."

"Ducks?" Suddenly the revelation hit her. Daniel was at the bridge in Central Park. Her bridge. "Thanks, Eduardo!" Amanda said, kissing Eduardo on the cheek and starting off. "Wish me luck."

"Good luck," Eduardo yelled. And before he could say anything more, she was gone.

STARLIGHT WEDDING

***

Entering the park, Amanda could feel her heart pounding. What if Daniel wasn't there? What if he didn't show up? What if the dress really was just a delivery? She wouldn't know until she saw him, of course, and even then there was no guarantee he hadn't changed his mind. It had been weeks since she'd last seen him. Weeks since she'd told him she never wanted to see him again. It was practically a lifetime. She had been cruel, of course. But that was then. Now she felt completely the opposite. But was it too late? Had she missed her window? The doubts raced through Amanda's mind as she came to the bridge and scanned across it. It was empty, of course. What's more, there were no ducks in the water below. Daniel must have gone elsewhere in search of a better place, if he'd even come at all. Moving to the edge, Amanda looked down at her reflection. How pathetic she must have looked running all this way for nothing. How foolish to think he'd be here. Amanda was still berating herself when she heard footsteps come up behind her. It was probably just another couple, she thought. The park had been littered with couples since she'd arrived, yet another cruel reminder of how alone she was. Yet when she turned, there he was—staring back at her with an enigmatic, undecipherable expression.

Amanda's breath caught in her throat. He was actually here. Now all she had to do was say what she came to say. But where would she begin? How do you tell someone you love them after pushing them away?

"Looking for someone?" Daniel said, finally, with the hint of a smile.

"As a matter of fact," Amanda began, "I seem to have lost my delivery guy."

"Your delivery guy?" Daniel asked, raising an eyebrow. "How terrible."

"Yes," Amanda agreed. "I wasn't nice, and I drove him away."

"Sounds tragic." Daniel shook his head, playing along. "Maybe he deserved it."

"No," Amanda admitted, "he was good to me. Even after I called him a Neanderthal."

"A Neanderthal?" Daniel feigned disbelief. "Sounds terrible."

"I know," Amanda said regrettably. "But I was so caught up in having the perfect life with the perfect wedding and what I thought was the perfect guy, I couldn't see what was in front of me. Daniel, I'm sorry. I really am. I did everything to push you away. I was mean and insensitive and stupid...but I love you. I do."

Daniel let the words hang in the air before continuing.

"I know."

"You do?"

"You wouldn't be here otherwise. But what about William? What about your Starlight wedding? Do you really want to give that up?"

"They're everything I wanted," Amanda admitted, "before I realized what was important. You were right. What good is the perfect wedding if it's with the wrong person?"

"And William?"

"Gone."

"And your wedding?"

STARLIGHT WEDDING

"Taken away. They gave it to the granddaughter of some rich woman named Helmslow."

"Helmslow?" Daniel thought of Caroline Helmslow and the gentleman he'd seen her cowering nervously with in the lobby. "How terrible."

"I guess it wasn't meant to be," Amanda said, doing her best to sound positive.

"And you're okay with that?" Daniel asked.

Amanda shrugged. "I guess. I have no choice."

"So now you're available to get married in a sub shop in SoHo? To a Neanderthal?" Daniel teased.

"Maybe."

Daniel looked at Amanda seriously. "Really?"

"If you want."

Daniel thought about what he was hearing. Is it possible that she had changed? Really changed? There was only one way to find out. Looking Amanda square in the eyes, Daniel held his hand out. "Deal."

"Deal?"

"Deal."

"If we get married, I plan it and you have to trust me. No questions."

"But…" Amanda opened her mouth to speak.

Daniel stopped her by putting his hand to her lips. "No questions. Do you agree?"

Amanda started to speak again, but Daniel covered her mouth again. "Do you agree?"

Amanda thought about it a moment. After a lifetime planning her wedding, it seemed the more she tried to force things, the worse they got. Not to mention, at this point, there wasn't anything she could do to save it.

Maybe Daniel was right. Maybe it was time to let go. It was a silly dream, a childish fantasy. What matters was what she already had—someone who loved her. "Fine," Amanda relented.

"Fine?"

"Fine," Amanda agreed, shaking Daniel's hand.

"Good," Daniel smiled, satisfied. "I was hoping you'd say that. And now that it's settled..." Daniel dropped to one knee. "I just have one last question." Pulling a ring from his pocket, Daniel held it up for Amanda's inspection. "Amanda Jones, will you marry me?"

"Really?"

"Really. I love you, and I want to spend the rest of my life with you. Will you do me the honor of being this Neanderthal's wife?"

Amanda couldn't believe it. He was actually proposing. After all this time and countless missteps, it was finally right. She was sure of it.

Taking the ring, Amanda looked at it a long moment before looking back at Daniel. "Yes. Yes, Daniel, I will."

CHAPTER NINETEEN

AS DANIEL ENTERED HIS PARENT'S apartment, he hadn't the slightest idea of how he was going to announce the engagement to his parents. With everything that had gone on with his father's sickness and the craziness of his and Amanda's relationship, it seemed odd to tell them that he was getting married to someone, let alone to someone they hadn't even met. Of course with his father in and out of consciousness, he might not even register what was said. Daniel was still mulling over the challenge when he saw his father sitting on the couch in the living room completely alert.

"Dad, what are you doing here?" Daniel asked, shocked.

"Reading the paper. What else would I be doing?"

"Mom!" Daniel called out to the kitchen. "Dad's in the living room!"

"Yes, I know dear," Evelyn answered, entering from the kitchen. "Isn't it great? He was feeling better, so he decided to come out of the bedroom."

Of all the things that had happened that day, this had to be the strangest. His father wasn't supposed to be moving about. He was supposed to be lying in bed, hooked to a machine. Yet here he was, reading the paper as if it were perfectly normal.

"So you're okay?"

"Why wouldn't I be?" he said it as if nothing that had happened over the last month had taken place. "I feel fine, so I'm up. No need to make a big deal out of it."

"But it is a big deal. I thought… Well, never mind what I thought. What about your medication?"

Evelyn took the opportunity to step forward. "Oh, he stopped taking it. The doctor said to ease off of it last week. I told you that."

"No, you didn't. You never said anything. So you're fine?" Daniel asked, once again turning to his father.

"As fine as I'll ever be. Now stop talking about it. Evelyn, can you get me something from the kitchen?"

As Evelyn moved off, Daniel couldn't believe what he was seeing. In the flip of a switch, everything was back to normal. His father was not groggy and disoriented. He was fine. Which meant Daniel could go back to his old job, or at least painting and sculpting, but first things first. He needed to tell them about Amanda.

"Mom, dad…" Daniel began as Evelyn reentered. "I

have an announcement."

"An announcement?" Evelyn asked. "Sound ominous."

"No, it's good. At least I think it is." Daniel sat across from Jack, thinking of what to say. "Over the last few months I've been seeing someone. Sort of. It's a long story, but well...I'm getting married."

"Married? But to who?" Evelyn asked. "We didn't even know you were dating."

"Well, I am."

"Do we know her?" Jack questioned.

"No, but you'll like her. She's feisty and smart like you, Mom." Daniel turned to his father. "And she runs her own business like you."

"Well that's great," Evelyn answered as supportively as she could under the circumstances. "Sudden, but great. Isn't that right, dear?" Evelyn said to Daniel's father before looking back at Daniel. "Do you have a date in mind?"

"Not exactly. She'd originally wanted to do it at St. Patrick's on the twenty-fourth, but unfortunately that date fell through. Apparently Caroline Helmslow got it."

"But that's only a few weeks away. I just got the announcement."

"I know. It's a long story. Regardless, we'll have to find somewhere else."

"Not necessarily," Evelyn answered. Evelyn stood up and quickly pulled the society section of an old newspaper off the table and handed it to Daniel. "It was just announced yesterday."

"What was?" Daniel asked. Daniel read the

announcement from the society pages announcing the cancelation of the impending Helmslow wedding due to "scheduling conflicts." Daniel wasn't sure what the scheduling conflicts were, but he was sure there was more to the story since in upper-class society this sort of thing rarely occurred.

"I don't understand. What does it mean?" Daniel asked.

Evelyn took the paper and pointed to the word canceled. "It means," Evelyn explained, "that the cathedral is available."

***

As Mayberry listened to the last of the dozen or so desperate messages on his answering machine from eager brides hoping to take Caroline's place on the twenty-fourth, he couldn't believe it. He'd expected some response, but ever since word had gotten out in the newspapers, his phone had been ringing off the hook. Apparently every knocked-up bride in Manhattan read the newspapers' society sections and was clamoring to say her I do's at St. Patrick's in Caroline's place. Mayberry had even found a couple waiting at his door when he'd shown up in the morning for work. He felt like a rock star holding the last golden ticket, not that he knew what to do with it. The truth was there were too many potential brides to go through, and it was giving him a headache. Mayberry knew he should just pick one and get it over with, but with his phone constantly ringing, he hadn't had a chance to make a decision. He hadn't even had a chance to go to the bathroom. He'd gone so far as to lock his door and turn down the lights just to throw some of the less tenacious women off.

Talk about a time he'd like to go on vacation. The whole thing had been physically and mentally exhausting. Of course he blamed Browner, not that he had said anything. The fact of the matter was it was Browner's fault to begin with, as he was the one who had caved to all of Helmslow's demands. If it weren't for him agreeing to everything she asked, none of this would have happened. Still, Mayberry refrained from saying, "I told you so." No, he decided, he would just go about his business, filling the spot, and give it to the least demanding bride he came across. After that he would go home, take a hot bath, and dream of his next vacation. Leaning back in his chair, Mayberry raked the mini sand garden on his desk and pictured himself in the Caribbean. What he wouldn't give to be there sipping drinks and listening to the waves. Mayberry closed his eyes and had just started dozing off when he heard the knock at the door.

"Mr. Mayberry?" It was a man and clearly one too stupid to get the hint, Mayberry thought. What's more, the annoying visitor had the audacity to let himself in. As the door opened, Mayberry immediately knew he should have bolted it shut. It was Carl. Or fake Carl to be precise. "What do you want?" Mayberry growled. "And don't even think about asking for the twenty-fourth because it's not happening. I have a list of brides a mile long and neither Amanda nor you are getting it."

"That's fair. But let me explain," Daniel asked, walking further into the room. "After that you can make your decision."

"I've already made my decision," Mayberry growled. "So it won't do you any good, Carl, or fake Carl, or whoever you really are."

"It's Daniel. And you're right, I shouldn't have lied. I'm sorry. I'm not Carl. I'm nothing like Carl. I was just trying to help Amanda by pretending to be him and I shouldn't have. It was wrong of me."

"You cost me my job, a job that I was only able to get back because of Carl. So thank you for your apology and goodbye."

"I understand." Daniel turned to leave then stopped, knowing if he didn't convince Mayberry to change his mind Amanda would never get her Starlight wedding. Spinning around again, Daniel tried to think of what he could say to change Mayberry's mind. "You know, there's no one on the planet that wanted that day more than Amanda," he began. "She may not have been engaged, but it meant everything for her to get married here at St. Patrick's on the twenty-fourth. It was her lifelong dream, which is why she booked this church so far in advance, even before she had a fiancé. And then she thought she had a fiancé. She even found the ring he was going to propose with. But when the night came, he proposed to someone else."

"Those are the breaks," Mayberry replied unsympathetically. He'd heard enough. "She lied and she got what she deserved, and there's nothing that's going to change that. So thank you for your time and now you can leave."

Daniel watched as Mayberry returned focus to the

mini rake and sand garden on his desk. So that was it. It was over. There was nothing more he could do. Daniel turned to go again and suddenly realized something he hadn't noticed. Everywhere he looked, there was a picture of a beach, or sand, or some tropical destination. Daniel realized that, just like Amanda, Mayberry had a dream; only his dream was in the sand, sun, and surf.

"Is that what you love?" Daniel asked, eyeing the sand on Mayberry's desk. "Beach vacations?"

"Maybe."

"I figured," Daniel remembered his own childhood. "When I was five, my family went south every summer. My father started Evelyn's cleaners, and we were expanding into warmer climates, so I spent most of my summers in the Caribbean. While he worked, my mother would take me to the ocean. I still have fond memories."

"Is that right?" Mayberry asked, disinterested.

Daniel nodded. "In fact, we still have a house there, and it just sits there empty most of the year."

"What are you saying?" Mayberry asked, not knowing where Daniel was going.

"I'm saying it'd be great to have someone to look after our beach house from time to time, say...five or six times a year."

Mayberry sat up in his chair, warily intrigued. "Wouldn't that be expensive?"

"Not for us," Daniel responded. "We employ tens of thousands."

"Tens of thousands?" Mayberry's mouth dropped open despite his attempt to seem indifferent. "So this person could go whenever they wanted? To the

Caribbean?"

"Anytime they wanted: President's Day, Fourth of July, summer holidays... It would be their choice. Anytime they felt like getting away, they could hop on a plane and be there within hours, all expenses paid. What do you say?"

"And in return you get the twenty-fourth?"

"Not me. Amanda. I want to give it to her as a present. It would be a surprise. She couldn't know about it until the day it happened. I want to make it special, but I'd need your help." Having said it, Daniel pulled his keys out of his pocket, took one off the end, and offered it to Mayberry. "This one's for the beach house. And it's yours if you want it. What do you say, Donald?"

Mayberry looked at the key feeling conflicted. If he said yes, he would be able to feel the sand between his toes and bask in the glowing sunlight all year round, all expenses paid, whenever he wanted. It was a dream come true and too good to pass up. But it would mean he'd have to help Amanda, which was something he wasn't sure he wanted to do. She'd been a thorn in his side far longer than he cared to remember, and he'd soon rather forget her. It was a tough decision, and one not to be made lightly.

"Would I have full access to the house?"

"Absolutely."

"And could I come and go as I please?"

"It would be your house while you were there."

Mayberry weighed the decision, his mind wavering back and forth.

"But before you decide," Daniel added, "there is one

more thing." Daniel took a scrap of paper off Mayberry's desk and wrote a slip number down and set it in front of Mayberry, hoping to sweeten the deal.

"What's that?" Mayberry asked, unfamiliar with the terminology.

"That," Daniel smiled confidently, "is the location of the yacht."

CHAPTER TWENTY

AS DANIEL WALKED DOWN THE AISLE of St. Patrick's looking everything over, he couldn't believe that in just a few short hours the church would be packed, and he and Amanda would be getting married. The previous two weeks had been a blur. Once Mayberry had relented, Daniel had immediately dived into the process of transforming all of Amanda's scrapbook dreams into reality without her knowing. There had been so much to do in an impossibly short amount of time, but somehow everything had come together. Of course, keeping the details a secret from Amanda was nearly impossible. More than once mistakes had been made, and he was sure Amanda had found out. For a consummate planner like Amanda, Daniel could tell every second of not knowing was driving her crazy. It was like planning a surprise party for someone who knew it was coming and hated surprises. In the end, he had decided to enlist Margot, and together they attempted to convince Amanda that the only venue in New York available was the former deli space his grandparents had gotten married in. It was large, owned by his family, and most importantly, still available. After making it sound romantic and promising to transform it, Amanda had somehow miraculously agreed with the caveat that if she found something better they would change it, which of course, she did. Twice. Both times, Daniel voiced his excitement then secretly called each place, told them of his plans, and paid them a large sum to cancel. Left with no choice and a rapidly approaching deadline, Amanda reluctantly accepted the vacant space as the only option.

Meeting a smiling Mayberry at the top of the aisle, Daniel greeted the man who had been indispensable the previous few weeks, going above and beyond everything he was asked for. Sporting a healthy tan, despite not having left the city, Mayberry seemed like a man renewed. Just the freedom of knowing he could leave at any moment had somehow transformed him in ways Daniel couldn't have imagined.

"Is everything set?" Daniel asked, shaking Mayberry's hand.

"Everything you asked for," Mayberry informed him. "All we need now is a bride, a groom, and a minister, ideally at the same time," Mayberry joked. "How are we looking in here?"

Daniel turned and looked down the aisle at the sanctuary, amazed at how it had all come together. "It's everything she wanted. Thank you again, Donald. I couldn't have done it without you."

"I'm glad it worked out," Mayberry said. As he said it, Daniel detected a hint of pride in Mayberry's eyes and the shocking presence of emotion. "It's going to be a fine wedding."

"It is, isn't it?" Daniel agreed. "Most importantly, it's going to be the wedding of her dreams."

***

Amanda closed the scrapbook for what seemed like the millionth time and looked at herself in the mirror. It was time to go and she knew it. She'd kept the driver waiting long enough. Daniel would be waiting and the minister would be waiting, along with what few guests who were able to attend on such short notice. It would be nothing like her Starlight fantasy, that's for sure. She wasn't even going to wear her mother's veil. But at least she was having a wedding. It wouldn't be in a church decorated with roses and chrysanthemums like she'd imagined or at St. Patrick's liked she'd hoped, and it wouldn't have nearly as many guests as she would have liked, or her parents. But Eduardo and Margot would be there, Chloe and Henry, and of course, Daniel. Most importantly, she was marrying someone she loved, and a few hours afterward, the Starlight Comet would appear like it had thirty years before, making it all the more special. Setting the scrapbook down, Amanda took a deep breath, grabbed her purse, and made her way to the hall where the limo driver waited.

***

Sitting in the back of the limo, Amanda couldn't help but feel like a little girl playing dress up. Here she was in a puffy, white wedding dress, staring wide-eyed at the towering New York skyscrapers that passed outside the window. In a few minutes it would all be real. She would be starring in her own wedding, and despite it being a scaled down version of the dream she'd spent a lifetime planning, she knew everything would be perfect. At least she hoped it would. For weeks, Daniel had transformed the former deli space without allowing her to see it. It had been torture waiting, of course. She'd thought about sneaking over numerous times over the last few weeks and had even gotten into a cab one time and driven halfway up town. But in the end, she'd felt guilty and asked the driver to turn around. She'd honored her promise, but as someone used to stressing over the details, the anticipation was killing her.

"Are we almost there?" Amanda asked the driver impatiently, pressing her head against the glass trying to see up ahead.

"Just a bit further," the driver responded. "One of the roads was blocked, so we had to go around."

"Really?" That was a surprise, Amanda thought. No wonder it had taken so long. Manhattan traffic was always slow, but today it seemed like forever.

"Are you sure you're going the right way?" Amanda repeated, pressing her head harder against the window. "Because I don't see anything."

"Just a few more blocks, ma'am," the driver assured. And it seemed no sooner had he said it, than the limo pulled to a stop at the destination.

"Here we are," the driver proudly confirmed, opening his door and stepping outside.

Amanda looked out her window at the former deli

space and felt a rush of fear. There was no one inside, at least no one that she could see. The lights were on, but the place looked deserted. Surely it must be some kind of mistake. Amanda could feel her heart racing as the driver suddenly appeared outside and opened her door.

"Are you sure this is it?" Amanda repeated for what felt like the millionth time as she exited the limo, her eyes scanning anywhere and everywhere for signs of life.

"Yes, ma'am," the driver assured, stepping out of the way.

"But there's no one here," Amanda fretted. "It's supposed to be a wedding, but there are no guests, or groomsman, or anyone!"

"Just follow the carpet, ma'am," he said.

"What carpet?"

"Inside. You'll know when you see it."

"Carpet? You're sure?" Amanda asked doubtfully. As confident as the driver seemed, Amanda wasn't sure whether to believe him.

"That's what I was told, ma'am. Good luck," the driver said before turning and walking away so fast it seemed he was trying to run away from her before she could ask another question.

"Good luck?" Amanda asked herself, returning her gaze to the empty building. Why did she get the feeling the driver was saying it just so he could leave as soon as possible.

"Okay. Thank you," Amanda said doing her best to appear relaxed as she headed inside. Upon reaching the entrance, Amanda could feel her insides churning. In the history of bad ideas, this had to be the worst. She knew she shouldn't have trusted Daniel to do the planning. Trusting a man to do anything was asking for trouble, especially when it came to weddings. Grabbing the door handle, Amanda turned it, half expecting the door to be locked, but surprisingly, it opened. Well that's something, she thought.

"Hello? Is anyone here?" Amanda called out, stepping inside. "Daniel? Anyone?" Amanda's heart sank. The whole thing was downright terrifying with no end in sight. "Follow the carpet," she remembered aloud. And to her surprise, there it was—a three-foot-wide carpet roll, stretching the length of the floor to a hall, which seemed to lead nowhere. All right, here goes, she thought. Taking her first step, Amanda stopped and looked around, waiting for something to jump out and grab her like in a horror movie. Relieved to be wrong, Amanda took another step. It would be the first of many she surmised, as there didn't seem to be any end in sight. With each step, her panic grew, along with the fear that she'd come to the wrong place. To make matters worse, just when she was about to give up—it ended: both the carpet and the building. She had walked clear to the other end of the building with nothing even resembling a wedding in between. Amanda's heart sank. It was time to face reality—carpet or no carpet, she was in the wrong place, which meant, like it or not, she was going to miss her own wedding.

Amanda collapsed into the wall as the realization hit her. What was she going to do? The limo was surely gone by now, which meant she'd have to take public transportation in her dress again, but to where? Somewhere in Manhattan there was a wedding missing a bride, but she didn't know where. Amanda groaned in frustration. How could this happen? She knew she shouldn't have trusted Daniel. She shouldn't have trusted anyone but herself. Amanda followed the last few yards of carpet with her eyes again. It was a dead end. The carpet had led her nowhere. Then suddenly it hit her — maybe there was more. It was the end of the building, yes, but maybe there was something more on the other side. Nothing else made sense. At the very least, she could try it. There was no harm in that. Maybe it was what she was supposed to do all along. So, armed with little hope or expectation, Amanda opened the door and looked out and saw the last thing she expected to see — St. Patrick's Cathedral.

It was across the street and looked stunning with its giant spires and perfect architecture. What's more, every inch of the cathedral's immaculate detail was lit by sun and on display. Flowers and recently laid carpet bordered by roses and chrysanthemums covered the steps and sidewalk where Daniel stood smiling back at her. Thinking she was dreaming, Amanda shook her head, trying to wake up. When that didn't work, Amanda scanned the street around her only to find it closed with barricades blocking traffic on both sides. Behind the barricades, policemen stood guard, keeping people out. Amanda looked down again, following the trail of carpet with her eyes and saw that it crossed the street and went up the curb and stopped directly in front of Daniel. That's when it hit her—this was all for her. Daniel had somehow made her dreams a reality. Amanda's breath caught in her throat as the enormity of what he'd done registered. Daniel had actually found a way to give her the wedding she had always dreamed of.

Daniel descended the steps to meet her. Moving toward him, Amanda grinned as she made her way to the center of the street as cheers erupted from people behind the barricades, making her feel like royalty.

"You did this?" Amanda asked, coming face to face with Daniel.

"I just followed directions," Daniel admitted before nodding to the crowd. "I hope it's okay. I invited a few friends."

"Of course it's okay. It's unbelievable."

"I wanted you to be happy," Daniel said, relieved. "And I wanted you to have the wedding of your dreams."

"It is! But how?" Amanda asked, glancing over Daniel's shoulder to St. Patrick's. "I thought it was impossible."

"I guess it was meant to be," Daniel answered cryptically, glancing up to heaven. "I guess someone up in heaven's looking down on you."

"My mom," Amanda answered as a tear fell from her eye.

"It must be," Daniel said, holding an arm out for Amanda. "Now if you'll join me inside, there are a few people who'd like to see you."

As they walked to the front of the church, Amanda felt like a fairytale princess. It was beyond anything she had ever imagined. And with so many photos flashing from the onlookers, she felt like a movie star walking the red carpet.

Reaching the doors, Amanda stopped to look at the sky. Out of the corner of her eye, she could see the beginning of the Starlight Comet appearing on the horizon. "There it is!" she said, pointing to its location.

Daniel turned and looked with her. "Is it everything you imagined?"

"Better," she said breathlessly.

"And what about me? Am I what you imagined?" Daniel asked, stepping in front of her.

"No," Amanda admitted. "You're better, too."

Inside, the church was filled to capacity, and it was decorated exactly as she'd imagined. Amanda saw everyone she'd wanted to invite, as well as people on Daniel's side, and they were all standing, staring at her and Daniel. It was really happening. She was actually having her Starlight wedding.

"Well?" Daniel asked, gauging her reaction.

"It's perfect," Amanda responded.

"Then if you'll excuse me..." Daniel said, pointing to the front where Father Browner and the wedding party waited. "I'll meet you there."

As if on cue, Eduardo approached to take Amanda's hand. "Are you ready to be walked down the aisle, young lady?"

Taking Eduardo's hand, Amanda soaked in every moment as Daniel made his way down the aisle to Browner and turned to face her. It was all so overwhelming, Amanda didn't know what to say, but one thing was certain—she was more than ready. She'd waited her whole life for this moment.

"I'm beyond ready."

As if on cue, the organist began Amanda's favorite song as she and Eduardo took their first steps down the aisle. As they walked, Amanda took in all the faces staring back and realized her Starlight wedding had begun—and it was better than she'd imagined.

CPSIA information can be obtained at www.ICGtesting.com
Printed in the USA
LVOW07s0850280615

444164LV00001B/52/P

9 780996 141222